The Seventh List

Grant Finnegan

Set in Linux Libertine

Production by Hourigan & Co.
hourigan.co

Find the author online
grantfinnegan.com

v. 2014-08-01

About the author

A voracious reader of action thrillers, **Grant Finnegan** began his literary journey more than ten years ago by writing his first story. He then began *The Seventh List*, inspired by the question, "what would you do in your life if you knew the date it would end?" He is currently working on a new action thriller concerned with life's challenges and meaning, and how we cope with change. Grant is divorced with two teenage children, and lives near the beach in Melbourne, Australia. You can find him online at grantfinnegan.com.

The Seventh List

Prologue

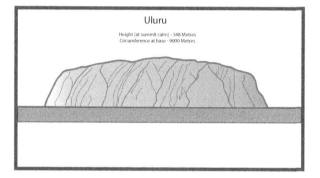

Uluru

Height (at summit cairn) - 348 Metres
Circumference at base - 9000 Metres

Uluru.

It's without doubt Australia's most revered and recognisable natural landmark. If you live on that very large island, you have either been to it, or seen its photograph, most likely.

Her fame stretches all around the world, making Uluru one of Australia's most popular tourist attractions, visited by tens of thousands of people every year, most of whom will walk away awed by the jaw dropping beauty and sheer size of the thing.

If the dictionary had pictures for words, the one for 'gargantuan' would have a photo of Uluru.

Only when you are standing close do you come to realise how unbelievably enormous she actually is, and how Uluru completely contradicts the flatness of the surrounding desert. She's an enigma, and a mighty one at that.

Three hundred and forty-eight metres high, 9000 metres in circumference at its base, 'Ayers Rock,' as she was previously more commonly known – is actually a giant piece of hardened arkose sand. She is the tip of a kilometres deep reef of arkose, as if she were an iceberg, the ice replaced by the reddish, rock-hard sand.

Uluru is a very special place, especially for those who have worshipped and adored her, for longer than most have inhabited planet Earth: the indigenous Australians.

* * *

Most of us have secrets by the time we reach adulthood, and we continue creating them as we grow older, some more than others.

Some secrets we will all spend the rest of our life trying to forget, and hope they are never discovered.

Uluru has secrets as old as time itself. Only a handful of locals in this present day are privy to them, for a very good reason.

You see, reader, if these secrets became public knowledge, to the outside world, it could threaten the very existence of Uluru itself, not to mention that of the people who live around her.

They could threaten you and me.

These secrets have remained safely shielded from the light of day for thousands of years.

Until now.

0:00:01

Late 2012.

The Russian glanced down to his Rolex, a custom build, made especially for a man with a wrist akin to a tree trunk. He grew anxious for his next appointment to get under way, keen to discuss the matters at hand. The watch, rumoured to cost over a million, matched the money choking his opulent office. Crammed with priceless antique furniture, it was as if Buckingham Palace had held a garage sale, and he had purchased everything except the kitchen sink.

The walls of the office overlooking Khokhlovskaya Square in downtown central Moscow were full to the brim with artwork most would only see in one of Europe's premier museums or art galleries.

Vadislav Privaca had money to burn. As CEO of Pravicon Industries, Russia's second-largest mining and resources company, his current personal wealth was a cool 39.25 billion dollars.

Vadislav was the undisputed model of the modern Russian billionaire, who, like many others, had taken full and very profitable advantage of the end of communist Russia in the early 1990s.

He was 6'6" in height, with 130 kilograms of proportioned weight and a big barrel-chest. His thick, black hair was trim and well kept. His teeth were straight and very white. Coupled with an impeccable dress sense, his looks made him the pin-up boy of the Moscow super-rich.

To round off his overpowering aura, Vadislav's eyes were a result of a rare congenital condition – *aniridia*. The irises of his eyes were as jet black as his hair, and staring into them was nothing less than disconcerting.

Most avoided it where possible.

His favourite films were the *Godfather* trilogy. If he had a ruble for every time he had watched them, he could double his wealth.

Vadislav's personal secretary, Mikita, ushered in his appointment. 'Siamko Tudiu,' she announced, even though the two men knew each other well.

Vadislav nodded, waving her off. Mikita was relieved – she would not have to stand in the same room as her boss's personal thug. She hated the way he looked at her. He was as grotesque as a gorilla.

Siamko wondered, not for the first time, if she was the hottest woman he had ever seen.

Vadislav greeted his morning appointment in his usual fashion, with a flick of his large, meaty hand. Siamko stared at his cup of tea. If there was one thing he hated, it was this God-awful English Breakfast tea. But he would never dare show his disdain, and had suffered through countless meetings sipping what he compared in his imagination to warm camel's wee.

Contrary to his thoughts on tea, Siamko's grey, dull eyes were alive. His ears wiggled with excitement and, as they had long ago been hacked off in a street fight and re-attached by a backyard surgeon, this was something of a feat. His most recent trip to Mexico City where he had, in addition to blowing Vadislav's money on broads and blow, uncovered more evidence of Vadislav's obsession: the Akashic Record.

Eighteen months earlier, Vadislav had learned, from the underground movement of whackos across the world, of the Akashic Record, a book that can tell you the time and date of death of anyone living, right down to the second. Some believed the Akashic Record was the second of three books in the set of three known as the Akashic Records; the first, a register of previous lives and the third, you guessed it, of future lives.

Many dismissed such things as a complete load of rubbish, but Vadislav was convinced the Akashic was not, and exhaustive research pointed to an ancient Mayan connection, leading Siamko, on Vadislav's behalf, to Mexico City.

Siamko leant forward in anticipation. 'This lead is like no other. The last place you'd ever have thought – but I'm sure it's correct.'

'Where is it?'

'Australia.'

Vadislav placed his cup back on its saucer. He rose to his feet and towered over his subordinate, buttoning the jacket of his customised Armani suit. 'Call me when you get there, comrade.'

0:00:02

Ross' mind drifted to his rear view mirror. He watched the dust storm his truck created on the dirt road, and wondered what other storm was coming up on his horizon, metaphorically speaking, that is. Something in the way Jimmy had asked him to come over had him worried.

The eyes, aqua-blue, had come from his mum for sure: a true copy. They were set between a healthy nose, a relaxed and great smile. His mop of blond hair, generally kept at a crew-cut, was similar to his father's well-kept mane. At 6'4", his height also came from his pop. Ross was a respectable 102 kilos, near perfect for his height. He was a keen Australian Rules football fan, and had played for the local competition most of his life. His job, flying helicopters, was what his Dad did for the same company he worked for, and ensured he kept in good shape.

Ross generally found romance around every corner, if he was looking. His robust, country-boy looks, coupled with a friendly, easy-going nature, was a sure-fire hit with the opposite sex. But his love of flying helicopters was an Achilles' heel for a long-term relationship. His restless nature, his need to fly choppers all over the world, came well before the thought of getting hitched.

Ross hit a pothole and the F150 pulled to the left. The 1991 Ford was one of Ross's favourite things in life. He corrected and slowed to turn on to the Lasseter Highway. A few minutes later, he made the easy turn into Giles Road. Another twenty metres or so and the gates of Merrigang were before him.

Jimmy's place.

His father's name was Bernie, but he was the spitting image of Australia's rock legend, Jimmy Barnes. Long ago, Ross had called him Barnesy and the nickname Jimmy was born.

Some five acres of desert, a mixture of native trees with a large cluster of them surrounding the small house, Merrigang was named after the Aboriginal word for the dingo. As he came through the gates, his Dad's kelpies, Curly and Razor, raced from the shed. They knew the familiar F150 well, and loved their owner's son.

Ross opened the ute door and patted the dogs who were jumping over each other to get at him. He had to push them away to get his feet on the ground. He nodded to his old man, standing on the top step of the veranda that flanked two-thirds of his house, front and sides.

'Jimmy.'

'Roscoe.'

'How are you Pop, all right?'

Jimmy nodded over at the F150. 'Time for that leap-year wash, huh?'

'Sure.'

The two men stood uneasily, one at the top of the stairs, the other at the bottom. A few seconds passed. This is getting weird, Ross thought.

Jimmy took a step back and waved his son up to the veranda. 'We need to talk, son.'

'Jesus Christ,' Ross muttered under his breath. Jimmy never called him 'son' unless it was serious.

Damn serious.

14

0:00:03

Mikita watched Siamko stride off down the hall, throw open the door to the central office area of Pravicon Headquarters and disappear from view. There was nothing she liked about Siamko. She often wondered what stank more, his body odour, his cheap cologne, or his halitosis. He would stare at her, as most men did, flashing those sand-coloured, awful teeth.

Mikita believed Siamko was beast in a human suit, albeit a short one. Apart from those ugly ears, the over-large head and beady eyes too close together, his body resembled that of an ape. His arms were thicker than his legs, his shoulders too wide, his torso big but solid and always struggling to be constrained by his hideously cheap suits. The rumour around the executive office at Pravicon was that Siamko utilised a 'third sock', as if it were a cricketer's box...

The thing she hated about him most of all was simple and succinct. He was an old fashioned, sexist thug, who, she was sure, did whatever Vadislav demanded – anything.

Mikita was the antithesis of Siamko.

Beauty, personified.

Standing a mere 5'2", her curvaceous figure, sparkling green eyes, and blonde hair with an almost perfect, year-round tan, had men eating out of the palm of her petite, little, hand.

Vadislav was introduced to Mikita in Paris – at a Gala Ball held by a friend and business partner. As their conversation broke the five-minute mark, he discovered her Russian background, at the seven-minute mark; her love of Moscow, and by the ten-minute mark, Vadislav had found his new personal secretary.

Mikita stole one more glance down the hall and with no one around, pulled her compact out and, partially hidden by the neat pile of files on her desk, checked herself in its mirror. She flicked her thumb across the keypad, using her free hand to casually tidy her hair.

The little screen flickered. *Report.*

New location: Australia.

Repeat.

Mikita could not believe it either.

Australia. Report over.

She snapped the compact shut and made her way back to Vadislav's office to clear the items from morning tea. She picked up the custom-made china cups and jug, placing them on the ludicrously expensive silver platter – another Sotheby's relic, circa 1700, from the Italian Royal Family. She stole a very secret grin as she picked up the sugar bowl. This little item was actually Mikita's own, a faultless replica of the one Vadislav had purchased from some over-priced South African auction house. This one, with the world's most efficient microchip bug, was only a year old, and made on the shores of the Mediterranean Sea...

0:00:04

Ross walked up the three steps of the veranda. Against the house sat the outside couch, the place he'd spent hundreds of hours sitting with Jimmy and their collective mates. The couch had weathered storms, some in the sky; it had seen a shit-load of magnificent Territorian sunsets, lived through the dust of wirly wirlies and survived to perform its job, some near twenty years on – perfectly.

Jimmy was already in his 'spot', the armrest displaying an indentation that would match his bicep and forearm (the right hand would be holding a can of Carlton Draught, Jimmy's favourite beer for as long as Ross could remember). Unless he was away flying, no one ever dared sit there.

To the right of the brown corduroy couch was the sleekest portable fridge ever built. When your best friend owns the pub not far up the road, you're assured of one thing – a perpetual supply of beer; the esky was rarely, if ever, empty. At night it locked up as if it was a bank vault. Ross sat on his habitual side, stealing a quick glance at his father as he walked past him.

The setting sun bathed Uluru in a postcard-perfect orange hue. No matter how many times the Taylors had seen it, (probably thousands), they still loved watching the changing colours at this time of night and the sunset never failed to shut at least one of them up for a few seconds. Tonight though, the alarm bells in Ross's head were going bananas. There hadn't been *this* much silence since the day his mother died.

That had been a dreadfully hot day, the day his mother passed away, the tarmac at the airport had appeared to be melting at the corners, the smell invaded Ross's throat, stuck to his clothes. His mum had been ill for weeks. It had struck her down hard. What was harder, the quacks had no idea how to cure it. When Ross reached his old man that fateful day, he experienced Jimmy's silence going on longer than he could stand. Then his father said, 'Nineteenth day of February 2002. Three forty-four and forty seconds,' and Ross saw something he had never seen before, his father crying. He knew at that moment – his mother was gone...

Ross finished the can of beer about 10 times quicker than normal.

'Thirsty, boy?'

Ross only nodded and helped himself to another. He was very thirsty, and very nervous.

Bernie Taylor was famous for being able to tell a good yarn. After telling Ross of sleepless nights, waking up in pools of sweat, migraines more powerful than a stick of dynamite, Jimmy came to the crux of the matter, the reason he wanted to see Ross tonight.

'February eighth, 1971. We flew the Huey out of the base at Nui Dat, in the Phuoc Tuy Province. I was one of the first Ninth Squadron chopper pilots to fly a Huey, converted into a gunship. The orders were to medivac a bunch of soldiers who had taken a beating and were in all sorts of trouble.'

Jimmy sat forward and rubbed the nape of his neck and then continued:

'It took two long hours to arrive at the rendezvous point. The scene was horrifying, for Christ's sake, men blown into pieces, death in every direction, mayhem. The last remaining soldiers still in one piece – were doing the best they could to fight off the enemy. Our machine guns onboard buzzed endlessly, spraying anything below that looked like the Vietcong. Son,' Jimmy shook his head in despair, 'they were fucken everywhere. Then, out of nowhere, we we'd been hit. We were close to the ground and the chopper lurched to one side, and I mean hard. A second later, my co-pilot's head exploded; glass, bits of his brain and blood flew across the cockpit, all over me.'

Jimmy took a long swig of beer.

'I got the Huey on the ground and thought; at any second that little fucker of a sniper who took out my co-pilot would do the same to me. I heard shouts and then the last surviving men were at the chopper. Six soldiers scurried into the cabin, fuck, arms and legs flying in all directions. Suddenly, six became five. A young fella took a direct hit just below his Adam's apple, blood showering the other guys and the interior of the Huey. Shit.'

Jimmy closed his eyes and muttered, 'I still to this day remember the God-awful sound of a human skull hitting steel and cracking open like a walnut.'

The story dragged on for another thirty painstaking minutes. Ross was drifting off by the time Jimmy finally drew it to an end. 'When the chopper crashed, I was knocked out. When I came to ... there were these voices, coming from ... somewhere.' Jimmy leant forward and made eye contact with his son. 'I was told ... that day was the day I was to die. But if I agreed to a certain deal, I would be allowed to live much longer.'

Ross's beer nearly fell out of his hand. 'What the hell?'

'I thought of your pregnant mother, and of you. The choice was easy.'

Ross nodded; atrophy, possibly, setting in. He wasn't sure he knew what the fuck his father was talking about.

Jimmy leant forward. 'Son, I chose to live, to take care of you all.' He hesitated, wiping the top crease of his forehead. 'But, I knew one day, I knew this day would come.'

Ross frowned. 'What day?'

Jimmy could see the fear in Ross's eyes. 'I'm sorry, son.' There was no easy way to say what he had to say, so he just came straight out with it. 'I have a brain tumour. It's too deep for them to be able to do anything about it ...'

'No bloody way,' Ross shouted, standing up and putting his hands on his hips in protest, kicking his beer over. 'How long, how long do they say you have?'

'A month, maybe two.' Jimmy closed his eyes and swallowed hard.

Ross walked to the railing of the veranda and shook his head. 'Fuck, this is not happening,' he shouted into the desert. Eventually, he looked back at his father.

Jimmy waved him back to the couch. 'There's something else I need to tell you, Ross.' His eyes narrowed. 'Come on, sit down.'

0:00:05

Adam rolled over and gasped in horror. He was due at work in twenty-one minutes. He bounced out of his bed and in one fluid move was in the shower a few seconds later.

'You're going to be late again,' his father called from the kitchen.

'No, I'm not.' Adam flew past his old man, snatching a piece of toast from his plate as he whirled past on his way to the front door.

His words to Burnum were accurate; he made it in time. When you work at the Uluru visitor centre, ten minutes from your home at Old Yulara, it would take a disaster of biblical proportions to screw it up.

Adam's favourite movie was Crocodile Dundee, but only because he was an extra, chosen for the part due to his height and lean body. The fact that he was a good-looking man with strong cheekbones, now tipping the ruler at 6'1", subtle brown eyes and a good tight crop of black hair, had him receive even some fan mail for a couple of years after the movie was released.

He clipped on his nametag. Soon the place would be buzzing with tourists from all over the globe, getting in before the sun's heat overwhelmed them. Talking of hot ... there she was,

Erin, sitting behind the reception desk. Adam had two loves, playing Aussie Rules for the local league, and the woman casually regarding him from a few feet away behind the reception desk.

He'd always liked her, though never crossed the line. He was too afraid of Ganan, her father and his old man's best friend.

Erin had recently returned from a five-year stint working overseas and, to Adam's relief, had left her boyfriend behind. Adam dealt with the quick shot of adrenaline pulsing through his veins with a long, deep breath, quashing his caveman desires.

'Good morning, Adam.'

'It is, Erin.' Adam urgently wanted to slap the blush out of his face. 'Good morning to you, too.'

'You look a little rushed.'

He cocked his head for confidence. 'Not really, just a small problem with my alarm, and setting it properly.' He smiled.

Erin smiled back, Adam fought hard not to buckle under the heavy weight of his inhibitions. Her dark-brown eyes sat above a beautiful smile, teeth just visible between her full, luscious lips. Her muddy brown hair sat comfortably around her sleek shoulders, her face, perfectly proportioned, and her skin a light, coffee brown, with absolutely no blemishes. She was well on the way to her goal of running the visitor centre; soon she would finish her part-time courses and become the 2IC.

Adam was a mess when she wore those small, circular gold earrings, and he could smell her beautiful, alluring perfume.

'Adam,' Erin glanced around to ensure no one was in earshot. 'The fathers are off again this weekend.'

Burnum and Ganan were two of the most respected elders in the Pitjantjatjara, who share Uluru Kata Tjuta National Park with their fellow traditional owners, the Yankunytjatjara people, and the whitefellas, the *piranpas*. Proud of their heritage, prouder of their rock, the men had quietly embraced what the *piranpas* had brought to their doorstep: television, microwaves, the Eurovision Song Contest ... but one thing had never changed, as long as Adam and Erin could remember – their insatiable need to get away into the desert, regularly, like clockwork. Most trips lasted around two to three days at least, some longer.

The crux of the matter was this – no one could ever be sure where they'd go. Rumours Adam first heard when was about sixteen, had some believing they were sneaking off to Alice Springs to 'live a secret life'. At around four hundred kilometres driving distance, Adam was pretty sure that was bullshit.

However, he'd still wanted to know. At eighteen, his burning curiosity forced him to take action. One particular weekend, Burnum mentioned that they were venturing off to a place called Bobbie's Well. Adam hatched a plan to secretly go to Bobbie's Well and see if they were actually there. He even created an elaborate story of getting lost as the back-up plan, so when he walked 'in on them' – they wouldn't suspect anything.

Well, he'd made it to Bobbie's Well, but they were nowhere in sight.

When Burnum had arrived home the following day, Adam wasted no time asking his father how the weekend at Bobbie's Well was.

'Quiet and peaceful,' was the response, not one word more. He never found out where Burnum had really been. It was a complete mystery and ten years later, still was.

Erin was staring at him now, a hint of amusement in her eyes. He realised he'd been a million miles away. Wake up, Adam. He smiled nervously. 'Okay, so the fathers are away this weekend...'

23

Erin blinked those beautiful eyelashes.

'I was just thinking about having a few people around our place on Saturday night, would you like to come?'

Adam could not help but blush, it felt a deep tomato red, he wanted to speak though his lips wouldn't move, eventually, they did, 'Sure, I'll drop in, great.'

Shut up Adam, he thought. You're overdoing it!

He smiled and slipped away – a drink of water high on the agenda.

0:00:06

Achban relaxed in the outdoor chair and breathed in the perfectly blue, cloudless day. Ramat Ha Sharon resembled a ghost town this morning.

Sitting on the outskirts of Dan, north of Tel Aviv, Israel, there was no shortage of them, if required.

Ghosts, that is.

He liked it quiet. His past – littered with the haunting sounds, always loud – Bombs, Gunfire, and Death.

Quiet was good – good for the soul.

Retirement from the Israeli Army had been strange for Achban. Army life was all he had ever known, but he discovered retirement came for a reason. A life-changing reason, a reason so powerful, it must have come straight from the inbox of God.

Achban, upon retirement, was in demand in the private security sector. He earned big money with much less risk of getting his head blown off. Being a former heavyweight of the IDF, his connections ran deep, as deep as his reputation for being one of the most formidable, and reliable, hard-asses the upper echelons of the Israeli army and government had ever seen.

A call from an old friend asking Achban if he was interested in something a little left field caught his curiosity. The money was good, but it was more than the money – it was as if fate were giving him a forceful nudge and he'd known right away he had to find out more about the contract.

Achban ventured to a secret location where under heavy guard, he met with a few of Tel Aviv's wealthiest men. These men had formed a secret society, known as The Society Akashic.

The TSA formed for one purpose only. To find what many believed was nothing more than a fable, a legend.

The second book of the Akashic Records, better known in the group as the Akashic Two.

Legend had it, in certain circles, the Akashic Records held information about every living soul on the planet. Achban at first scoffed at the fable. However, the members of the TSA were adamant it existed and very much prepared to bankroll a worldwide search, for at least five years to start with. Even without Achban, they had a covert military backbone, and millions of shekels to spend. Achban joined the TSA a short time later.

A couple of years had passed, with no strong leads. Certain members of the TSA grew frustrated, though Achban held steady and asked for patience.

Not one week later, a contact at the Mossad delivered very interesting news. Another organisation was searching for the records. Certain members of the TSA were deeply concerned to say the least. For Achban, this was fantastic news. His middle name was 'Infiltration', running agents in deep cover. He was the best in the business.

Achban slipped his sunglasses down over his eyes, as he pulled the outdoor chair from the shade into the sunlight. His thinning grey hair did not protect his head from the heat, but Achban loved the sun all the same. His olive skin was dark and weathered from a lifetime in the desert. His body – apart from the receding hair – was coping well with middle age. At 5'9",

Achban was no giant, though his perfectly proportioned, muscular body had always taken good care of him when required.

His dull brown eyes were set within a relatively attractive face, a square jaw with dimples which appeared when he smiled. Achban had known decades ago, marriage and a commitment of his strength to the Army were never going to work hand-in-hand, he had been single for as long as he could remember.

Dania, Achban's second in charge at the TSA, had called an hour earlier with significant news. She'd wanted to discuss it in person, not even wanting to give him the slightest hint over the phone. Achban had prepared mint tea and waited out in the delightful morning sun. He'd just popped inside to find his hat, when he heard the familiar sound of Dania's beloved, but clapped-out Fiat, pulling up his steep driveway.

'Shalom, Achban,' Dania said, stepping out of her car.

'Shalom, Dania.' Achban ushered her down at the outdoor table. 'Mint tea?'

'Yes, thank you.' She could not contain her excitement. 'I have promising news.'

Achban sipped his iced tea. 'Tell me,' he said.

Dania sat forward. 'Our undercover agent confirms the potential location of the second book.'

'Where?'

Dania sat back in the chair and grinned. 'Hope you like long plane flights.'

Achban raised his eyebrows and smiled. 'I would fly to Jupiter if it meant I could get my hands on that book, Dania.'

Dania sat forward and sipped her tea. She looked over the brim of the cup. 'Where was your cousin's latest consulate posting?'

Achban gave her a strange look.

'Chonen? He's in Australia.'

'Well, I hope he has a spare bed for you.'

It only took Achban a few seconds to understand what Dania was implying

'Well, well, well, Australia, of all the places in the world.' He finished the contents of his cup.

'You'd better call Chonen then, tell him we are coming over for a visit.'

'It has already been arranged,' Dania winked.

0:00:07

The smell of stale beer drowned the pitifully small room. The squat, deep in the heart of Sydney's inner-west, was better suited to rats than to human beings. Its only occupant lay across a dirty mattress that sat amongst litter and dirty clothes strewn across the bare floor.

Brett rolled over. His skinny body, in desperate need of sunlight and a decent feed, greeted the cold floor with a gasp. He slowly opened his eyes, his eyeballs felt stiff and sore. His throat was drier than his bank account. He stumbled to his feet, venturing into the bathroom to wash his face. He looked in the mirror and agreed with himself; he looked like absolute shit.

An hour or so later, he left the flat and headed for the local TAB, wasting what was left of last week's unemployment benefit (which was two-fifths of nearly nothing) on the horses. Back in to his normal rhythm, losing, Brett left himself just enough cash for four schooners. This, to him, was lunch. He headed next door to the pub.

Nursing his first schooner at the bar, his bloodshot eyes toggled between the old television in the corner showing a replay of yesterday's rugby match, and the tasty, young, curvaceous barmaid, busy behind the bar. She poured beer like no other.

Paying no attention to the world which went on behind him, he felt a light tap on his shoulder. He was about to say, Who the hell are you? – when his sluggish brain registered the face. 'Well, I'll be fucked,' Brett shouted, not caring about offending anyone around him.

'G'day, mate.' The tall figure smirked, towering over him.

Stuart Moore was an old mate from the parachuting club, one of Brett's hobbies since he was old enough to drive a car. Stuart nodded to the barmaid, *beer please*. The two men had not seen each other in many years and looked each other over.

Brett, the last time Stuart had seen him, was the pin-up junkie: skinny, pale, and gaunt. He hadn't changed at all, Stuart surmised. Maybe his hair was a little thinner, a lot shorter, but still as scruffy and unkempt. Brett's eye sockets were hollow, his arms chicken-bone thin. His aqua-blue eyes were out of place, too serene, too nice, for such a shit-bag package.

Brett shot a glance up and down the man-mountain standing before him. He was a big motherfucker, Brett thought. No doubt about it. At 6' 6", he had certainly not shrunk of late, looking the picture-perfect ex-state league rugby player he'd been for the last five years. Stuart's Torres Strait Island ancestry was never more prominent than today. His dark eyes spoke of a man who could take care of himself in almost any situation, though his overall demeanour was most of the time soft, friendly, and approachable.

'Still jumping?' Stuart asked, handing a ten dollar note over to the barmaid before taking a long sip of his beer.

Brett shook his head. 'Not since the last time I was bloody arrested.'

Stuart laughed. 'Shit, that's right, I saw you on TV when it went down. You have either got big kahunas or no brains. The North Sydney Harbour apartment block, man that is what, only fifteen storeys high!'

'Correct-o-fucking-moondo my friend, the toast of the BASE jumpers of Sydney for a week.' Brett revelled in his own infamy. He straightened his bony back,

'I enjoyed being arrested and locked up for a day – not.' He let out an overcooked sarcastic laugh, the barmaid nearby wishing it were legal to shoot dickhead customers.

'Tool of the day,' she muttered.

'And what about you, ya big bastard, any jumps lately yourself?' Brett added.

Stuart shook his head. 'Too busy, would love to though – I bloody miss it.' He took a bigger swig of his beer this time and rested it back on the bar. 'What about you Brett, you working at the moment?'

Brett, halfway through another gulp of his near empty schooner, shook his head. 'Na, can't fucken find anything I like.' Stuart responded with a nod and a thought then came to him.

'Hey ... I have a lot of work on right now. Do you want a job?'

Brett looked at the television for a second. 'Are you still landscaping, that's what you do right?'

Stuart nodded. 'Flat stick, brother. We've expanded the business, now doing a lot of work in Canberra. I am up there most weeks – Monday to Friday – come home Friday night. Big money, brother ... you interested or what? I need a labourer, one just walked out on me on Friday.'

Brett's eyes lit up. He nodded for another two beers, Stuart deserved a beer on him.

Stuart took the second schooner and chinked it against Brett's. 'We've got contracts with many of the embassies up there; we start work on the grounds of the Israeli Embassy next week.'

Brett inverted his smile raising his eyebrows to complete the surprised look his scrawny face was looking for. 'Wow, well

I got nothing goin' on here, when do I start?'

Stuart was pleased he had filled a hole in his team; labourers were bloody hard to keep hold of these days. 'Mate I will pick you up in the morning.'

Brett was well on his way to getting half-cut by lunch.

'Can't fucken wait!' he said.

The barmaid grumbled under her breath across the bar.

0:00:08

Driving to Achban's house, Dania looked forward to the adventure of travelling to a place she had only seen online. The mission was twofold: gather hands-on information about the history and geographic footprint of the local Aboriginal people whilst covertly watching the Russian's every move. If Siamko got close, this was fine with Achban. The Israelis would bide their time and at the right moment – take the Akashic Record from the Russians.

For these two highly decorated ex-soldiers, the mission was challenging. They had never set foot in Australia, and knew nothing on the local culture and what to expect.

Dania reflected for a moment how she came to where she was at that very moment, on her way to Achban's, and on her way to a far off foreign land.

Years ago, Dania had wanted to start a family; the decision to retire from the armed forces was never an easy one, but the biological clock was ticking louder and louder every day. And, as a member of the *Magav*, the Israeli Border Police, she had seen her fair share of misery, death and destruction. Dania's husband, Tavas, was also a soldier in the IDF. She shivered, gripping the steering wheel just a little tighter, now thinking further back into her past, of that fateful day which changed her life in the most tragic of ways. The urge to lie down over-came her, as she recalled the army personnel at the front door, solemn looks gripping their faces.

She had seen it before – hell, she had had to give the same look at countless front doors herself many times before. 'Dania, I am sorry. Palestinian militants destroyed the M-113 Tavas and his crew were in today. No one survived,' one of them whispered to her.

The heartbreak Dania felt at losing her soul-mate fell inwards. Her body could not cope. She miscarried 72 hours later.

Dania had known Achban for years, more acquaintances than friends. When he was looking for a second in charge, and heard Dania had not worked for a long time, he made the call.

Dania savoured the task at hand. It was good to be back in action again, and now she was completely committed to their mission: to find the Akashic Record, Book two.

0:00:09

'Knock – knock,' Adam shouted from Ross's front door.

'Come – in – dickhead!'

Adam dumped the six-pack of beer and two bags of chips on the kitchen bench. 'I have feelings, you know.'

Ross grinned, cracking open two cans of beer, sliding one over to Adam with enough force for the cold ale to splash over Adam's hands.

'How many bloody times have I told you not to bother knocking, twit?'

They headed out to the backyard, where two very unfashionable '80s banana lounges – relics of a bygone era where gaudy, multicoloured designs seemed to be the fad – sat decaying by the world's poorest excuse for a fishpond, the water and fishes so long gone, Ross wondered if they'd ever been there in the first place.

The cheap plastic squealed under their collective weight. Ross had purchased the chairs from a tourist desperate to offload them, for half a dozen cans (for both) many years ago – stating his wife had demanded they had to go – and they had served the two men on nights like this ever since.

Mates for over thirty years, the boys had known each other since childhood, since Jimmy's family had moved to Old Yulara.

Bernie Taylor had become close friends with Adam's father, and the two sons followed suit. Even though Ross had travelled the world for nearly a decade, only returning to Old Yulara permanently a few years ago, their friendship had remained strong. They sat in silence for a moment, taking in the view. Ross's backyard, you could say, stretched all the way to Lake Amadeus, thirty-five kilometres away.

The boom from the twin engine of the Qantas Boeing 737, which had just taken off from Connellan Airport and was climbing into fading light, roused the men from the few moments of silence.

Adam looked over to Ross. 'You told your brother, yet?'

Ross's expression went dark. 'Nope. I haven't spoken to that asshole in years,' his lips snarling, 'fuck him.'

Adam wondered if he should have asked.

Ross saw the withdrawing look in his mate's eyes and returned to his controlled self.

'Sorry bud, he is just a prick, and I wouldn't know how to tell him. It's been that long; I have no idea if he's alive or dead.' Ross took a welcome swig from his can. He nodded to Adam. 'How'd your old man take the news?'

'Pretty upset, but he still went away this weekend.' He met Ross's gaze. 'I thought they would have wanted to spend it with Jimmy, all of them.'

Ross shrugged, staring at the ground between him and Adam as if it would give him some answers. 'Well, you know the Elders; they need their desert-fix.'

Burnum was revered as the 'main-man', the undisputed leader of the Anangu, though it was never made official that's how everyone treated him. Ganan was the next one, as widely respected as Burnum, and Derain rounded off the trio. Derain, a little younger than the other two, had only been an official Elder for just under a decade, basically, he was still doing his apprenticeship. Ganan and Jimmy were friends as well, though not nearly as close as Jimmy and Burnum were.

Considering the news of Jimmy's demise was still fresh in their minds, the decision to still piss off into the desert looked strange to many.

The weekends away were a topic Adam could bang on about for hours. He just did not get it. At least now they were talking about something other than Jimmy, and Adam thought this would be better. 'Two times recently they said they were going to a specific place, and like before—' Adam reflected on the matter for a second. Risking castration, he some time ago, sneaked up to the location and realised the old men, once again, like the other time he had checked on them – were not there.

Ross sat up, no mean feat on the clapped-out banana lounge. 'Did they say where they were going this weekend?'

Adam shovelled the last of the potato chips in his gob, spraying bits at Ross as he spoke. 'Britten Jones Creek.'

Ross frowned. 'Christ, that's over a hundred kilometres away.'

Adam wiped the side of his mouth before taking another gulp of beer. 'That's right chump. Hope they make it – they took Ganan's bloody old truck. It's running pretty rough these days.'

Adam caught a glimpse of his watch. 'Erin's invited us, if you're up for it, over to her house for a barbeque – just a small group of friends.' The animation in his eyes, the nervous clench of his jaw – Ross could tell – the boy was whipped! Adam had recently made no secret of his heart flutters for Erin.

'You right, mate?'

Adam jumped, startled. 'Yeah, just a little nervous, you know.'

Ross laughed. 'For God's sake, let's put you out of your misery.'

Ross pulled the truck out onto the dirt-track just out the front of his house and turned to his love-struck friend. 'I just have to stop in at Jimmy's.' He looked Adam up and down.

Adam was breathing tightly, his hands tapping the dashboard. 'O-okay,' was all he could manage.

Ross snorted, 'hold yourself together man, you're embarrassing!'

Adam shook his head, nodding profusely. Finally, he squeezed a smile out of his face as if he were shitting a watermelon.

For the first time in a week, Ross roared with laughter.

The ghost gums surrounding Jimmy's house gave Merrigang, at night, that disturbed, uneasy feel, especially when there was a bit of a gale blowing across her. The place seemed to ooze – haunted – the feeling when the hairs on the back of your neck prickle – for no apparent reason at all.

Ross drove into the property, turning the engine off as soon as he pulled up. He quietly entered the house. Jimmy was sound asleep – even from the front door he could hear his old man's snoring. It sounded like the Ghan Train powering through the desert on its way from Adelaide to Darwin. He checked on him anyway, before making sure all the doors and windows were secure. He closed the front door carefully and double-checked he had locked it. He got back to the truck and jumped in.

'How is he?' Adam asked.

Ross smirked. 'Fast asleep, the Ghan Mark II.' He was about to start the car when nature called. 'Damn,' he whispered, opening the door and hopping out.

'What is it?' Adam whispered back.

'Need to take a whiz, back in a minute.' Ross jogged off. It would be far easier to take a slash behind the shed than go back inside Jimmy's place. Finishing the task, he pulled his zipper up; glancing around to ensure the hairs standing on the back of his neck was the cold breeze, not his sixth sense... 'What the fuck?'

Ganan's four-wheel drive, with a tarp draped over it, sat hidden behind Jimmy's shed.

0:00:10

The infinite darkness injected the men's veins with a dull, eerie sting. The air was cool and crisp, permeated with a hint of must. Not a trace of wind, the air still and calm, carrying with it no sound; the outside world snuffed out.

Ganan's floodlight bathed the path ahead in a soft, pale yellow. On this current setting, it would last around 10 hours, enough time to get to and from their current destination safely. The second setting though, ate the power as if it was a child in a candy store – the second setting 10 million candle power – enough to light up half of Old Yulara.

Before the invention of the modern torch, the elders who walked these same paths, used fire to light the way. The key was to take enough accelerant to last the trip, which was obviously quite hazardous, although not nearly as hazardous as being stuck there without any light at all.

The Elders remembered the haunting stories, part of their training when you became one of the chosen three, of times when the light had run out to earlier Elders.

The nightmarish stories laid down three basic, but very important rules.

Rule number one – Take enough light for the whole trip, always.

Rule number two – Stay on the 'path.'

Rule number three – Stay. On. The. Path.

They recounted the story about the elder who, around a hundred years ago, decided to do what no other had done before, or had done since. Not only did he go off the path, but he went it alone. His curiosity to explore the unknown (and lack of respect to those who had taught him) cost him a slow, agonising and painful death, and trauma to the other members of his party.

With only a limited supply of crude kerosene, and with a poor sense of direction, the irresponsible man soon become helplessly lost. In the end, he could only pray the others would find him before it was too late. His screams grew louder, scarier, and more desperate. Eventually they became a high-pitched shrill, the darkness telling him of his impending fate.

A slow death.

The problem was – the two men knew – if they spent too long searching for him, they too would run out of light and meet the same fate as he eventually did. Your last few hours of life totally blind in the infinite darkness, your only friend your own voice.

The men sat around a small fire, the silence – palpable. Ganan, who rarely showed his true feelings, struggled to keep a lid on his growing frustration. Derain was sometimes a whinger, he banged on about little things a little too often for Ganan's liking. When you reached the pinnacle of the top three elders of the Anangu, this was a position which came with power, influence, and foremost, respect. It was not a place to reach – to spend the latter half of your life moaning as if a child. However, Derain was different, that was for sure, Ganan thought looking over to him.

Derain had brought up the issue of the truck; the decision not to go back for the shed keys was a sore point for him. There was something in the wind tonight, something telling him this decision would be the precursor to events ahead which spelt trouble.

Burnum sighed, shifting in his seat. Ganan knew there was something else on Burnum's mind, more than the moans of the third elder – who should have known better. He spoke quietly. 'Something troubles you.'

Burnum looked into the darkness through the shimmering haze of heat coming from above the flames of the small fire. 'Jimmy's not in the book,' he said.

0:00:11

Ross and Adam arrived at Erin's house. The get-together was in full swing, the stereo thumping with the bass turned all the way up, the hypnotic smell of a barbeque working overtime to feed the hungry mob, people talking, laughter. Adam walked through the gate, Rosco a few steps behind, to the cheers of the small crowd.

Erin turned to see who had commanded such an entrance.

Adam almost pulled a muscle in his neck; stopping dead in his tracks, he could not recall a more beautiful sight. Ross nearly knocked him clean over.

'Well, hello boys.' Erin gave them both a light kiss on the cheek, her soft lips just lightly touching their skin. Both men's faces turned a light shade of salmon, Adam more so than Ross.

'Looks like things are going well h-here,' Adam mumbled, his nerves getting the better of him.

'Where have you been?' She smirked, meeting his eyes. 'You're late.'

Ross put his hand up, as if asking permission to speak. 'My fault, Erin, we had to check on Jimmy before we got here, sorry.'

'Hey, it's fine, Ross.' Erin put her hand lightly on his shoulder. 'Is he okay?'

Ross just nodded, unable to speak.

Adam, fully recovered from his little spasm, knew it was time to jump in and lift the mood. 'Time for a beer, bro?' He flung his six-pack of beer in the icebox and without turning, threw one over his shoulder, shouting, 'Incoming.'

Ross flung his left hand up and caught the beer. After many years of practice, the boys had mastered this little act, a boyish habit they seemed not likely to break anytime soon.

Erin headed back to the barbeque. 'Ross, I'll catch up with you...'

'Before you go,' he interjected, 'Can I just ask where the elders have gone to this weekend?'

'They said they went to—' thinking for a second, the light in her eyes suddenly bright, 'Britten Jones Creek, yes, that's where.'

Ross tilted his head. 'Cool, good to see they still enjoy it. I guess Ganan took the truck?'

Erin's face showed no effort to cover anything up. 'Yes, of course he did.' Someone waved her over to the barbeque and she headed off. 'Britten Jones Creek is too far to walk.'

Ross and Adam did the rounds, catching up with many friends. Later, they sat on a bench, bellies full of the delicious late dinner, a couple of beers having washed it all down. The night sky was crystal-clear, the temperature dropping as the time ticked on. Both admired the endless blanket of bright stars, the view mesmerising. The odd orbiting satellite meandered across the rich sky; in these parts, you saw them often.

'Are you okay?' Adam asked Ross, seeing his stare up into the atmosphere dragging on just that little too long.

Ross sat up. 'I'm okay, just daydreaming.' He could not stop his mind wandering back to that bloody truck sitting behind that damn shed. Where were those old fellas?

Erin walked up to the bench through the dwindling crowd, squeezing her way between them and getting cosy. 'So guys ...

46

are we in for a big night?' she asked.

The boys looked at each other with contrasting expressions.

Ross went first. 'Not for me, need to see Jimmy first thing in the morning.'

Erin swung around and looked at Adam, her eyes sparkling in the evening light.

He hesitated, more from being nervous than anything else. Erin looked more beautiful than ever. 'Er, I might stick around for a while, I think.'

Her face lit up.

The Uluru visitor centre Staff Mutual Admiration Society meeting was, Ross rolled his eyes, back in session. He could not pick a better time to leave these two admirers alone. 'I'm out of here.' Ross stood and gave Erin a kiss on the cheek. 'Thanks for a wonderful night.'

'My thoughts are with your dad,' she whispered.

Adam stood up as Ross walked in the direction of the back gate, shaking his outstretched hand. Adam pulled Ross's arm in closer. 'It's about time you pissed off,' he whispered with a killer grin.

Ten minutes later, Ross pulled the truck up onto the side of Giles road, not more than fifty metres from Merrigang. He didn't want to risk waking the old man. He pulled an old torch from the glove box and carefully closed the driver's side door, making no sound. The dark never fazed him, though tonight, something felt wrong, very wrong. 'Damn it' Ross cursed; the torch batteries, flat.

The wind rustled the ghost gums dotted around Merrigang, the large branches swaying back and forth, enough to cause anyone the jitters. Brittle, dry bark crunched under his feet as if it were deep-fried, combining with the sound of a distant, whinging hound to give Ross the creeps. He turned the corner of the shed, his breath short, and sour ... and when a small marsupial sprang from a tiny hole, nearly peed himself. Ross tasted the bitterness of adrenaline tricking down the back of his throat. 'Shit,' he whispered to himself, taking an extra breath to regain his composure.

He crept to the corner, quickly looking behind to ensure no one was there. 'You've got to be joking,' he gasped.

The truck was gone.

0:00:12

The smell of freshly brewed coffee wafted through Jimmy's house. Ross had no doubt this infectious aroma would rouse his father from his sleep, it always did.

'Good morning, Ross,' Jimmy said moments later, shuffling into the kitchen, patting Ross on the shoulder and walking straight to the coffee plunger.

'Morning Old Man.'

Jimmy poured himself a coffee, sitting down at the breakfast bar and looking out the window. He looked pale; his face had aged considerably in the last couple of weeks. Ross turned his attention to breakfast, muttering, 'Where the fuck is the Vegemite?'

Ross took the tray of toast and jug of coffee out to the veranda. Jimmy sat on his throne and smiled faintly as Ross put the tray next to him on the esky. Jimmy finished his toast and reached the bottom of his large coffee mug soon after, no words spoken. He held the empty mug out in his son's direction. Ross poured him another and said matter of factly, 'What's with Ganan's truck, then?'

Jimmy coughed heavily and dropped the near-full cup of coffee, clean out of his hands.

'Shit, Dad.'

Jimmy, reaching out and placing his left hand firmly on Ross's shoulder. 'There are secrets only known to but to a few.' Jimmy's hand gripped Ross shoulder a little firmer. 'I have very little time left here, so I feel the time has come for you to know.'

Ross had to fight the urge to laugh, but the old man seemed so serious. He waited while Jimmy shuffled off inside, returning a few minutes later with a glass of water and some pills.

Jimmy swallowed the pills and took a long drink. 'There are forces which exist around these parts that are beyond the comprehension of humanity.'

Ross had never heard this tone from Jimmy, as if the pills he had taken had turned him into someone else.

'You are not to repeat what I am about to say, ever, understood?'

Ross sat stiff, kind of shitting himself. 'Okay.'

Jimmy wiped his eyes, looking over to the shed before turning his deadly gaze back over to Ross. 'Did you tell anyone about Ganan's truck?'

Ross shook his head.

'Right, this a good start.' Jimmy was obviously relieved.

'What's going on?' Ross asked nervously.

Jimmy shrugged. 'They didn't need to use it, so they left it here.'

Ross cocked his head. 'Where is it now?'

'I moved it into the shed.'

Ross frowned. 'Why hide it in the first place?'

Jimmy sat forward. 'Son, the fellas venture to a sacred place ... and no one can know.' He sat back. 'Not even Adam.'

Jeez, it would be hard to keep quiet about Adam's favourite subject – besides Erin, and that stupid bloody movie. Ross forged ahead. 'So all this time, when the Elders go away for the weekend, they're going to the same place?'

Jimmy crossed his arms. 'That's all I can tell you – for now.'

'So where do they go, Barnesy?'

Jimmy looked coolly at Ross. 'When the time comes, which will be soon I imagine, you'll find out.'

0:00:13

'How was your flight, Comrade?' Vadislav enquired from his vast penthouse high atop Central Moscow.

'Too long and the vodka tasted like petrol,' Siamko mumbled, nursing his monumental headache.

Vadislav closed his eyes and shook his head in despair, picturing another wasted trip to a foreign land. The lack of any clear progress was annoying. 'What is your plan of attack then?'

Siamko was to meet with a couple of tour guides, ones not found in the usual pamphlets, ones who were a little 'left of centre'. They were experts in the sacred sites of Indigenous Australia.

Vadislav's roaring voice snapped him out of the moment. 'This book is important, Comrade.'

'I—'

'The Romanov is in Singapore for repairs and alterations. We'll send her along with her crew to Australia to help you.'

The Romanov was his undisputed pride and joy, aptly named after Russia's second and final imperial dynasty. At one hundred and fifty-three metres, the Blohm + Voss private yacht was the world's third largest, costing Vadislav a small fortune – 334 million American dollars. He'd then, surreptitiously, spent an extra 50 million on additions the outside world would never hear about, or see...

The 22-man crew lived on the Romanov all year round. The captain, Ivon Krutek, was one of Vadislav's most loyal and longest serving men. Every crew member had experience in either the military, or intelligence circles, hand-picked by Vadislav, each one with a different speciality. The crew enjoyed living in comfort aboard the Romanov, travelling the world and taking care of whatever business Vadislav requested.

The billionaire also had a fleet of state-of-the-art helicopters. All regional offices worldwide had their own chopper and so did the Romanov. The Romanov's helicopter was one of the sleekest, quickest, and youngest in the Pravicon fleet. The Eurocopter EC175-SSS, comfortably sat eight, with a cruising speed of 275 km/h, and a range of just over eight hundred kilometres. It, too, had modifications which were hidden from view.

Siamko hoped he hadn't missed anything. The phone, stuck to his sweaty ear, was dead.

0:00:14

Jimmy lay on his bed, motionless, save for his tired eyes scanning the faces of his friends. He had deteriorated quickly. Sweat trickled from the crease lines on his forehead. He was dog-tired and so desperate for an extended sleep; he had considered asking someone to knock him out.

Burnum stood beside the bed. At three inches over six-feet, Burnum towered over his sick friend. Burnum dripped confidence, strength, and above all, supercooled-calmness. With strong shoulders, muscled, and often on display due to his love of shirts with the arms cut off, he was a formidable leader. His wiry silver hair, remarkably full for a man of his vintage, sneaked from the sides of his trademark Akubra, which he rarely took off his head.

Burnum leant down and waited for Jimmy's eyes to meet his. 'Tell me what to do,' he said quietly.

Jimmy took a long breath, turning up to his friend's gaze. Burnum's brown eyes bore down on Jimmy, though they were always friendly, always approachable.

'We all know one day, our time here is up,' Jimmy whispered, his tone tinged with regret.

Ganan paced the room. He was close to a full foot shorter than Burnum. He was also lighter in weight, gangly, with a weathered, narrow, rat like face.

'Why'd you leave the truck outside last night, you bloody twit?'

'I lost the key to the shed, that's all.'

Jimmy shook his head. 'Risky. Get another one cut before you go, eh? Ross saw the bloody thing.'

Ganan and Burnum shared worried looks.

'If there's one thing I can tell you...' he said. Jimmy looked at them with narrowed eyes. 'The boy can be trusted.'

Jimmy could tell there was more to their silence than this. 'What?' he barked, 'what else is on your minds?'

Burnum patted his old friend's hand but it was Ganan who spoke.

'Jimmy, you're not in the book.'

0:00:15

Achban and Dania arrived without incident at the entrance of the subtly fortified Israeli Embassy in Canberra. As the chauffeur opened the car door, Chonen and the Israeli Ambassador made their way down the steps.

'Chonen, shalom, good to see you,' Achban said, greeting his cousin with genuine enthusiasm.

'Likewise,' Chonen said, embracing Achban and kissing Dania's cheeks. He stepped back. 'Achban, our Ambassador to Australia, Salis Talman.'

Achban shook the Ambassador's hand before turning to his aide. 'Salis, my colleague and friend, Dania Radwan.'

Dania smiled as she took Salis's hand.

'Come.' Salis signalled his guests to walk the steps with him. 'We can have some tea in our courtyard at the rear of this lovely building – as you can see, we're currently undergoing some extensive landscaping of the consulate grounds.'

Achban tapped his cousin on the shoulder. 'Promise me the tea is not the same as the over-boiled petroleum they served me on the plane, Chonen,' he joked.

'So tell me,' said Salis, carefully placing his teacup on the saucer. 'To what do we owe the pleasure of two highly-decorated retired members of the IDF visiting this faraway land?'

Achban had not made it to a high rank by not keeping his cards very close to his chest. Even Salis would not be 'in the loop' – with missions like this one, loose lips – sunk ships.

'I was in need of a good holiday.'

Only Dania could have recognised the hidden sarcasm.

Achban smiled at Chonen. 'What better place than the country my cousin has been speaking so highly of since he came here?'

Dania glanced out over the grounds, impressed with the condition of them, and the plush, almost oasis feel of the compound. The grass was a luscious, British-racing-green; the garden beds a kaleidoscope of flowering plants, the large overhanging trees providing shade, and ambiance. She noted a group of workers still completing the far end of the compound, surrounded by tools, dirt and potted plants.

At the other end of the compound, the workers chipped away at the last section. They would be finished by tomorrow. Brett glanced up to the consulate building. 'Check the hottie, checking us out.'

Stuart took a quick glance up to the rear deck of the consulate, spotting Dania and agreeing she was quite the stunner. 'But I don't think it's your sex appeal they're talking about,' he said.

Chonen addressed Dania. 'So,' he smiled, 'do you intend to see the wonderful beaches, here in Australia?'

Dania pictured herself lying on a towel on one of the ubiquitous Australian beaches. 'Of course, can you recommend a good one?'

The chatter amongst the four Israelis remained light-hearted, trivial, and rather mundane, affairs of the state, blah, blah, blah... Salis rose to his feet. 'I must leave now for my next appointment. Achban, Dania, it was a pleasure to meet you.' He shook their hands. 'I wish you a safe and pleasant holiday in

Australia.'

When he had gone, Chonen took a sneak peek down the hall. There was no one in sight. 'Do you think he suspects anything?' he whispered. The three formed almost a huddle. 'Salis is a very sharp, intelligent man. I have no doubt he is wondering why you are really here.'

Achban shrugged him off. 'With the Foreign Affairs conference in Tel Aviv next week, I'm hoping he won't have time to focus on us right now.'

Achban's plan was to recruit a couple of locals who could assist in scouring the long list of Aboriginal sacred sites, while keeping their mouths shut. He had enough cash to guarantee it; though should the recruits threaten to blab, or blow their cover – he would simply blow their brains out.

Chonen smiled. 'I spoke to the guy in charge of landscaping the grounds the other day. We chatted for a little while, and when I talked about one day wanting to see some Indigenous Australian sites myself, he told me that he and one of his friends knew a fair bit about them. His friend actually grew up around one of the big ones. I think they are the sort of people we are looking for.'

'Achban, Dania...' Chonen looked down to the two workers, standing somewhat awkwardly. 'These two gentlemen have lived among Aboriginal people and know where most of the sacred sites are.' He turned to Achban confidently. 'They have agreed to assist us, and keep it most certainly – confidential.'

Achban sized them up. The taller one was far smarter than the other, but the little fellow was crafty. 'What we are asking of you is complete secrecy.'

'We can keep our mouths shut,' Stu said.

Achban took one last glance at the candidates and turned to Dania to gauge her thoughts. She seemed far from convinced, but Chonen was no fool and they had to start somewhere, time was of the essence. She gave him an accepting nod.

Achban gave the two men a final once-over. 'Very well. Go on with your work, we'll be in touch.'

'Righto,' said Stu, turning away, but Brett had a bright idea. He put out his hand.

'Any chance of a bit of advance?' he said.

0:00:16

Dusk was Ross Taylor's favourite time of day. He loved the cooling breeze, the ambience of the dimming light, the harsh dry heat diminishing to a low, manageable nuance. The way Uluru became more subtle, more majestic as the sky above turned purple and the millions of pinholes of light began to appear on the dark blanket of the sky.

He sat on the couch at Merrigang and stared out across his father's property, feeling ill at the thought one day he would be sitting here alone. Even though he'd lived away from Jimmy for many of the last ten years, he'd always remained tight with the old man. He was glad, more than ever, that he'd decided to return to Old Yulara permanently. It was good to know he always had a job to come back to, a perk of the strong friendship between Jimmy and John Kelsey, their boss.

But even dusk today could not bring him the usual hypnotic feeling. He stared over to Uluru; his mind not escaping his father's comments from a couple of weeks ago ... the secrets, the revelations. The burning light of curiosity often shone too bright in our boy Taylor; it was something he could not control. Ross was very keen to find out more.

Burnum and Adam were in with Jimmy while he was awake and mildly coherent. When the patient drifted off to sleep, they joined Ross on the veranda.

Father and son didn't worry about the need to strike up any conversation with Ross. They knew in times like these, people needed silence to reflect and get their head around the situation at hand.

After a time, Burnum quietly cleared his throat. 'You contacted that long-lost brother of yours?'

Ross answered in hushed tones, as if he wanted to make sure his father didn't hear what he was saying. 'The truth is, Burnum, I promised Dad I'd call him weeks ago.' He shook his head. 'But I just can't.' He sat back and flicked his chin at Adam and then the esky.

Adam passed Ross a can.

Ross turned to Burnum after his thirst had been well and truly quenched. 'I suppose I had better call him now...' He closed his eyes and took a deep breath. 'Now that the old man's not faring too well.'

Burnum agreed, but Ross guessed there was something else going on in that silver-haired noggin ... it was the way he was staring at him, something in his eyes. Not one to hold back, Ross said, 'Something on your mind, friend?'

Burnum ingested the slither of attitude, and stared out into the purple sky. 'You saw Ganan's truck.' He stretched out his arm, putting his weathered hand on Ross's shoulder. 'My friend, I have known you and your father a very long time. You are part of our family.' The Elder turned to Adam. 'Please, go and check on Jimmy, son.'

Adam sprang to his feet, disappearing through the front door.

Burnum leant forward and drew a long breath. 'Your father is one of the most important people around here, Ross.' He turned and looked down the hallway, making sure they were still alone.

Almost instantly, the sky darkened. A sudden gust of wind

threw the desert sand up and into Ross and Burnum's faces. Curly and Razor came running to the porch from their kennels down near the shed. Ross looked out over Merrigang and the horizon beyond, twitching, as if someone had walked over his grave. A thick pole of lightning cut the darkening horizon. 'Jesus, did you see that?' he muttered. In a matter of seconds, the sky had filled with menacing cloud.

A massive bolt of lightning crashed down, this time far closer than the other one a few seconds ago. The accompanying thunder nearly blew Ross's eardrums out of his ears.

Burnum watched the violent storm approach, his wiry silver hair swaying in the wind, his dark-brown eyes wide and frightened. 'No, they are too early,' he moaned.

'What?'

'They're coming for him...' Burnum shouted.

The flyscreen door of Merrigang burst open, the hinges almost snapping. It was Adam – panic written all over his face. 'Guys come quickly, please.'

'What's going on?' Ross shouted as the thunder grew louder, the wind hissing through the surrounding trees and into the house.

'Jimmy,' Adam screamed, dialling for the ambulance. 'He's not breathing.'

Ross rushed to his father's side and administered CPR. Jimmy's heart gave Ross the faintest of beats after seconds of feverish work. Burnum and Adam paced the room, neither possessing the ability to stay still for one second.

Jimmy opened his eyes, just. He made a strange sound from deep within his throat, snapping Ross from his focus on how close the wailing sirens were getting. Jimmy opened his mouth, at the same time making a hand signal; he wanted is son to come closer. Ross bent down and held his old man's hand.

'My time here is nearly over,' Jimmy managed.

The distant sound of the ambulance siren drew closer.

'Burnum,' Jimmy groaned, looking up and around the room, his hoarse voice struggling to hold a note.

'I am here, Bernie.'

The sirens were almost upon them.

'Take him,' Jimmy moaned, his gaze wild.

Burnum was taken aback by his friend's dying wish. He leant forward as the ambulance screeched into Merrigang. 'I don't know if this is a good idea my friend.'

In a last ditch effort, Jimmy caught a handful of Burnum's shirt and pulled the Elder closer. He took a painful gulp of air, opening his eyes and looking directly into Burnum's. 'It is my last wish ... I ...want him to see it ... see why...'

Jimmy's face, along with the rest of the room, turned a flashing red and blue. The ambulance was upon them. Burnum looked back down to Jimmy, the intent in Jimmy's eyes never stronger. He closed his eyes and took a deep breath, reaching out and holding Jimmy's cold hand. 'If this is your wish, I will see it done.'

Ross heard the ambulance doors fling open, followed by the heavy footsteps of the paramedics coming up the stairs.

Burnum looked over to Ross. 'You're coming with us, to ... Uluru.'

Ross had no idea where the elder was talking about. 'Where?'

The paramedics burst through the bedroom door.

Dania worked around the clock to map out the 'top two hundred' Aboriginal sacred sites across Australia. The sites were,
so it seemed to them, indiscriminately littered across the conti-
nent; from as far west as Broome, Western Australia where the
desert meets the Indian Ocean, to Port Arthur, on the southern tip of Tasmania, where the land bites at Antarctica; from
the far north of Queensland where the planet's oldest rainfor-
est continued to grow uninhibited; to sites dotted all the way
from Adelaide in South Australia, across and further south to
Lake's Entrance in southern Victoria. The Northern Territory
appeared to have a concentration of sites. Only towards the
end of the laborious task did reality sting Achban like a fine
paper cut to the tip of your tongue. They may have to go to all
of them...

'At least places like this "Oola-roo" have an airstrip close
by, Achban,' Dania said, relieved.

'Thank God for that,' Achban shouted from the kitchen,
busy preparing their lunch.

* * *

The boys could not believe what had gone down. Out of nowhere, this dipstick asks if it's true they knew about Aboriginal

culture ... they'd been bragging they knew a bit, but truth was, it was not a lot ... but old Chonen, who looked like a poof to Brett (though every man did, unless he smashed a slab every weekend) seems convinced at their stretch of the truth, and offers them fifty grand each to help them find—

'What the fuck's it called, again?' he said.

Stuart could not remember the name, but he could hear the 'ching-ching' of the cash coming their way, and a bonus if they leave Australia with it safely.

Brett was inadvertently showing Stuart how never to eat a pie. Stuart was a tough son-of-a-bitch, growing up in Redfern in Sydney's west, he had seen it all – but this? He looked away and shook his head. 'They obviously did not have etiquette classes on eating in the joint.'

Brett wiped pie off the side of his face and took a ridiculously large swig from his bottle of soft drink. His Adam's apple worked hard to take it all down.

Seconds later, Brett burped louder than Stuart had ever heard anyone do before. He swore he heard it echo off the nearest building close to a hundred metres away. 'Bloody Hell, Taylor, you are such a pig,' he shouted.

'I know, just the way they like it,' Brett said, laughing ... proud as punch. Being a tool, the easiest things get you off.

'You're all class, Taylor.' Stuart checked his watch. 'Come on, back to it. We're almost done and then it's time to take a little paid "holiday".'

Brett's retort was cut short by the lamest ringtone Stu had ever heard ... some hip-hop tune you'd beg the radio station never to play ever again.

'Hell-o?'

There was silence for a few seconds.

'Hello?' Brett was about to look at the number on his screen to see who to abuse, and then—

'Brett?'

'Who the hell is this?

'Brett...' This time the voice was clearer and substantially louder.

'Ross?' Brett's tongue went into a momentary spasm.

'Yes.'

Ross found it hard to speak. He was not scared of Brett, far from it; he just hated the prick's guts. Calling him was the last thing on earth he ever wanted to do. He cast his mind back to the day of his mother's funeral, the last time the proverbial shit – had hit the fan, and hard.

The wake was typically Australian: lots of mourners, beer, wine, and soft drink (plus those God-awful egg-and-lettuce sandwiches cut into triangles). Merrigang packed to the brim; Jimmy had to open his big shed to give the smokers somewhere to get their fix, out of the rain. The weather was awful, the storm had not wavered for hours, the rain coming down in sheets, a constant thud of thunder, the dark, windy sky dotted with lashes of lightning. Ross sat on the porch, watching it all with Adam. They'd slipped out to avoid the constant and overbearing condolences.

Brett, recently released from another spell in jail, actually appeared human for a change. His skin a normal dark pinkish colour rather than looking like a piece of blank A4 paper. His near anorexic body had finally put on some welcome kilograms, the bones looking less prominent and pronounced as they had always done before.

Jimmy had asked Ross to keep an eye on him; he knew Brett had a tendency to over-drink, and when he did, it spelt trouble.

But trouble was already on the way.

The first thing Ross and Adam heard was the shouting. When a fight erupts, the shouting is distinctive. The men surrounding those punching on revert to their ancestors the cavemen and turn into idiots who think they are at the boxing, the need to egg on the two men fighting, an apparent necessity. Ross was in no mood for this shit tonight, not on his watch. When he burst through the door, his heart sank. Brett was on the floor – knocked out cold.

Archie, their cousin up from Adelaide, pointed with his chin. 'Your asshole brother is a fucking loser!'

A few metres away: another horizontal pair of shoes. 'What the hell happened?' Ross shouted over the ruckus.

One of the locals fronted Ross. 'Brett lunged at Cobar with a syringe, and stuck it in his neck. Archie punched Brett a second later and by the looks of it – knocked the little prick out.'

The story went rather simply; Brett was being a smartass. Cobar told him to respect his deceased mother's memory and to go to bed. Brett found Cobar's words offensive. He would have 'no blackfella speak to him as if he were a second-rate citizen...' and so the story went on.

Ross heard in much detail later ... in court ... how, without warning, Brett had lunged at Cobar with a full to the brim syringe of high-grade heroin. The needle went straight into the side of Cobar's neck and Brett had nearly squeezed the needle all the way to the end. As Cobar shrieked and went heading for the deck, Archie, witnessing the mayhem from the side gave Brett a classic 'haymaker', decking him so hard, Brett's feet momentarily lifted off the ground.

He was out before he hit the floor.

Both men had been taken to the Resort Medical Centre. If the ambulances had taken a minute longer, Cobar would be dead.

Brett had woken wondering why he was handcuffed to the bed, not even knowing where he was. But he certainly knew where he was about seventy-two hours later, back in the same cell at Long Bay he had shared with Bubba for the previous four years. You could say his little stunt at his mother's wake had totally fucked up his parole.

Cobar woke from his induced coma around the same time Bubba had welcomed Brett home. The entire town of Old Yulara breathed a collective sigh of relief.

But not the local undertakers, who'd arrived from Alice Springs to pick up the body of Janet Taylor. They had more pressing matters to mess with their heads on that day.

The body of the late Janet Taylor had grown wings – vanishing – into thin air.

0:00:18

The shrilling sound cracked Siamko out of his self-induced alcoholic coma, at who knows what time. He rolled over and fumbled with the handset before wobbling it to his ear. 'Hello?'

'Hold for Vadislav.' Mikita, her tone clipped and razor sharp.

'Fffff-u-c-kkk,' Siamko hissed under his breath.

'Siamko?'

There he was: God on the line from Moscow. 'I am here Ffladisav.' Hell, Siamko, you are in deep shit now.

'I see your behaviour when travelling afar has deteriorated, comrade.'

'Vadislav I can exp—'

'That's enough.' Vadislav was good at cutting people off, especially his employees. 'Stop drinking my time away, and get me the damn records.'

'Vadislav, I have been—'

'Bullshit, Siamko. Call me back when you have sobered up, or you might just find yourself—'

The line went dead.

'That bloody fool,' Vadislav shouted, slamming his fist on the desk. He stormed out of his office.

Mikita watched Vadislav trounce down the empty corridor and disappear. As soon as the door slammed shut, she picked up her device, dialling the number succinctly, without even looking at the keypad, her eyes on the door.

ST in Sydney, drunk, and nowhere near finding the book.

Dania looked out across the Australian landscape and smiled, sliding her Mossad-issued Blackberry back into her hip pocket.

0:00:19

'Brett, I … I have some bad news about Dad.'

'Who? Listen man, I don't have a fucken dad. Who ya talken 'bout dude?' Brett's scowled. 'Oh, you must be talken 'bout *your* old man, right?'

Ross wished he could put his arm through the line, grab Brett by the throat and squeeze it very, very hard. 'Fuckstick – listen to me…' Ross hissed, his anger rising. 'Dad's on his deathbed, Brett. He has asked to see you; he wants to bury the hatchet before he dies.'

For the first time in a long time, someone had squeezed through the cracks of Brett's fortress-of-assholeness. He nodded to Stuart. 'I'll just be a sec, meet you back there.' He turned and sat back down on the bench and took a deep breath.

Ross could hear him breathing. He wanted to wait a little while longer, hoping the news would sink in and find the Brett, pre-drugs; almost a lifetime ago.

Brett's conscience flickered. If it were not for his old man, he'd still be in Long Bay. His father had convinced Cobar's family to settle for Brett pleading guilty to a serious assault charge, not attempted murder as originally planned. He'd ended up only spending thirty-six months in jail, though upon release made no attempt to contact Jimmy or Ross … he just couldn't.

What would be worse Brett thought: crawling over a mile of broken glass naked, or, fronting up to Old Yulara? Country folk, especially up there, were like elephants; they never, ever forgot.

'Shit,' Brett whispered, his mind imploding with contradictory thoughts. 'I'll call you after work tonight; see if I can get up as soon as possible.' Brett pulled the sweaty phone off his ear and stared at the screen. He hung up.

He arrived back at the work site a little paler than the pasty white he already was. The call had spooked him. Memories of the carnage of a few years ago, the death of his mother, the fight, the court case, the bashing he received when he arrived back in Long Bay Jail – it all came back, and fast.

Stuart grabbed him by the shoulder. 'You okay ... Champ?'

Brett took another couple of seconds, as if he were in a trance. He blinked hard, shaking his head. He looked up to Stuart. 'Yeah, I'm okay, just got some news 'bout the old man, that's all.' He went on to tell Stuart about the call from his brother, the one he hadn't spoken to in over three years, about his old man with only days to live and how he did not want to go back to Old Yulara but felt that he had to ... a part of him wanted to go to spit in his brother's arrogant face.

They went back to work. Brett had swung his shovel a couple of times when a thought struck him. He grabbed Stuart by the arm. 'Come here, I have an idea,' he whispered, a fat grin on his face. 'Mate, come with me to visit the old man. While we're there, we can suss out the area for the Israelis, check out what was going on with the blackfellas and see if we can find out anything which may lead them to this bullshit artefact they're looking for.'

Stuart thought the idea through. The next job wasn't scheduled to start for another ten days ... this may work, hell yes. 'Ripper idea, brother,' he said.

Later that afternoon, Stuart called the Israelis. If they were going to earn the ridiculous amount of money these strangers had offered, they would have to appear to be working for it. He told Achban they needed some travel money as they were off to check out things at Uluru. The Israelis already knew of the place, the best-known Aboriginal site the world over.

'Yes, a good start,' Achban agreed. And he and Dania would travel to Uluru with them and see what the big deal was all about.

Brett, for some reason, was not as excited as Stuart was with the news of the Israelis tagging along.

0:00:20

Abelia Cohen was one of the brightest undercover agents Israeli intelligence had ever bred. A true professional, fiercely loyal, ruthless, and cold-blooded – at the flick of a switch. All of this tucked neatly into a package better suited to the front cover of a women's magazine or a Paris catwalk.

Abelia's focus finally showed signs of faltering in the summer of 1997. Two fellow Mossad agents, close friends of hers, were caught and detained in Jordan for the attempted assassination of the Hamas leader. The incident caused a political tsunami, both men literally on the brink of the firing squad many, many times.

Fortunately, they were eventually released.

However, for Abelia, it struck a nerve. She felt it was time to take a step back from the high octane danger which had been part of her life for a long time.

The world is indeed a small place, they say.

One sunny Sunday afternoon, at a three-year-old's birthday party, the son of a friend from the ISS, Abelia was lightly bumped from behind. She had been trying to eat a piece of birthday cake on a flimsy paper plate ... hard while standing up. She knew it was an honest accident, though as human instinct commands, you must have a quick look to see who the person was.

Achban Honi.

Though she had never officially met him, she knew who he was. There was hardly anyone in the IDF, or Intelligence, who did not know of Achban Honi.

He knew who Abelia Cohen was too. Achban had served alongside her Uncle Eli in the '60s.

They talked for quite a while that afternoon. It took another two meetings before Achban convinced her to come over to the TSA. He had cut a deal with the hierarchy of the Mossad; if she didn't like the change of pace, she could always go back. The next day the deal was done – Abelia Cohen was now on secondment, to the TSA ... indefinitely.

Achban had discovered through a couple of other active Mossad agents, Pravicon Industries was under investigation for some bizarre activities in Africa and the Middle East. The Mossad realised early, terrorism was not on the Pravicon agenda. They grew curious as to why Pravicon employees were attending ancient rituals, getting involved in black magic ceremonies and, allegedly, using human sacrifices. After some prodding around in Moscow, Achban (utilising the ancient art of the small brown, flat, paper bag full of rubles), learned that Vadislav Pravica was personally overseeing these activities; as well as searching the world, for an ancient, mythical book...

The Akashic Record.

Achban knew what to do from here. The TSA would devise a plan to get someone into the inner sanctum of the Pravicon Empire and see what was going on.

* * *

Vadislav shouted Mikita into his office, forsaking the inter-office phone system. Mikita dipped her head around the office door, steeling herself to meet Vadislav's cold aniridian eyes. He nodded for her to enter.

78

Vadislav let out a long, drawn-out breath, not looking up from his notes once.

'Is there something you need to tell me Mikita?' Only after 10 seconds of ear-splitting silence did he look up and meet her green eyes

Vadislav stared at her. It was as if he was in a deep trance. Shit, he may have had heart a attack and was dead. 'Vadislav?' Mikita had a sting of concern. 'What is it?'

Vadislav slowly, methodically, leant forward, not for a second taking his black eyes away from hers. 'Mikita,' he said, almost whispering for effect. 'Do *you* have something ... to tell *me*?'

Mikita's years of training kicked in. She had learnt the art of suppressing any visible sign of compromising her cover. She took charge, staring back at him, her tone a little arrogant. 'What,' she took a long, deep breath, as if she was getting annoyed, 'are you talking about, *Vadislav*?'

The man-mountain behind the desk seemed to be growing impatient. This was getting a little awkward.

Mikita held her glance and position perfectly, though deep, deep down, she was starting to wonder ... what if...

He sat back in his chair, ensuring it reclined all the way ... not taking his eyes off her for a second.

Suddenly, he flipped the chair forward (for maximum effect: what a show pony) returning to the upright position. 'Well,' he said, reaching down into his desk drawer and reached in...

Mikita gasped ever so lightly, the first time in a long time.

Vadislav quickly pulled out ... the large ... white envelope.

'You are very thoughtful, Mikita...' Vadislav's face brightened, a smile erupting. 'Valya always seemed to forget my birthday ...'

Holy guacamole. Holy fucking guacamole.

'I have never seen so many names and signatures on a single birthday card, either,' Vadislav gushed.

Mikita remained composed, smiling ... though inside her head she was nearly collapsing with relief.

'You have been good to me Mikita,' Vadislav grinned. 'And very hard working.'

'Thank you, Vadislav.' Mikita's eyes glowed.

Vadislav pushed his chair back and stood up. 'Well, I would like to reward you.' He walked around to the front of his desk and rested against it. 'And send you on a little break, sort of "work holiday?"'

'Great.' Mikita flushed. 'The Greek Isles would be nice.'

Vadislav broke into loud, unabashed laughter, nodding at Mikita before looking out his office window. Something clearly had amused him, not that Mikita had any idea.

'That does sound like a lovely destination, Mikita,' Vadislav said before adding, 'Maybe next time.'

'Where are you sending me?'

He looked down to her and grinned.

'I want you to go to Australia and pull Siamko back in line.' Before Mikita could react his tone went more serious.. 'I will also brief you on another mission ... when you get there.'

0:00:21

Jimmy had been rushed to the Uluru Medical Centre, his condition now stable, his heart weak though still beating. The decision was to keep him admitted for round-the-clock observation for at least a week.

Burnum and Adam returned to a familiar place, the front porch of Merrigang, where they found Ross sitting where he was often – on his old man's couch. Clouds drifted across the evening sky, the balmy wind flowed through the ghost-gums and across the knee-high grass, and then into the homestead, continuing its course through the open front door. Adam made some coffee, joining his father and Ross with three mugs. Ross thanked him for the coffee. Ross could not stop staring at Uluru.

Burnum narrowed his serious eyes. 'It's time to discuss what I know you both want to talk about.'

The boys shared a glance, part curious, part amused.

Burnum closed his eyes and inhaled an extended breath. 'For thousands of years, we have called this place home.'

He stood still and seemed to gather his thoughts.

'For thousands of years, we have been guarding a secret. Since the whitefellas came, it has been the rule; only a few men know at any time.' He ran his hand through his silvery hair. When it was something important to talk about, Burnum could take all day. 'It is safe to say the gatekeepers have made sure it remains this way. We know how sacred Uluru is to the Anangu. But what the world does not know, what even the greater part of the Anangu don't know—' Burnum wiped his eyes with his bandana. 'Is, Uluru is sacred for another reason, a secret reason.'

Without letting Ross say a word (and he was aching to ask about a thousand questions), Burnum told the boys how everything changed when the first white man came. He talked of the struggle to keep them out of the sites, the sacred ones – they climbed all over the rock as if they were ants...

A smile crept across his face when he spoke of Jimmy; along with other whitefella locals he had helped the Anangu to change the view of the authorities and the tourist operators. Eventually, the sacred sites were fenced 'off-limits' and the wishes of the spirits finally respected.

'Do you want me to show you why Uluru is so sacred?

Adam stepped up to the plate. 'I'm ready, Dad. But show us where? What are you talking about?'

Burnum placed a hand on his son's shoulder. 'To the *Seventh.*' He smiled at Ross. 'As Jimmy often called it.'

Adam was still a little confused. 'The Seventh? The Seventh what?'

Ross nudged Adam with his elbow. 'The Seventh sacred site, you nim-wit.'

* * *

'Vadislav, I implore you, this is not necessary.' Siamko breathed heavily into the phone. Mikita, listening on the sugar-bowl bug, was relieved the bug did not pick up the stench of his breath.

'How long did you think I was going to sit by and watch you waste my time, and not to mention – your travel allowance?'

82

Vadislav cared little about the money. Hell, he would struggle to spend his fortune in his lifetime, but Siamko spent it fruitlessly, and what's more – making no clear progress on the mission. And prostitutes could have big mouths for one thing. 'Mikita leaves for Sydney tonight.'

Siamko looked out the window and wished he were somewhere else. He fancied Mikita, who wouldn't? But he really didn't want Vadislav's little eye candy looking over his shoulder.

0:00:22

Burnum had hardly slept. He'd never taken anyone to the place, other than the chosen ones.

The boys put together a quick, early morning breakfast, eating in silence in order to get on the road sooner. As they left Merrigang, Ross noted the darkness. It was still a few good hours before dawn. Apparently it was forbidden to go where they were about to go, in daylight, and that was about the only thing Burnum would tell them.

Their first destination was the rear lot of the Uluru visitor centre; here, cars and four-wheel drives would sometimes stay idle for weeks at a time, hardly anyone ventured out there. Suffice to say, Adam's car would be safe there, incognito. With the car securely locked and Adam's backpack fastened, Burnum surveyed the greater area surrounding the visitor centre. Even at this time of the night, he would take no chances. With a quick nod to the boys, Burnum leapt into action, sprinting off in the direction of Uluru.

Like three rabbits running from a wild dingo, they scurried together across the open land between the visitor centre and Uluru. Even living within close proximity of the rock all these years, Ross had never ventured this close at this time of the night ... he felt as if he were trespassing.

Only when Burnum approached the women's sacred site on the southern tip of Uluru, did he slow down to a canter. Adam caught up to him and pointed beyond the fenced-off area. 'Ever been in there, father?'

Burnum gave him a quizzical look before shaking his head. 'No, of course not.' He jogged another ten metres before flipping his head back in the direction of his son. 'Woman's place. Only selected Anangu women are allowed there.'

Ross could feel the power of the rock as he drew closer to its walls. It was if a powerful force reached out to him and plugged into his senses. He had always believed the rock had powers beyond human comprehension, though he kept these thoughts to himself.

Burnum kept a vigilant eye on the Lasseter Highway, the main road between Old Yulara, the Resort, Connellan Airport, Uluru and the Aboriginal settlement of Mutitjulu, to the west of the rock. There was always a chance someone was going between these many places, even in the early hours of the morning.

Burnum broke back into a steady run and headed towards the walking track surrounding the rock. He picked it up just after the Women's place and headed to the calm beauty of the Mutitjulu waterhole.

Adam and Ross were giddy with excitement. They had only slept a few hours between them, the thought of what they were about to see was enough to keep them awake for a week. The walking track came to a sharp bend fresh from the Mutitjulu waterhole car park. As Burnum approached the bend, Ross and Adam had fallen into the rhythm of the run. They were surprised when Burnum came to a sudden stop. The boys shared a glance. Bloody hell, he was fit for an old bloke, he had hardly broken into a sweat.

Burnum waited for the boys to regain their composure,

nodding towards the fence which cordoned off a small bushy area beyond the corner of the track. The small sign, which said politely, 'Keep Out', was meant for the tourists, *not* Anangu elders. Burnum slid under the fence, having done it many times before, and directed the men to follow. The bushes were thick with sharp branches throughout.

Adam went next, Ross behind him. A branch scratched Ross's face as he moved through. The foliage must have been over ten feet thick; he struggled to get his body through, and when he did it the bushes seemed to close behind him. Whatever was beyond here would remain hidden.

He came through to find Burnum and Adam standing upright in a small enclave, waiting for him. Uluru rose hundreds of metres above, it was an incredible sight to see it this close. Ross saw a crack between two massive boulders, barely wide enough for a child to squeeze through.

Burnum turned and went straight to it, pushing into the crack and turning his head sideways. He had already taken off his Akubra and was struggling to squeeze this through even in his hand.

Adam slipped off his backpack and pressed his body into the narrow crevice. Ross pushed the backpack through to Adam before making his own way through, his gut pushed hard up against the rock, and he swore he would give up the beer ... again.

They were now in a crevice, no wider than a closet. It went on for about five metres before ending in a slightly more open dead end. There were cracks in every corner, a couple of them large enough for a man to squeeze into.

'This is it,' said Burnum, bending down and shining his torch up into one of the large cracks.

Burnum crawled up into it. The other men followed.

The tunnel opened up into a small dead-end cave, just big

enough for all three to huddle together. Burnum waited until Adam and Ross had settled. 'Close your eyes,' he whispered. Satisfied they were not looking, Burnum reached up into a small crack above his head.

The first sensation Ross felt was the smallest whiff of a breeze. It was not only the breeze that caught his senses, but the temperature of it; super-cool, as if someone had just opened a refrigerator. He did not want to disobey Burnum, he knew what a privilege it was for a him to be shown the sacred things, but shit, how much he wanted to open his eyes.

Burnum put him out of his misery. 'Open your eyes now,' he whispered.

For a second they were puzzled, nothing had changed. Burnum sat with his poker face ... then something caught Ross's eye. He swung his head around and gasped. Shit – that was not there a second ago. A hole had appeared behind Burnum. Ross had to look twice, to make sure he was not seeing things.

Burnum grinned, stepping into the hole, turning back to the stunned young men. 'Coming?' he said before moving another metre in and looking back again.

Adam and Ross stayed close to the elder. Suffice to say, they were silent; they could not believe what they had just seen, and now, where they were.

Ross moved further in. A thought struck him for six ... he'd spent years of his life flying around Uluru, marvelling at its infinite beauty, showing thousands of tourists every year one of the world's greatest landmarks. Now ... he was *in* it.

0:00:23

Achban lifted the Sydney Morning Herald back up to eye level and threw in one last comment. 'This is great news, huh. You sure it's accurate and credible?'

'Ramat Ha Sharon confirmed the information just a moment ago. It is, I can assure you,' Dania smiled as his eyes slowly lit up, 'no joke. Abelia is currently en-route to Australia.' Dania was unconvinced. She did not share Achban's positive, glass half-full attitude to the news. For there was another piece of information from TSA headquarters she had to share: the Romanov was coming into port in Australia, most likely – Darwin.

This little of nugget of information snapped Achban out of his relaxed, jocular mood. The newspaper had barely hit the table. 'Call Ramat Ha-Sharon back and tell them, code: Football.'

Dania reached over and picked up the Blackberry ... it was time to call in the team.

* * *

Going by Ross's watch, they had been walking for over thirty minutes. He was keen to know when dawn would arrive outside.

'We take a break soon,' Burnum said. 'When we get to the cave we call the 'Deep Valley of the Poisonous Snake.'

The tunnel eventually began to level out. Ross was relieved, the last section had been quite steep and his calves burned hot. He was looking forward to a rest soon ... although God knows when, Burnum was a bloody machine ... he had not missed a beat. He dared not mention the need for a rest, for fear of looking like a pansy; he would wait for Adam to mention it first.

Burnum slowed down as the tunnel began to widen out. Up ahead, his torch seemed to be hitting something, something that did not reflect the light back, as it had done for the entire trip. It was as if the tunnel wall had ... disappeared.

Ross felt the change of circulation. Previously it had been shallow and quite cold; now it was flowing much more and a little cooler.

Burnum pulled up and Adam nearly collided with his father, who reacted in a strange way; he held up his right arm rigidly, as if it was a boom gate at a train crossing instantly closing. He did not want Adam, or Ross, to step another centimetre beyond him. He lightly pushed Adam back a step.

'Turn your miner's torches off now.'

They reached up and flicked their miner's torches off.

Burnum flicked the secondary switch on his big torch. Ten million candlepower, it was a seriously powerful beam.

'My friends welcome,' his torch was pointing upwards. Language rolled from his tongue and Adam nodded gasping, his bottom lip – jelly. For Ross's benefit, Burnum translated. 'What you see before you is called the "Deep Valley of the Poisonous Snake."'

Ross froze in utter disbelief, his jaw – limp. It was the most mind-numbing sight he had ever seen.

0:00:24

Mikita arrived into Sydney in the middle of the night. By the time her head hit the pillow, it was pushing 2.30am. The flight was long and boring, her mind spinning with one perpetual thought: her ticket was one way.

The meeting with Siamko was scheduled for 8.30am. They met at the hotel restaurant, where the frenzy of the 'all you can eat' breakfast was in full swing. Mikita thought half the occupants should spend more time on the treadmill, rather than going back for a third serving...

Mikita might have felt like shit, jetlagged, but Siamko *looked* like it, another bender for sure. He was an utter disgrace. He stank of booze and looked un-showered, his tight little chin covered with a two-day growth. Even the waiter placing the coffees on the table turned up his nose.

The meeting was short and annoying. Mikita wanted to be elsewhere; more sleep high on her agenda. Siamko, luckily, had little to say. He had found a couple of tour guides they would soon meet when he travelled up to Darwin. The Romanov was already in port – at Darwin, and Siamko would meet with the crew there to further their plans. Mikita left the restaurant relieved with being away from his awful stench.

Siamko watched her disappear into the lift and as the doors shut, he stole a glance over to the corner of the room where a man sipping tomato juice with the Sydney Morning Herald held high enough to shield his identity, dipped it enough to give Siamko a old fashioned wink, and a matching grin before folding his paper and leaving, fast.

Ivon Krutek, captain of the Romanov, loved nothing more than a Bloody Mary over breakfast, and he'd be a busy man for the next twenty-four hours.

He followed Mikita to a safe house in suburban Woollahra, in Sydney's leafy east. There, he watched her enter the terrace house with Chonen Baram from the Israeli Consulate, and less than thirty minutes later, exit and disappear into the night in a cab. Before Mikita had travelled fewer than five hundred metres from the house, Ivon called Vadislav and confirmed their suspicions.

0:00:25

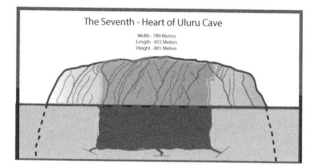

The Seventh - Heart of Uluru Cave

Width - 789 Metres
Length - 855 Metres
Height - 801 Metres

Complicated words bounced around the inside of Ross's head. His eyes told his brain what they were seeing, though his mind could not construct the vision into words to form a sentence. The only thing his mouth could do was to mutter and gasp, cough and grunt. He had whacked Adam on the arm at least three times.

When Burnum had hit the secondary lamp switch, the 10 million-candle power burst the darkness, revealing a prodigious, inner world – a cave big enough to swallow the central township of Old Yulara in one gigantic swoop. Burnum was slowly panning the torch around the massive cave. The distance between the wall they were abutting and the wall on the other side was easily five hundred metres. The cave was about as wide as it was long. Unbelievable, Ross thought.

Burnum grunted to them, panning the torch downwards. More gasps came from his two guests, Ross carefully leaning over just a little bit more, attempting as best he could to see the bottom of the abyss. He slapped himself in the face, to make sure he was not dreaming.

Burnum smiled. 'I felt the same way when I first saw the Heart of Uluru Cave.'

Burnum had been coming here for the last thirty years, every time the three elders would 'go away', so to speak. Among the Anangu community, only he, Ganan, and Derain knew of the existence of the Secret Heart of Uluru, the Seventh site. 'There was only one whitefella who knew of the Seventh, as far as we know. Bernie Taylor...' Burnum rolled his shoulders. 'Now there's two.'

* * *

Ross suddenly felt the weight of the rock bearing down on him, relieved when they reached a larger opening in the tunnel. Burnum slowed to a halt. 'This part here is a resting place.' He grinned at Ross. 'Your dad called it the Junction.' Burnum panned the torch around, the light dipping into at least six separate tunnel entrances.

Adam was like a kid in a candy factory. 'Where do they all go?' The look on his face told the other two he wanted to explore them all.

A frown fell over Burnum's face. 'We only know where one of them goes.' He slipped his water bottle back into his backpack. 'The others, I wouldn't risk finding out.'

Ross felt the cool water replenishing his reserves, a wave of contentment washing over him. His legs were still a little sore.

'Burnum, how can you go at this pace for so long, you are one fit man for seventy-eight.'

Burnum smiled, staring at the water swilling around the see-through water bottle. He shook his head, the smile growing wider. 'Who said I was seventy-eight?'

Adam cocked his head. 'What do you mean, "Who said I was seventy-eight"? Are you saying this is not your true age?'

'I am not seventy-eight, son.'

Adam was not convinced. 'Hold on, I was told you were fifty when I was born.' He turned to Ross for conviction. 'Which means if I'm twenty-eight, he's seventy-eight, right?'

'Adam, Ross.' Burnum stood up and stretched. 'The Heart of Uluru – when you start coming here, it makes you feel a lot younger. You see, if I did not lie about my age, people would not accept how fit and young I look – that I'm as old as I truly am.' He looked down the long, dark tunnel. 'It would raise questions. This could lead people to think up all sorts of things. It could threaten the exposure of the Seventh.'

Ross let out an elongated whistle. Wow, he thought. Now the secrets are coming out thick and fast.

Burnum put his hand on his son's shoulder and rubbed it gently. 'Adam, Uluru is truly sacred, because of the Heart.' He looked over to Ross to ensure he was paying full attention. Burnum tapped his forefinger under Adam's chin, his son's eyes once again met his own. 'The stories of Uluru are all true, but beneath these, is the story of the Heart. Only when white man came, was the decision made – the story of the Heart, along with its existence, and what lay hidden within it, would be buried in secrecy, with only the three most senior elders to know from that point on.'

He stepped back and felt as if a weight had been lifted off his shoulders.

'This is the way it has been.'

Satisfied he had explained himself and the boys were now well rested, Burnum slipped on his backpack and adjusted the Akubra stuck to his head for optimal comfort. He was about to give the marching orders when Adam, still appearing as if he had seen another ghost, slipped off the rock and stood up straight, holding up his hand to signal for Burnum not to move another inch. 'So, how old are you, father?'

Burnum inhaled slowly through his nostrils, which flared as he did so. 'I'm twenty years older than you think I am.'

0:00:26

Brett knew his entrance might not go unnoticed. He was, his heart felt, entering hell on earth: the public bar at Chris Ox's Old Yulara Hotel. Brett was not on Chris' Christmas card list, and the feeling was mutual, to say the least. Chris was a prick of unimaginable proportions, in Brett's eyes. He'd always felt Chris treated him like the black sheep of the Taylor family. Which, in fact, he was.

But there was no way to avoid confronting Chris and trying to make peace. If he did not come to see his father's best friend, his time at Uluru would not go well.

The noisy bar fell silent in a matter of seconds. 'Well, look who we have here,' Chris said, turning to see who had commanded such an entrance.

Stuart followed Brett up to the bar. He sized-up the publican – one big bastard. Even he would struggle to take the man hovering behind the bar down – unless he had a shotgun or was coming from behind with one hell of a big shovel. Chris's arms were as thick as Brett's legs, probably both of them combined. The veins under the skin in his forearms looked like garden hoses. Stuart glanced down to Oxy's hands and thought Chris was holding a standard size glass. It was not. It was a pint. Hands big enough to crush a basketball. They looked to Stuart like a bunch of fat carrots.

The amazing thing was, even with a neck as thick as a gum tree, the man's face was as normal and non-descript as you would ever see. A full head of short brown hair matched his slightly bushy eyebrows, which sat above big, saucer-shaped brown eyes. His chin looked as if it belonged on a teenager, small and innocent. Stuart could have sworn the publican flared his teeth like a pit-bull, if only slightly, at the sight of Brett, revealing a mouthful of well-kept teeth.

'Hello, Chris,' Brett whispered.

'Here to see the old man, I guess.' Chris looked down at Brett as if he were a dog – in need of a bullet.

'Yes, I am,' Brett muttered, the eyes of the entire room making him uneasy.

Brett took a long, dry, deep breath and began the speech he had practiced a hundred times in the last three hours. 'I came here to tell you Chris, I am a changed man. I will not make any trouble for you, or anyone else.' He stole a look around the room before turning back to the man behind the counter. 'And ask for your forgiveness, for what happened a few years ago.'

Chris's eyes narrowed. He rested both big hands on the counter and looked Stuart over. 'And you are?'

Stuart ignored the venom in his tone and stepped forward. 'My name is Stuart, mate, pleased to meet ya.' He held out his hand for a shake.

Chris turned his attention back to Brett. 'Your father's not well, he'll be glad you're here.' He pulled two schooners from the rack. 'You two look like you could use a beer.'

As he placed the beers in front of them, the usual noise of the bar slowly returned. 'I'm seeing Jimmy tonight.' Chris looked down to Brett. 'You can come with me if you wish.'

Brett took another swig of beer, the thought of fronting up to the old man making his stomach turn. 'Thanks Chris, I would like that.' Like a hole in the head...

Chris picked Brett up as promised, right on time. The drive to the Medical Centre was awkward, and quiet, luckily for Brett, it didn't take long.

The glass doors slid open. 'Well, I'll be dammed,' whispered a man in a white suit to the woman behind the counter.

Chris and Brett walked in, Brett a clear three steps behind. 'Don't be shy, lad,' Chris bellowed, a hint of a mock-Scottish accent in his tone. 'You remember Ian, don't you?'

Brett did not want to look the doctor in the eye.

The floodgates in Dr Ian Petersen's memory burst open; the mayhem surrounding the moments Brett and Cobar had come in, the mob of angry locals outside, shouting for Brett's head, Jimmy himself almost wanting to lynch his own son. Crikey, it had been a tense forty-eight hours; before Cobar woke up and Brett dragged off to Alice Springs...

Ian, like Oxy, was a man of strength, and forgiveness. Oxy had called him to let him know Brett had arrived in town, and to let Jimmy know he was coming. 'I'm glad you came, Brett.' Ian reached out over the counter to shake his hand.

'Thanks Ian, it's good to see you.'

'Brett, allow me to introduce my assistant, Tania.' Ian smiled down at her. 'Tania, this is Brett Taylor, one of Jimmy's sons.'

Tania caught the whiff of Brett's aftershave, Brut 33, for sure, she thought. Yuk. His shirt was cheap, probably purchased from Best and Less for $4.95. The minute pieces of toilet paper strategically placed on two spots of his neck indicated the boy knew not how to use a razor, or he had shaved with a butter-knife. 'Nice to meet you,' she said quietly, deciding she would nod rather than shake his hand.

Ian stepped towards the hallway. 'Jimmy is a little tired but it's okay to see him. I think it's time, Brett.' Ian could easily read Brett's ashen face. He was shitting himself. This, you would expect. The last time these two Taylors were together, the proverbial shit was all over the fan.

* * *

The three men had just emerged from another ubiquitous tunnel, the ceiling suddenly disappearing. Adam and Ross knew they had entered a massive cave. It was the air, it was different … so was the sound, there was none at all.

Burnum had already stopped, not five metres in. This time, he turned on his powerful torch with the beam facing directly down, the light so bright it made the boys squint.

When his eyes adjusted, Ross almost fainted. Adam let out sounds you might hear on a movie that you hid from your mother in the bottom of your drawer.

'Home of the Carpet Snake,' Burnum announced, matter-of-factly.

'Fuck!' Ross said, louder than intended. His voice bounced off some distant cave wall; so far away, it took seconds to reverberate back to him. He and Adam broke into wild laughter.

'Is this for real?' Ross gushed to Adam.

Burnum cleared his throat. 'Time for that rest, come over here, boys.'

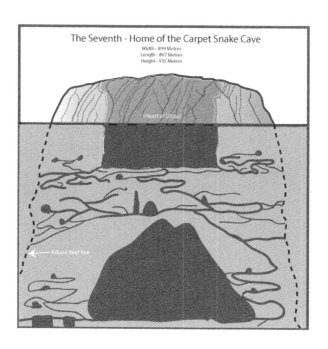

The Seventh - Home of the Carpet Snake Cave
Width - 899 Metres
Length - 867 Metres
Height - 935 Metres

(Heart of Uluru)

Arkose Reef line

0:00:27

Brett's face had turned an ashen grey. For the first time in five years, he would come face to face with his father, now, only a few feet away.

Chris noted Brett's sullen expression and quietly wished Jimmy's youngest son was not such a troubled fuck-up of a man. It was quite fitting Chris would witness the first meeting between Brett and Jimmy in five years. The Pub owner, along with Jimmy's other close friend, John Kelsey, had helped Jimmy work through the loss of his wife and the torment of what happened at her wake, thanks to his youngest born. Chris had reflected on the fateful day many times in the hours since seeing Brett standing in his Pub, his stomach twisting itself into a knot each time ... the look on Jimmy's face when he knelt down to check if Brett's lifeless body still possessed a pulse; the mob of angry men trying to kick him as he laid motionless on the floor.

He was the toughest prick in these parts, Oxy, but even for a man of his ilk, it still struck too close to home. He could also remember Brett as an innocent kid, begging Chris for just one more raspberry lemonade, his favourite drink as an eight-year-old...

Tania slipped out of room number five – Jimmy's room. 'He's awake, though a little tired.' She looked over to Chris's

103

warm face and felt a stab of sympathy. Oxy had visited Jimmy twice a day, like clockwork, the telltale sign of a true friend. She caught Brett's anxious gaze. 'I don't know how long he can stay awake.' Turning back to Ian, she said, 'I would suggest he gets in there sooner,' she glanced at Brett, her expression a little terse, 'rather than later.'

Ian led the way but Brett was still standing back down the other end of the hall. Either his shoes had stuck to the floor all of a sudden, or he could not walk the plank...

'Get down here, laddy.' There was that stupid Scottish accent Chris would lay on Brett to try and soften the mood. It worked well – not.

'Okay' he whispered awkwardly, his legs working in slow motion.

Ian patted Chris on the back. 'He's all yours.' Casting a dull glance at Brett, he walked back towards the reception desk.

Chris decided he couldn't wait for Brett anymore. He pushed the door open and strode into Jimmy's room. Brett heard him announce, 'Brett's here, Jimmy.'

At the door of the hospital room, Brett took a long, nervous, shallow breath. The room had gone silent. Fucken hell, this is it... The door felt far heavier than what it was. When it finally opened enough for him to see inside, Chris was standing at the end of a hospital bed, arms crossed, eyes locked on him. Brett crept into the room.

Jimmy sat up in the bed. Jesus Christ, Brett thought, he looks like he's aged twenty years since I last saw him. Jimmy was pasty pale, his eyes – grey, his lips an unnatural shade of purple; all of this seem to extenuate the wrinkles around his eyes, nose and forehead. For a split second Brett felt as if he were looking at a ghost.

Thanks to you arsehole, he'll be one soon...

'Come here, son,' Jimmy said with affection, holding out his hand. Brett shook his dad's hand. Jimmy pulled him closer and gave him an awkward hug.

Chris patted Jimmy on the left foot. 'I'll be out the front with Ian, hit the button if you need me Champ.'

Seeing your son for the first time in five years would pull the heartstring of any father. Add to this the prospect knowing it would be the last time.

Jimmy could not stop staring at Brett; his first clear emotion was one of sorrow. Sorrow of how he, as a father, had failed in not guiding this boy through to a better place in life.

All it took was for Brett to complete one sentence and Jimmy's heart twitched a little – in the wrong way. He recalled the havoc his youngest son wreaked on him all those years ago. It was one of the worst days in Jimmy's life, when half the population of Old Yulura wanted Brett's scalp. He pushed the thoughts back – for now.

'I am glad you're here, Brett.' He waved his hand around the room. 'As you can see, I'm not faring too well.'

Brett remained passive; he was still coming to terms with being in the same room as his old man. 'I'm sorry, Dad.' He sat awkwardly on the edge of the bed, emotions of all kinds swelling up inside him.

'What happened in the past is in the past,' Jimmy said forthrightly. He sat up a little more and held out his arms for his son, an awkward, but heartfelt man-hug resulted, Brett patting him on the back as lightly as he could.

Bernie had always struggled to connect with Brett; Janet seemed to have the 'direct-line' to him, knowing how to talk to him and what would work to get through. Everything changed when he was sixteen and took speed for the first time. He spent his seventeenth birthday in jail in Alice Springs, grand theft auto and knocking out a policeman, taking the poor guy's front tooth with him, to boot. After that, Janet knew – she had lost him for good.

But Jimmy made an effort tonight. Something inside him told him this may be one of the very last chances to speak to his youngest son. After a while, Brett began to relax and open up. Eventually, they were able to share a laugh.

For Brett, it felt great, but he was still wary. 'So,' he smiled. 'Where's my brother?'

Jimmy's eyes went to the window, the night sky infinite save for the distant stars and the odd flash of car lights. 'He went to Alice Springs.' He looked back to Brett. 'To organise some things for me. He should be back tomorrow night.'

Brett nodded. An awkward silence appeared in the room.

'You working son?'

Brett's eyes lit up. He took a deep breath and gave the old man the story of how he'd ended up working for Stuart, and what they had been doing since. Jimmy was impressed. Brett normally couldn't hold down a helium balloon for more than fifteen seconds, let alone a job for more than a month. He really hoped things might turn around for him.

Brett was thinking about telling Jimmy about the side-project with the Israelis. He couldn't work out if he should or not. But Jimmy had kept some whopping secrets about Brett to himself many times before. If Jimmy had wanted to, he could have seen Brett remain in jail for most of his life. And with him dying and all ... why not?

Bugger it, he thought. 'Dad,' he turned to make sure they were alone. 'Can I tell you a secret?'

Jimmy frowned, catching his breath. He wiped his face with a small face towel, taking a long, painful breath. He closed his eyes. 'Don't tell me,' opening them a moment later and meeting Brett's. 'You haven't killed someone?'

Brett was too simple to find the sentence offensive, he thought his old man was taking the piss! Hello Brett? He was dead serious, you goose.

Brett burst into laughter and shook his head. 'Na, Dad, nothing like that.'

'Okay, I can keep a secret, what is it son?'

Brett spewed out the secret as if the words were bullets from a machine-gun. He'd never been offered such an obscene amount of money – to him it was a million dollars – and it had all gone to his dim-witted head.

'Israelis—'

'In Australia—'

'Paid us to help them find some top-secret—'

'Aboriginal artefact—'

'What the hell was it called – the Bashic, or Akakashic, Record?'

Suddenly, only one heart continued to beat in room number five. Jimmy collapsed; he would have fallen out of bed if it were not for Brett catching him. Alarms went off.

'Fuck,' Brett shouted, as he reached for the nurse come-here-real-quick button. But it was Ian who came bursting through the door a second later, followed by Chris. 'What happened?' Ian shouted, lunging for Jimmy.

Brett fell back, panic now setting in. 'We were just talking.' He stepped back and hit the wall. 'And he just collapsed.'

The colour of Jimmy's skin had, in seconds, turned a darkening purple. As the light in Jimmy's eyes faded, his hands lunged for anything which might assist him in living. He caught the bottom of Chris' shirt sleeve and tugged harshly.

'Shit, Jimmy,' Chris muttered; turning to Ian, 'Help him, please.'

Ian went to work, ripping open the hospital gown. He swung around and studied the monitor. His own heart sank with what he saw; the heart rate so low, Ian knew any second it the heart would probably stop.

Jimmy grabbed at Chris's shirt again, this time getting a fistful of chest-hair. He pulled him closer. With one final gasp, Jimmy's fading voice gave it all it had left. 'Tell Ross it's in danger.'

Chris had no idea what Jimmy was going on about. He pulled back enough to look deep into his mate's watering eyes. 'What, Jimmy? What do you mean?'

The veins in Jimmy's neck were close to bursting. He pulled Chris down so his lips were touching Chris' right ear. 'The Heart—'

From the other side of the bed, Ian put his hand firmly on Chris's shoulder. 'Enough Chris, we need to try and save him.'

Tania arrived with a portable defibrillator on a trolley. 'Give us some space, mate. We'll give it everything we have.'

Chris stepped back and looked over to Brett standing against the back wall, his face pale, but with an expression Chris could not read.

Jimmy's heart ceased beating a moment later.

Chris stepped away from the bed, nearly falling back over the chair.

The two medics tried in vain to bring Jimmy back. Ian waved his hand at Tania: enough. He met her eyes and spoke quietly. 'He's gone, turn it off.'

Chris placed his hand firmly on the young Taylor's shoulder. 'I'm sorry.'

Brett looked up to him. Chris noted there were no signs of sorrow in Brett's eyes, no tears, no emotion, nothing.

Tania pulled the curtains around Jimmy's bed and said, 'Come on, I'll make you both a coffee.'

Alone in the room, Ian picked up the clipboard hanging on the end of the bed, checking his watch before he wrote the last note to go on the file of Bernie Taylor: his time of death.

'We'll miss you, Jimmy.'

Ian flicked the light off and headed to the kitchen.

Jimmy's room was deathly silent, pardon the pun. The night sky cast a faint grey shadow over Jimmy's body. Something moved in the corner of the room, in the darkness. A second later, a whisper from the same corner.

'Time to come home, Bernie.'

0:00:28

The paintings on his office walls moved a millimetre to the left with reverberation from the big Russian smashing the top of his desk with his cantaloupe-sized fist. 'You sure?' he shouted into the microphone of his desk phone, for the second time.

'Yes, Vadislav,' Ivon said bluntly. 'I believe most probably – Mossad.'

The paintings on his office wall all moved one millimetre to the right. At this rate, Vadislav's desk would be in pieces in a couple of minutes. 'Fucken Israelis,' Vadislav spat.

Ivon could tell the big boss would be after nothing less than blood. Female. Israeli. Blood.

* * *

It was luxurious. Well, sort of. Three stretcher beds, all with pillows and blankets, a card-table with chairs, gas lights, a small gas stove, all the assorted grub to make a decent meal, cans upon cans of stews, canned vegetables, coffee, tea, sugar – all of this in a small open cave, off the jumbo-sized cave Burnum called Home of the Carpet Snake.

Burnum pointed to a camp-bed for each of his two guests and told them to rest. He need not twist their arms; they were beat. Ross fell asleep seconds after his head hit the pillow. Adam followed suit, his body exhausted from the trip thus far.

Burnum studied the flames of the fire. It was one of his simplest pleasures, watching a fire burn. He loved the way it was alive; the flames swaying, flickering, and moving, the bright, orange glow giving off subtle warmth, the small, straight plume of smoke rising directly above the tips of the flames. He always felt at home in front of a fire – especially in the Seventh.

Later, Adam shuffled out and stood on the other side of the fire. To him, this was all so surreal; his mind took a few seconds to remind him he was not outside, but hundreds, upon hundreds of metres below the surface of the earth. He joined his father in staring at the fire for some time. Eventually he said, 'Should I wake Ross?'

Burnum nodded and his eyes fell back to the fire.

In the cave, Adam picked up his miner's torch and clicked it on. He gave Ross a shake.

'Not now Melinda, I'm too tired.'

Ross smiled and Adam realised he was awake, and just being a smart ass. Ross opened his eyes. 'White with two thanks.'

Adam shone the torch right in his mate's face. 'In your dreams, flower pot.'

Burnum made stew as Ross and Adam feverishly discussed the cave system they were now deep within. Burnum would only interject when the discussions fell off the tracks, or the summation one of them would make was incorrect. Ross asked how the names of the big caves he had seen so far had come about. Burnum talked of the stories he was taught when he was chosen to become a gatekeeper, well over fifty years ago. 'We lost an elder down in one of these parts about ten years ago.'

The statement caught Adam and Ross by surprise. They sat up straighter, their eyes a little wider. 'His wife was Annie, from up our road.'

Adam went to say something though Burnum waved his hand quickly.

'No, Adam – he didn't move to Broome as everyone was told.' Burnum's expression was serious. 'When you agree to take on this job, as one of the three, it comes with the agreement—' He rubbed his chin with his thumb and his index finger for a few seconds. 'If you die down here, no one can know that you did. Nothing is to expose the existence of this place to the outside world.'

The story of the old fella's unfortunate demise within the Seventh Place scared the living daylights out of Ross and Adam. They walked in complete silence for the next section of the journey. It was as plain as day to them both that they were again heading further into the earth. The tunnels were indistinguishable: how Burnum could remember one from the other was incredible.

An hour later after leaving the Seventh 'Bed and Breakfast', they came to the next cave – Deep Hole Cave.

Deep Hole Cave was as its name suggested: well over two hundred metres deep. They would have to traverse a narrow ledge, the cave ceiling less than six feet above them, with the path in some sections literally no wider than a grown man's footprint. The length of the harrowing ledge was about 100 metres long.

Burnum allowed them to digest his explicit instructions and before he turned to the path, only ten metres away, he allowed a long pause to make the most important point to the two. 'This is where he left us.'

Burnum was spot-on with his description of the Deep Hole Cave. It took them about thirty minutes to navigate the narrow ledge. Ross was still coming to terms with the harrowing pathway, the only way across. When Burnum said the pathway was only as wide as his feet, he was accurate to the centimetre.

Add to the experience, pitch blackness, save for the pissy little light his miner's torch offered. Shit, Ross realised – they had to come back this same way to get home.

When they'd made it and were about to move on, Burnum turned and looked down into the deep pit of the cave.

'Are you okay, Dad?'

Burnum turned to his son. 'He is still down there, his body.'

Ross overheard Burnum's words. The thought of the poor man's body still down there was unnerving to say the least.

0:00:29

The three men sat in the foyer of the Pioneer Outback Hotel. The air was thick and muggy, the tension palpable. Chris sat on one chair, and across from him, Brett and Stuart shared the sofa. It was the day after Jimmy's death. The conversation between them – disjointed; it came in spits and spurts, all three of them wishing they were elsewhere, far away from each other.

Mysteriously, Ross's phone was stone cold dead. It had been off for the last thirteen hours. Brett had been quite vocal about this; he was dumbstruck as to why his big brother would have turned his mobile off. Chris was more laid back about it. He said the phone's battery may have run out, his phone may have broken down, hell – he may have had it stolen, who knows? The bottom line was: they could not get hold of him to tell him Jimmy was … gone.

Chris checked his watch; enough was enough, he would prefer to eat a razor blade sandwich than sit with Brett and discuss why they could not get hold of Ross. To shut the little prick up, he said Jimmy had been in and out of the Medical Centre many times in the last five weeks and Ross probably assumed this latest visit would be yet another false alarm. Chris rose to his feet, relieved he was getting out of the foyer. 'I'll see you later, boys.'

When he'd gone, Brett let out a sigh of relief. 'Shit, that was awkward.'

'Tell me about it. That guy certainly has something up his ass.'

Brett leant a little closer to Stuart. 'Some really weird shit went down before the old man kicked the bucket, bud; you're not going to believe it.'

Brett went through the events with surprising clarity; how Jimmy was aching to talk, about anything, how it felt as if Jimmy had forgiven him for the past and how, in the end, he had decided to tell him about their little project ... and at that exact point, Stuart nearly exploded.

Brett grabbed him firmly by the arm. 'Chill the fuck out and let me explain,' he whispered. 'Dad could have had me committed to double the jail time, he had that much shit on me – but he chose not to. He knew how to keep a secret. And anyway, he died, didn't he?'

Stuart calmed down enough for Brett to tell him what had happened seconds before Jimmy went into a complete and one-way meltdown.

It was full on, Stuart thought. Very, very intriguing indeed. He looked at Brett with narrowed eyes. 'So if I have this correctly,' he whispered. 'You tell the old man we're helping the Israelis look for an ancient Aboriginal artefact – then the old man has an instant spaz-attack? Then, as they're trying to save him, he says something to the big bastard about some Aboriginal thing, and it being in danger?'

Brett caught a glimpse of a busload of Japanese tourists making their way through the entrance doors to the hotel. Phew; a couple of them were hot.

Stuart yanked his shirt arm angrily. 'Are you paying attention, fuck-face?'

Brett, itching to swing his head around to perve at the tourists, nodded quickly, hoping the sooner Stuart shut up about this shit, the sooner he could try and chat the Japanese girls up.

As Stuart reflected on what he had just heard, a large open grin materialised.

'What?' Brett said, spotting the grin.

'Jesus, Brett, you have no idea.' Stuart leant over and came right up to his ear. 'Wait until Achban hears about this. This is major stuff.'

'If you say so...' Brett sat forward, preparing to stand. 'Now, I have other business to attend to.'

Stuart watched him meander over to the group of Japanese tourists. The two girls he had been watching were staring at him as he walked over, giggling to each other. Stuart wondered why they would show any interest in such an ugly prick as Brett. Were they out of their minds?

Brett grinned. 'Ladies, camitchee-wa.'

* * *

Ross and Adam, both a little shaken by the experience of traversing, in near pitch-black, a ledge better suited to a rat, could hardly believe they were about to do it again. Burnum shone his torch down into the abyss and said it was probably the same in depth. Fortunately, the path was considerably wider than the previous, treacherous cave ... this one was about a foot across. Ross thought it was still a little hairy, though a shitload better than the last one.

Burnum shared the last little nugget: 'Oh and one more thing.' He turned and winked. 'The ledge may be wider, but the track is a lot longer.'

Adam and Ross exchanged rolling eyes. Ross turned to the elder. 'How much longer?'

Burnum adjusted his backpack, jeans, hat and bandana before looking over to Ross as if the answer was the least worry on his mind. 'Oh ... about double.'

117

Ross's heart sank, before his head told him to toughen up and cease being a girly-man.

After shuffling along the ledge and making it to the end, they arrived at another fork in the tunnel, or so Ross and Adam thought.

What they walked into was a vast underground honeycomb of caves, which appeared to stretch in every direction for as far as their torches carried the light. Shadows appeared across the entrances to what seemed to be tunnels, which stretched into the inky blackness. Spooky? Fuck yes, Ross felt nerve endings he thought he never had: prickle underneath his skin, this place gave him the creeps.

Burnum took the first step into the area and spoke in a whisper. 'Stay close,' he leaned in further for effect, 'and I mean, real close.'

Burnum was still within spitting distance of Adam, who responded with a twinge in his voice, 'So does this part have a name?'

'This is Spirit Land.'

Ross saw the jolt in Adam's body. He grabbed Adam by the arm, pulling him in close. 'What did he say?'

'Spirit-land.'

Burnum's instructions to stay close were suddenly fulfilled. Adam and Ross lurched forward, nearly knocking the elder over.

'Turn your torches on full,' Burnum muttered.

Ross fumbled for his miner's torch, clicking it over to full power,

'All of them,' Burnum said.

As Ross pulled the spare torch out of the side pocket of his backpack, Burnum flicked the switch on his big daddy and the area exploded in a sea of white, grey shadows appearing in all directions, with inky darkness everywhere else.

Ross's breaths grew short and spasmodic, before an awful, almost surreal feeling engulfed him.

Someone was watching him.

No, many people were watching him.

'Farck,' Adam gushed. 'Did you hear that?'

Ross was about to ask him what he was talking about. Then, swallowing uncomfortably, he also heard the distant sound. He clenched the torch in his left hand, his knuckles turning a pasty white.

The journey through Spirit Land continued for another ten horrific minutes. Ross and Adam were beside themselves, the area gave them the creeps. Burnum remained passive; it seemed to be all in a day's work for him. He strode, as he did, five feet in front of the others, not a care in the world. 'Stop,' he barked suddenly, stopping precisely where he stood.

The two stood close to the elder. Ross had counted to fifteen before hearing a sound a that sent a shiver down his spine. He and Adam caught each other's horrified eyes.

It was the sound of a man's voice, far off in the distance. He sounded as if he were in pain.

'Turn your torches off – *now*,' Burnum hissed.

'B-but, why...?' Adam whispered.

'No time for answers, just do it.'

Adam's torch was the last one to go off. When it did, Ross had a sick feeling of vertigo, combined with a level of fear he had not experienced before.

Burnum whispered, 'Stay still and don't say a word.'

Ross fought with the desperate need to turn his torch back on and run like the wind back towards daylight. As the seconds ticked over, he heard the distant moaning growing louder. He wondered if Adam would think any differently of him if he wrapped his arms around him right now.

What happened to Ross next was beyond surreal. He would

later wonder if it had ever actually happened or if it was all a dream.

He felt the air around him move, then, something brushing lightly past, as if it were circling him. He clenched his teeth and twisted his eyelids shut so tight they hurt. The voices were now so close he could hear them, though not understand a word they were saying. As if the voices were on a fast-moving locomotive, they brushed past his ears and sped on.

The voices began to taper off in the other direction.

Burnum tugged on his arm and said reassuringly, 'When I turn on my torch, do not panic. But when I start running, keep up.' There was a short pause before his voice lightened. 'Or else they will be back.'

Ross opened his eyes when Burnum turned on his torch. He did not have time to recover from what had just happened – Burnum took off and ran like the wind. Ross and Adam did precisely the same.

Burnum only slowed when he had been running for at least five minutes, running upwards into a narrow tunnel which had about five 'S' bends. When they came out into a small, flat, innocent looking cave, Burnum finally slowed to a stop.

Ross and Adam pulled up too, switching on their miner's torches and bending over to regain some composure. Only after about two minutes of panting and breathing did Ross look up at Burnum. 'What was all that about?' His voice raspy and shallow.

'He was an elder who lost his way down here over a hundred years ago,' Burnum said.

Ross raised his eyebrows. 'Are you trying to tell us,' his eyes darted to Adam for a second, 'that he is still alive?"

Burnum shook his head so subtly, Ross nearly missed it. Ross could feel his windpipe constrict to the width of a garden hose. 'He's dead?'

Burnum nodded. He breathed in through his nostrils, a sympathetic look washing over him. 'Sometimes, he sees the light, well his spirit does, and he thinks he is still alive.' He dipped his head in sorrow. 'The only way to stop him is by turning all the lights off.'

Ross was no less rattled. 'I felt him brush past me,' he said.

Burnum rested his hand on Ross's shoulder. 'Anyone who dies in, or on top of the rock,' he turned to Adam to make sure he was also listening, 'their souls are trapped down here in Spirit Land – forever.'

The two men took in what they had just heard. The only thing they could think at that moment was how much they dreaded returning through Spirit Land on the way home.

Burnum was about to move on but Ross caught his arm. 'Hold on, there was something else.' He took a deep, uneasy breath. 'I felt something brush past my shin; I could have sworn it felt like a child, a baby, maybe...'

Burnum rubbed his eyes, nodding a moment later. 'That was probably her.' He looked back up the tunnel that led to Spirit Land. 'The baby girl who went missing here, thirty years ago.'

0:00:30

The Elder told them it was time to move on. He mentioned it may be a good idea to run, as Spirit Land was still close. They did not hesitate. As they ran with him, Burnum struggled not to laugh, the next surprise was going to knock them for six. They were fifty metres from the Heart of Uluru. 'Keep up guys.' Burnum turned back. 'Did you hear something?'

Ross and Adam dropped back into third gear and ran harder. 'Have we come far enough yet, B-Burnum?' Ross moaned, the combination of running and being scared out of his wits threatening to pop a valve.

'Just a little bit longer, come-on,' Burnum shouted. Ten metres from the heart of Uluru.

He could see it coming up – the black hole ... of all black holes. Ross and Adam were too busy looking behind them for the ghost of the trapped Elder. They had no idea they were nearing the end of a tunnel.

Three metres from the Heart of Uluru.

Burnum burst through the end of the tunnel. He was now in the Seventh place, the Heart of Uluru. He came to a stop. 'I saw something behind you, quick.'

Ross and Adam crossed into the Heart of Uluru without even knowing it. They huddled behind Burnum, looking back from where they had just come. Only when they heard Burnum's deep cackle, did they realise he was taking the absolute piss out of them. He'd been pulling their leg the whole time.

Burnum flicked the switch of the torch to full-blast. 'Welcome,' he said between breaths of laughter, 'to the home of the Devil Dingo Cave.' He lifted the torch high into the air as if it were a trophy and he was standing on a podium.

Ross gasped, slipping his backpack off and not caring where it landed. He tilted his head upwards, watching the very end of the torch's blade of light.

The last two 'large' caves were not as enormous as this one. This giant was at least another third bigger. Ross realised why it was called the Heart of Uluru. It must have to have been at least a kilometre high – regulation height for the choppers he often watched heading over to the Olgas from Merrigang. He knew his heights and, by Lord, this was the biggest – forget gargantuan, super-gargantuan – cave he had ever laid eyes on.

Burnum let his arm down and turned to Adam. 'Check this out.' He swung his torch down and across. 'The official name for this cave is the Lair of the Devil Dingo,' he proudly explained to his guests, rolling it off in Language for Adam's sake.

'Wow, this is beyond unbelievable,' Adam squealed, as if his voice box had returned to pre-teenagehood size and output.

Ross thought for a second he had dribbled out of the side of his gob, then realised his lips were flapping on their own. It was dumbfounding to think this cave was deep below Uluru and only a handful of people knew of it.

'Come this way.' Burnum shuffled through the men and off towards the other side of the cave. 'I have one last thing to show you...'

Burnum led the men to the other side of the enormous cave. He gave them both a turn of the big torch, allowing them to explore the vast expanse. He had seen it so many times now; it

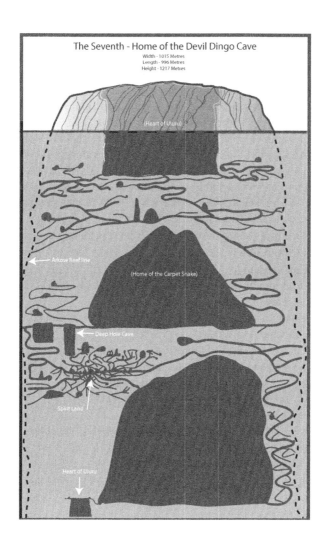

The Seventh - Home of the Devil Dingo Cave

Width - 1015 Metres
Length - 996 Metres
Height - 1217 Metres

(Heart of Uluru)

← Arkose Reef line

(Home of the Carpet Snake)

→ Deep Hole Cave

Spirit Land

Heart of Uluru
↓

was as if he were in his second home. (Actually, he felt more at home here than on the surface.)

Ross felt a strange sensation. Déjà vu came to mind; it was if parts of this cave were a carbon copy of some of the areas surrounding the outside of Uluru, hundreds of metres far above. The air was getting cooler, this was for sure, and Ross slipped back into the sweater he had long discarded.

Burnum cleared his throat, the prelude to the much anticipated speech he had rehearsed many times during the journey into the Heart. 'Uluru will always be a sacred place to the Anangu. But what not all of them are aware of,' he shook his head with a small grin, 'is that we've been hiding something down here since humanity began walking on this planet.'

Ross and Adam shared a look. What was he talking about?

Burnum slowly rose to his feet and spoke in his language.

Ross's Anangu did not extend beyond a few words. He turned to Adam, his miner's torch pointing straight into his face. 'The – what?'

Adam looked down to his feet, his mind was ticking, and then it came.

'Shiiit,' was the only word which slipped out of his mouth before he jumped off the rock and stood eye to eye with his father. 'Did you say,' quickly re-translating the words in his head, 'The book of the souls, birth and death?'

Burnum nodded.

Ross now joined in, flinging himself off the rock as if it were on fire. 'What is it, Burnum?'

'Come – I will show you.'

Now Ross was really feeling like all this was a dream.

Burnum led them through a narrow crevice which looked precisely the same as the one that took them from the bushes up on the surface into the secret entrance to the Seventh.

Ross crawled up the small tunnel and started to freak out

126

somewhat, for a few seconds later, they came to a dead end and were all huddled up together. Ross's head was spinning; he was pissed off with himself. Damn ... I must be dreaming all this, but it has been all so real, he thought.

Burnum reached up into a crevice, and once again, a black hole came into view behind the elder. He led them into the tunnel and at the five metre point, Ross was literally about to implode, desperately trying to work out if this was an actual dream, or not.

The three men came to another sudden dead end, save for the familiar mass of pitch black, dank air. Burnum turned on his torch (yes the bigger setting), showing them a narrow walkway, not any wider than fifty centimetres, that stretched for about twenty metres across another deep, dark and formidable cave. The air was foggy, or so it seemed. Burnum's torch could only make out about fifty metres before the light bounced back.

'We go across,' Burnum said. 'And take your time; you do not want to fall over the edge.'

Ross beat Adam this time by a second. 'How far down does it go?'

Burnum glared over to them, his eyes narrow. 'We don't know.' He looked over the edge and turned back to them. 'Could you see the top of the Lair of the Devil Dingo's cave with my torch before?' he asked.

Both nodded.

'Well, a couple of years ago, I wanted to know how deep it went.' He patted his big torch as if it were a pet. 'So I brought another big torch down with me one day. I turned it on full blast, and threw it over the edge.'

Adam and Ross felt their nerves go icy with anticipation of the answer.

'The torch just kept on going.' Burnum smiled and shook his head in amazement. 'Until it was the size of a pin-hole, then it was gone. You see,' he readied himself for the careful walk across; 'the name of the cave is Heart of the Earth. Maybe this then answers your question?'

Burnum turned the big torch off and began the slow walk across the narrow path. A few metres across he said as clear as a bell, 'Take your time, and don't look over the edge.'

When Ross reached the other side he let out an almighty gasp, obviously happy to have made it. Burnum and Adam were patiently waiting for him at a ledge about five metres in depth on the other side. To the left was a tunnel; the only way to proceed.

Burnum patted him on the back. 'Wait, we are here.'

He disappeared into the tunnel. Ross and Adam could tell he was close; they could hear him shuffling around and see his torch light dancing. As the seconds ticked away, they saw the yellow light was getting stronger and stronger from wherever he was. Burnum was lighting candles in a small cave, the flickering lights occasionally broken by his long dark shadow.

'You can come in now,' he said.

Adam was first; Ross followed his footsteps, his heart racing. Burnum was standing at the top end of a small, fully enclosed cave. Ross felt as if he were in someone's mid-sized caravan, the ceiling was as low, the walls – he wondered if they were man-made or natural – were flat and smooth. Rocks, fashioned as candleholders were dotted on both the left and right of the cave walls, all with candles burning brightly, bathing the room in an ambient light. To the side and rear of the cave were a group of rocks, about knee-height, flat on top with a big flat boulder sitting in the middle. Ross thought it looked like a cave dweller's dining table. As he stood at the entrance of the room, the opposite wall finally caught his attention.

As he stared, Burnum spoke quietly. 'Welcome, to the home of the *Seventh List*.'

The wall contained many shallow indentations. The holes were all the same size, same shape, all flat at the bottom, not more than forty centimetres square. As Ross' eyes adjusted to the light he realised there was something ... hold on, there was an object in every hole. Every cavity contained what appeared to be a large, dusty and very old ... book.

Adam gasped, tapping Ross on the arm. 'What's that on your wrist, man?'

Ross looked down and caught his breath. 'What the hell?' he said, holding up his hand and staring at the bizarre anomaly.

0:00:31

Mikita walked into the busy Red Salt Bar, in the Crowne Hotel in downtown Darwin, capital of the Northern Territory, and spotted the men sitting in a booth on the far side of the room.

Siamko sat there with a smart-arse grin as she walked up to the booth. She gathered the others were the 'tour guides,' Siamko had hooked up with.

'Glad you could join us,' Siamko sneered.

He turned to the two men and introduced them to Mikita. They looked her up and down as if she were the only female on planet Earth.

Men had been giving Mikita the once over since she turned 16. Even back then, she possessed the Goddess-type aura her maturity had only heightened. She knew it came with the territory. Just don't ever touch her, or else she would squeeze your neck in that little spot which would have you passed out before you head hit the ground.

Once they had stopped mentally undressing her and the drinks arrived, they got down to business – Darwin style. The guides crapped on about their expertise and background. All that they had to decide was where the search would start, and this seemed to be a debatable point.

'It comes down to a couple of locations,' the taller man said. 'The best place to start is a place called Kakadu National Park.'

The other could not stop talking about this world-famous place called Ayers Rock, 'smack bang, in the middle of the country,' was his quote. After another thirty painful minutes of debate and argument, it appeared the meeting had no end in sight.

Finally, one of the guides made a compromise. 'We'll flip on it,' he muttered, producing a coin.

'Tails it is, brother.' He grinned. 'Kakadu, here we come.'

0:00:32

The strange mark had appeared at the bend of the wrist, where the forearm meets the hand and possessed a jade-coloured glow, similar to that of the Northern Lights that dance across the top of the world on certain nights. Ross rubbed it, poked it, and even sniffed it.

Burnum stood beside him, staring at the beautiful insignia now etched into Ross's skin. It was perfectly round, the size of an average man's watch face. A thin line ran around the outside, with intricate lines and shapes creating a unique insignia.

Adam stepped closer and checking his own wrist, saw one had appeared on him.

'Anangu call it the mark of the soul,' Burnum whispered, 'not one is the same as any other.'

'The mark of the soul,' Adam said quietly.

Ross's was in awe of it. 'Why has it appeared?'

Burnum smiled. 'I will show you.' He took Ross's elbow, leading him away from the crevices and books. All three stepped back two metres. Burnum held up his wrist. His insignia had disappeared.

Ross and Adam in unison checked their wrists – nothing.

Burnum then stepped them the two metres back towards the wall and like magic, the insignias came to life, as bright as the sun at dawn.

'Wow,' said Ross.

Burnum pointed to the wall. 'It is because you are within range of the book. When you are close to it, your insignia appears.' He signalled for them to sit on the floor. 'I will give you the short version because I am keen to stay on top of the time. We'll have to leave soon, the journey back takes longer.' A strange grin fleetingly appeared. 'The mark of the soul appears when you are within range of the Seventh List.' Burnum rose to his feet silently, shuffling over to the wall of books and standing before it.

Burnum began chanting something to himself. The old man slowly lifted his arms, stepping forward and reaching into one of the crevices. Then, carefully, he pulled the book in this particular crevice out.

'Sit there.' He nodded to a flat rock, like a table. Ross and Adam slipped over and sat on the rocks surrounding it. Burnum, as if carrying the Christmas turkey straight from the oven, placed the book before them.

In the ambient glow of the candles, the book seemed as old as time itself. A strange odour engulfed Ross's senses; it was of leather, quite pungent, strong. The book's skin was dark, almost black, with small interwoven twigs, encased by the thinnest of threads, surrounding the front and side covers. Square in the middle of the front cover sat a beautiful piece of opaque glass or something similar, mysterious, dark and mesmerising. The book, Ross tilted his head to get a better angle, was no more than ten centimetres thick. He guessed the other dimensions to be around thirty centimetres wide with its length slightly longer again.

Burnum put both his hands carefully to each side of the book, making eye contact with both men. He tilted his chin and took a deep breath. 'This,' Burnum spoke in serious tones, 'is the Seventh List. It contains the name of every single living soul on this planet.'

Ross and Adam stared at the book. Ross knew, if Burnum said it did ... it did. But part of him could not help but think, How can the names of seven billion plus people fit into this one solitary book?

Burnum smiled. 'I know what you are thinking – how do so many people fit into the one book?'

Ross and Adam nodded.

'All I can tell you is this,' he touched the top of the book lightly, 'this book is one of a kind, and not ... from here.'

Burnum would provide no further explanation. 'Every person alive is in here,' he whispered. 'It has the time they are born, down to the second.' He met his son's wide eyes. 'And the second the person will die.' He placed his hand to the side of the front cover, getting ready to open it, this time turning to Ross. 'When a person dies, their name is no longer in the book.'

Ross looked down at the book, his mind racing. 'Are you telling me that you will be able tell me the precise second I am going to die?'

Burnum, the master of pause, stared at Ross' intrigued eyes for what must have been ten torturous seconds. 'Yes,' he whispered.

Adam whispered an obscenity, under his breath.

Burnum leant closer to Ross. 'So the question is, Ross,' a quizzical look appearing, 'would you want to know?'

Adam held up his hand. 'Ross, surely...'

Burnum turned to his son. 'It's Ross'choice, Adam, and he's a grown man.'

'Don't do it, brother,' Adam pleaded, shaking his head with vigour. 'You'll ruin your life if you find out.'

Ross acknowledged his friend but wasn't sure. Maybe he wanted to know. He wanted a couple more minutes to decide. 'What are all the other books, Burnum?'

Burnum knew what he was doing and was happy to play along. 'There are twenty-five other books, all identical to this one.' He nodded at the table, 'you could not tell them apart.' Adam began a question but Burnum cut him short. 'The other twenty-five are fake.' He looked back over to the books. 'It takes a long time to know the right one.'

'Wouldn't anyone eventually work out which one was the real one?' Adam asked.

Burnum nodded. 'It would take some time, but yes.' He pointed to Adam for effect. 'These books have never left this cave ... ever.'

Ross was more interested in the working model. 'Tell us more about the insignia. And how could I distinguish my name from the potentially thousands of Ross Taylors dotted across the globe?'

'If you know the precise time, including the second, this will tell you – you have the right person. But if two people are born at the precise second, then you have a problem.' He placed his hand around Ross's wrist. 'This is one reason for the insignia.' Pulling Ross's arm over to the book, he said, 'Let me show you how this works.'

Burnum carefully counted out pages in the book. When he arrived at the one he wanted, he opened up the rest of the book enough for Ross's hand to sit comfortably, inside. 'Hold your hand right there and don't move it an inch.'

Burnum counted to five and then whispered, 'Look at the front cover of the book.'

Ross leant to his side and whistled. 'Check it out, Adam!'

Adam stood and came around Ross's side. 'Wow.'

The small glass crystal in the middle of the front cover now clearly displayed Ross's insignia, the same one as on his wrists. Burnum asked both men to stand up and away from the table.

He opened the book.

Burnum rested his hands on Ross's shoulders. 'The only name on the page,' he nodded to the open book, 'is the name of the person with the insignia you just saw on the front cover.' He leant forward as whispered, 'Yours, Ross.'

Ross could see a single line directly in the middle of the 'page' – a few words and numbers. The rest of the page was dark, a mix of grey and black, though what had Ross spellbound was that the darkness around the one line of information – moved. Ross leant a little closer. 'The page is ... alive,' he whispered. The book's pages were not of paper; it was if he were looking at a tablet, a device of some sort. The book looked as old as Uluru itself, but the pages were from the next century.

Burnum leant closer into Ross's ear. 'So, are you going to have a look at your date of death?'

Adam went to make one final plea but Burnum raised his hand. For him, the choice was Ross's only, and one that Burnum believed every person on the planet should have a right to know, though as one of the Gatekeepers of the Seventh and its prized possession, that was not grounds for him to give that right to the greater world. His job, for a good part of his life, was to ensure the book remained safely hidden – 1969 metres beneath Uluru.

Ross took one last look at Adam; his face said it all: Do not – do it.

The problem with this situation was simple.

Curiosity ... killed ... the ... cat. Ross knew he may find out something he was probably better off never knowing.

Reader, would *you* want to know?

He may die in a week ... a month ... a year. How would he live until then? The questions raged through his mind relentlessly, though one continuously overrode all others ... Do I want to know?

Ross sat down and looked closely at the page. He started

from the left, his heart thumping violently against his ribs. A tsunami of adrenaline exploded in his bloodstream. He established it was his date of birth; he recalled his mother once telling him he was born at 8.30 am, or thereabouts...

Wednesday, 13 August 1973, 8:31:39 AM

Ross turned to Burnum. 'Hold on a second!' He looked agitated. 'How does a book, thousands of years old, list my details by the Gregorian calendar?'

Burnum nodded calmly. 'We only know what previous elders have told us.' He looked up and over to the wall of books as if he was consulting them. 'When the Gregorian calendar was adopted world-wide, the book changed to the same.' He looked down at Ross, who did not seem very convinced. Burnum offered no further explanation.

Ross looked again down to the page, this time, noticing the name after his date of birth,

Ross Timothy Taylor

Ross flicked his eyes shut and asked himself, one final time. Do you want to know when your life is going to end? Hindsight, until his death, would now be his greatest enemy. Against his better judgement, something billions around the world would never – ever do ... Ross looked.

It was sooner than he expected.

Ross let out a shallow gasp. He couldn't breathe.

Burnum patted him on the back. 'You are now one of only a handful who has ever done it.'

Ross, his mind still ablaze, fumbled in his backpack for his bottle of water. He wished for a second it was a bottle of bourbon. He turned to Burnum. 'You can find out about when someone else is going to die, can't you?'

Burnum nodded. 'All you need to know is the precise second, minute, hour and day they were born, and if you know this,' he looked down to the book affectionately, 'then you will know.' He waved Ross back over to the book and turned to another page, sat down and leaned into the book's page. 'All you do is call their name to the page, and the name will appear.' He looked over to Adam. 'Well, the long list of that name.'

'How do you know what page to go to?' Ross asked, colour slowly returning to his face.

Burnum shrugged, as if the answer were obvious. 'You call their name, Ross, and – bingo.'

Adam looked over to the wall. 'How many books are there?'

Burnum shuffled over and stood next to his son, 'Twenty six,' he said. Adam stared at the wall for a few seconds before the Elder decided to move things along.

'We must go now, get your things together,' he said.

Ross and Adam were ready to go. They stood at the entrance, and stood in awe of the far wall. Ross had aged about ten years, or so it seemed. The burden of his newfound knowledge was maturing, to say the least. Burnum picked the book up carefully and placed it back in the crevice from which it had come. He flicked on his torch and blew out each candle in quick succession. Time was now upon them.

They walked back to traverse the narrow walkway. Ross wondered how far down the abyss actually went, after hearing Burnum's story of throwing a powerful torch down there and it being reduced to the size of a pinhead before evaporating into the pitch-black, it could be more than two kilometres at least. He had seen similar torches at night from many kilometres away; and although the light was the size of an ant's dick ... he could still see it.

Burnum reminded them before taking the first step, 'Look straight ahead on the path and do not look anywhere else.'

They arrived back into the world's largest, secret cave, the Lair of the Devil Dingo, Ross and Adam still in awe of the magnificent sight. It was a confusing feeling, as if they were back on ground level and it the middle of the night, though no clouds, no stars, nothing. Although the trip had been life-changing for them both, Adam and Ross's hearts sank as they remembered they'd have to walk all the way back up to ground level. The mere thought was exhausting...

Adam shrugged his shoulders. 'All right, let's go.' He nudged Ross with a friendly elbow. 'We have a long way to go.'

Burnum stood dead still; a strange, relaxed laugh came out a moment later. Ross and Adam turned and looked back at him. 'What's so funny, fella?' Ross couldn't see the joke.

Burnum waved them back to where he was standing. 'Who said we were walking back up?'

Adam and Ross shared confused expressions. They had no idea what he was trying to insinuate. Ross panned his torch around the cave walls. 'Do you have an elevator hidden somewhere down here?'

Burnum shrugged. 'You could say that ... well, sort of.' He led them back into the small, tight area which reminded Ross of the entrance to the cave system up at ground level. Burnum sat on the floor, signalling for them to do the same.

'No,' he said to Adam. 'Leave your backpack on.'

When Adam and Ross were seated, he asked them to move even closer. Now, the three men's knees were all touching. Burnum took a long, careful breath. 'Before we go any further—' He stared intently at them. 'You have to tell me if you believe in the power of the Heart of Uluru, and the Seventh List.'

Ross thought about it for a second. Yep, he was in. Adam knew in his heart, yes, he did too. Burnum held out his hands, one to each of them. 'Hold my hands, and each other's.'

Ross and Adam did as they were told, both feeling a tinge of

140

awkwardness as they latched on to each other's paws. Burnum straightened his back and rolled his head around his shoulders, his breaths slowing, though getting louder. He closed his eyes and held his chin high in the air. 'Close your eyes,' he said seriously. 'And if you open them, this will not work.'

Ross did as instructed, Adam the same. Ross squinted hard, there was no way he wanted to open them and mess things up. Burnum's breaths were longer and louder, before he said, 'Repeat the following words – all at the same time.' Burnum's tone was now loud and very deep, rolling out a chant in language that seemed to the boys as old as the rock itself.

Ross waited for the signal though he realised he would just have to repeat it the second time Burnum would say it. When he heard the first letter come from Burnum's lips, he then spoke the words with him. Adam fell into line and by the time they had to the fourth repetition, they were saying it together perfectly, as a chant. Ross could feel a strange sense of vertigo rising up from the pit of his stomach.

Ross could smell the rock; it was now a scent which he was used to, a chalky, dank odour which he actually liked. The smell grew stronger as the chants continued. Ross had lost count after repeating the chant ten or so times. He felt as if he were drifting off to sleep.

A refreshing gust of wind brushed across his face. Either something was going on, or Adam had blown him a kiss.

He certainly hoped it was not the latter...

His hands were clenching Burnum and Adam's hands so tightly, he could feel the small bones under his skin begin to ache. As he and Adam recited the chant once again, they realised Burnum had stopped. They went another round before Burnum spoke quietly. 'You can stop now.' They did as they were told. Strangely, both men's eyes remained welded shut. 'You can open your eyes now,' he added.

141

Ross slowly folded back his eyelids ... what a relief. A second later, a massive wave of panic washed over him. The cave was light and, fuck, where did the wind come from?

Adam snapped his head upright, as if something above him had screamed his name.

Ross let go of the other's hands, falling back on his backpack as a result. A shudder ran through him as his eyes adjusted to what they were seeing high above.

The three men were back on the surface!

The power of the Heart ... Ross knew it was absolutely impossible. However, there was one issue with that thought ... and all he had to do was look up and see the night sky once again. It was beyond doubt: he was back on the surface.

Adam's lips were tighter than a fish's arsehole; he said nothing and did not appear to have the ability to do so anytime soon. It was the most overwhelming thing that had ever happened to him.

Burnum recalled the first time he had done it. It was one thing to believe in the power, but it a completely new level of understanding and acceptance to experience it first hand.

The night sky was blanketed with dark grey cumulus clouds. With no moon, there was little light, the perfect cover to get to the truck and right out of there. Ross had walked about ten paces when his phone suddenly started going crazy with sounds.

The annoying little screeching sound meant someone had tried to call but under the rock, his phone was without doubt out of range. Burnum had said it was pointless leaving it on. After about the twelfth ring, Ross knew something was seriously wrong. 'Fuck,' he hissed, fumbling to find his mobile in the side pocket of his backpack.

Burnum turned, annoyed at the sound and how it may blow their cover. Only when he saw the blood draining from Ross' face, the phone still stuck to his ear, did he realise something was very wrong.

'Jimmy,' Ross gasped, before breaking into a gallop.

0:00:33

'Crikey, where the hell have you been?' Chris said to Ross as he opened the fortified back gate to the Hotel. 'I've been trying to get hold of you for nearly a day.' He led Ross, Burnum, and Adam up into his apartment, locking everything behind him.

Only when they were all standing in Chris' lounge room did Oxy really let loose. 'What is the deal with your phone? How come it's been off this whole bloody time?'

Ross looked over to Burnum and Adam, knowing he could not tell even Oxy where they had been. 'What is going on, has anything happened to Dad?'

Chris averted his eyes from Ross's gaze. The air in the room suddenly went cold. Burnum touched Adam's arm to signal for him to follow him into the kitchen. 'We'll leave you guys to talk alone for a minute.'

Ross's eyes grew wider as his heart sank, watching Burnum and Adam disappear through the kitchen door. When the door finally shut behind them, Chris raised his arm and rested his big hand on Ross's shoulder. The only way to tell Ross was to come straight out and say it. 'Jimmy,' Chris closed his eyes momentarily, 'passed away ... last night.'

Ross's face contorted as the words sank in.

Chris then did something Ross had never known him to do before. He stepped forward and gave Ross a bear hug. Ross knew it was just as much for himself, as it was for Ross. Chris and Jimmy were good mates, a friendship as strong as the bottles of alcohol on the top shelf of Chris's bar.

Chris fell heavily to the couch. He was still coming to terms with the death of a mate. He mulled over the details of what had transpired in the last twenty-four hours; Ross was unaware his long lost brother was in town already.

Adam stuck his head in and offered a round of beer. Ross and Chris both nodded in response to the offer.

'One more thing.' Chris looked over to the kitchen door to make sure it was closed. 'There's something else I need to tell you about last night.' Chris leant closer and fell into a whisper, 'Jimmy said something to me the second before he –'

Ross cocked his head. 'Go on.'

'He mumbled something...' Chris looked to the floor. 'Pleading with me to make sure I told you.' He took a long drink and looked out into the night sky. 'Something like the ... Sewer List, or something like that, being in danger.'

Ross's eyes grew wide. 'The Seventh List?'

'Yes,' Chris said, confidently. 'That's most likely it. Mean something to you, then?'

Ross jumped to his feet. 'And you said he was talking to Brett at the time, or before...?'

'Yes.'

'Adam,' Ross shouted. 'Come in here.'

Adam opened the door. Burnum stood behind him peering over his shoulder.

'Take me to Jimmy's house, now.'

'Of course.' Adam was wondering what in God's name was going on.

Minutes later, the truck's bright lights came across the side fence just before the entrance into Merrigang. Ross had said nothing. Adam had gathered Jimmy had died, and was a little

146

concerned as to what was going on right now, however the answers would come soon enough.

As the truck slowed to turn, Ross saw Jimmy's house through the dirty, smudged window.

Fuck, was that someone on the front veranda? 'Dad?' Ross muttered.

Adam shuddered. 'What's going on, Ross?' He tried to get a glimpse of the house through Ross's window. 'You're freaking me out.'

As the truck lights swung through the front gates, bathing the veranda, in a blinding-white-light, it was undeniable. There was no one standing on that veranda, tonight. 'I could have sworn...' Ross muttered to himself, confused and a little embarrassed.

Burnum knew, now was not the time to speak.

But – he had seen him too.

0:00:34

Connellan Airport throbbed with activity, this late morning. It would remain busy until the hundred or so passengers had picked up their baggage, and made their way to the various accommodations at the Uluru Resort.

'Welcome to Ayers Rock.'

'Thank you, Brett.' Achban offered his hand, shaking Brett's firmly before doing the same with Stuart.

'How was your flight?' Stuart said, making a point of looking at Achban before resting his gaze on Dania. Her flowing, shoulder-length crop of mousey-blonde hair sat perfectly above her subtle round face; hazel eyes and a lightly tanned complexion. Her nose was a tiny bit on the wide side, though with full, deep red lips revealing a dazzling smile, it would be the last thing you would focus on. Standing just a little taller than Achban, her pencil mini-skirt revealed taut, fit legs below a loose, open neck shirt, her upper body perfectly proportionate with no hint of flab on her arms, or anywhere else.

'Fine,' Dania said neutrally. The air in the small terminal was muggy; it reminded Dania of some of the small airports back home in the middle east.

Most of the passengers now congregated around the baggage carousel, all very keen to snavel their bags and get on their

149

way. When Achban had spotted his bags, he turned to Stuart. 'You have the car?'

'It's out the front, I'll bring it round.'

A few minutes later, Stuart pulled the Land Cruiser out onto the Lasseter Highway, which would take them from the airport to the resort in under ten minutes. Passing Giles Road, it stretched off into the desert for a kilometre before coming to the township of Old Yulara.

Brett sat in the front with the big Stu; Dania and Achban in the back. Brett was nervous; he was not good at creating conversation. He decided to step out on a limb, turning and smiling to Dania. 'Where are you guys booked in to stay?'

Dania had not warmed to Brett in the slightest. There was something in those beady little eyes. 'Sails in the Desert hotel,' she muttered and looked out the window.

Brett let out a small whistle. 'Nice place,' he said.

The rest of the journey was in silence.

Once he'd pulled the Land Cruiser up in front of the luxury hotel, Stuart leapt out and carried the Israelis' luggage to reception.

'Thank you, Stuart,' Achban smiled. 'Much appreciated.'

Stuart knew brownie points never hurt.

The retired Army leader smiled faintly. 'I want you both to be back here in one hour. We will meet in my private suite.'

Five minutes later, back in the Foyer of their far cheaper hotel, Brett looked glum, staring towards the front door from his vantage point of the two dreadfully cheap and uncomfortable sofas. He was envious of his mate's ability to kiss-arse, and the lodgings of their current Employers.

Stuart sat forward, 'They want us back over there in one hour, my chum.'

He poked him in the shoulder. 'You got that?'

Brett scowled, 'Yes – Boss.' It was too early in the morning for him to think straight. 'You think those Japanese babes will be back for—'

Ross.

The sight of him cut the little ex-junkie's sentence clean off. 'Hello, Brett.'

When Ross had spoken to Brett on the phone a few days ago – the conversation was amicable. That was then – this was now. Jimmy was stone cold dead and Brett had been there. Ross tasted a really bad shit sandwich.

Brett stood awkwardly in the entrance, the doors refusing to close. Stuart had to give him a nudge to move him out of the path of a group of tourists wishing to leave the hotel.

Ross moved the few paces to the couches in the foyer. Brett reluctantly followed, a cocktail of emotions running around what was left of his brain. Only when they stood within two feet of each other did Ross sit down. Brett sat on the opposite chair.

Stuart looked from one man to the other. 'Do you guys want a coffee?'

When Stuart was out of earshot, Ross looked Brett up and down. He was in no mood for politeness. 'So you saw Dad, huh?'

Brett shrugged. 'Yeah, saw him last night.' He stared out across the foyer to avoid Ross's killer stare.

'What did you talk about?'

Brett turned his attention back to his arsehole brother. Who the fuck did this guy think he was? He took his time answering, staring down his brother, knowing the longer he took, the more he was going to piss him off. Eventually, he waved his hand in the air. 'You know—' He met Ross's eyes. 'Mum, prison, jobs. You know.'

Ross leant forward, absorbing the response. He wished he could spring over the coffee table and strangle the prick on the spot. 'Anything else?' Ross narrowed his eyes. 'Did you talk about anything else?'

Brett shrugged his scrawny little flowerpot shoulders. 'Nah, that was about it.' To his relief, Stuart appeared with the coffees.

Ross looked up at Stuart and thanked him but made no attempt to introduce himself. Ross's anger was rising. They had talked about something else, that lying bastard, he told himself. Jimmy had blown a valve, *the* valve … and as a result, his dying words to his best mate were to warn Ross of the danger.

The danger of the book … possibly under threat.

As the awkward silence returned, Ross knew it was useless trying to get anything out of Brett. They say time heals all wounds – bullshit. The wounds Brett inflicted upon their family would never heal, even now – with both parents now gone. Ross sculled the awful, lukewarm coffee, rising to his feet as he put the cup down. 'Meet me at Chris's hotel at three.' Ross barely waited for his brother to respond. 'We need to finalise the arrangements for Dad.'

Ross was about to head through the door when Brett snapped out of his daydream. 'Hey, Ross?'

'Yes?'

'Where were you the last couple of days, we tried to call you dozens of times?'

'Er – Alice. My phone battery stuffed up.' Ross hesitated so minutely, only someone who had the same family blood would pick it up. He disappeared through the doorway.

Brett fell back into the couch and replayed that look on his brother's face. The stupid prick, Brett thought. He never could put on a poker face…

* * *

Stuart knocked lightly. The door opened a second later and Dania led them into Achban's suite. Brett glanced around. Now this is where I should be staying, he thought.

The room was three times bigger than his digs, with a lounge area, a full size dining table, beautiful ... and a great view of the outdoor pool area, good for a perve... Stuart gave him a quick tap on the arm and he took his seat at the dining table across from Achban and Dania.

'Before we proceed,' Achban said, grinning – a little put on, but still a grin all the same – 'I have a gift, gifts for you both.'

Dania placed four small boxes in front of Achban, who was still smiling. 'Here you go,' pushing two boxes to each man.

Stuart and Brett smiled. This was a nice way to start, huh?

Stuart was first to open one of his two boxes, he let out a 'Phew' as he opened up the lid to reveal the contents. The big, expensive-looking watch reminded him of those divers' watches rich-people wore, the ones who paid him tens of thousands to re-landscape their gardens. He held it in his hand and admired the heaviness, the stainless steel band. This watch bloody rocked. He grinned over to Brett, whose face was also animated.

Brett thought the watch must have cost hundreds, a nice little thing to pawn if he ever needed some cash...

Achban cleared his throat, and the two Australians met his relaxed eyes. 'You like the watches I see. I hope you enjoy them, one each is for you both to keep.'

Stuart and Brett gasped at the same time. This business venture they had stumbled upon – was looking up.

Achban eyed off the other two boxes. 'Now, I want you to open the other two, but don't take them out.'

Stuart and Brett shared a frown, though did as commanded. They flipped open the small lids and revealed watches identical to the ones they had just been given.

'There's one slight difference to the watches I gave you both, and the other two.' Achban leant forward, resting his elbows on the table. 'You see,' tapping both of the boxes containing the second set of watches, 'these ones have built in GPS tracking chips.'

Stuart understood, but Brett was out of his depth. Achban picked up the blank look on his face. 'We can track anyone, anywhere in the world, once they start wearing it.' Achban was proud of the innovative technology the Mossad had created; it was the best in the world. He winked at Stuart. 'All the person has to do is put it on, the tracking chip activates via the movement it picks up.' He pointed to a laptop sitting on a desk to the side of the room. 'We track, here. We will decide together who is given these watches, okay?'

Stuart shook his head. 'Wow, unbelievable.'

Achban nodded. 'Now, let's get down to business.'

Achban, are you going to tell the two men their watches are also GPS chipped? No?.

You sneaky little prick.

Achban informed the two Australians his team was en-route from Sydney. A four-member team, straight from the Mossad on secondment to the TSA, were experts in these types of operations on foreign soil. They had entered the country via New Zealand on tourist's visas, posing as a bunch of Moroccan backpackers. They were due to arrive in twenty-four hours.

Dania then pored over mountains of information regarding Uluru, the Olgas, hundreds of different sites. Brett could feel himself nodding off. He zoned out. He was in a spa full of lovely ladies, snorting coke, with one of the many hundred dollar bills he was going to earn, thanks to these two wankers on the other side of the dining table.

Achban's deep monotone snapped him out of his daydream. 'Brett?'

Brett guessed it was at least the second time Achban had said his name.

'Do you have any news, updates you want to share with

154

us?'

Brett's face lit up. 'Yes.' He sat back in his chair. 'Do I have some good stuff for you!'

0:00:35

Burnum smiled. 'Your dad ... called it "The HR Knock List." '

Ross caught himself smiling, though the pain in his chest was still there. Shaking his head slowly, he turned and looked out towards the monolith. 'Jimmy sure did have a sense of humour. I assume HR stood for – human race?'

Burnum nodded, patting Ross on the arm. He let out a tired sigh, his mind drifted to his bed – he needed more sleep, soon. But there was something Ross and Adam needed to know, something very, very important – about the Seventh List.

Ross realised he had interrupted the Elder. 'Sorry, Burnum, I interrupted you, please go on.'

Burnum rose to his feet and walked to the edge of the railing. Save for a tuft of cloud high on the horizon, the sky was clear in every direction. The day was warming rapidly; a sudden hot gust of wind threw a thin line of reddish sand across the deck. Burnum wiped his face as he turned around to see the men. His mind rattled. Where do I start?

But when he began, the words flowed freely from his mouth, as if his mind went into autopilot. He only noticed a couple of times the gobsmacked look on his son's and Ross's faces, the shockwaves of what he was telling them clearly reverberating in their minds. They seemed to be shocked more by what he was telling them now than by the way they had arrived back on the surface from the Lair of the Devil Dingo.

Ross leant forward and studied the weeds under his father's decking, before finally looking up and meeting Burnum's eyes. 'So let me get this one hundred per cent clear...' He scratched the side of his head hard. 'Anyone who gets access to the book, can change when someone -' A dark blue flash of metal accompanying a whirlwind of dust, killed the end of Ross's question in an instant.

Chris's 1984 Nissan Patrol pulled up at Merrigang's front veranda.

* * *

'Do you believe him?' Dania flipped shut the file on Brett. 'He has spent twelve of the last fifteen years of his life in prison Achban,' she muttered, checking her Blackberry for updates. 'I'd rather not be relying on what they tell us.'

Achban knew Dania was thorough; it was one of her indelible qualities. 'Deep down, I don't trust him either; he is as dumb as they come – but sneaky. But my gut tells me there may be something in what he said, in what happened.' Achban sat back in his chair and ran his hand through his hair, it coming to rest at the base of his neck. 'His father lived around here.' He looked down to study his notes. 'He was very close to the Aboriginal community.'

The two Israelis sat and contemplated the situation for a few minutes in silence. Eventually, Achban said, 'Anyone who has a heart attack from finding out what we are looking for must know something about it.'

Dania agreed. 'Right. And don't forget this brother of Brett's too – he's still around.'

* * *

158

Chris jumped back into his truck. 'Three o'clock, right?'

'See you then. Brett should be there as well.' Ross wiped the dust from his eyes, watching Chris' old beat up truck rumble out of the front gate and wind its way back towards the township. He turned to Burnum. 'Now, where were we? You can change the date of someone's death, in the book?' Ross was still trying to come to terms with the whole deal. He stole a glance over to Uluru. Not only could the book tell you when you die, now – you could change the date of death also? 'Jesus,' Ross muttered, turning to Adam to see how he was faring.

Adam was in his own world of mental-torture. 'It's amazing, to say the least,' he whispered.

'So,' Ross turned to Burnum with a grin. 'Is there anything else about the book you want to fill us in on?'

Burnum's serious expression wiped the attempt at joviality from Ross's face. After a moment of silence Ross sat forward. 'What – don't tell me there really *is* more?' he said.

Burnum took a deep breath, yes – there was more. He looked over to the Rock for what seemed to be almost a full minute, before turning to the men and coming straight out with it.

'You can add and take off the years of someone's life, by the number of 26.'

Adam did what he did best. He screwed his face up and blurted out the question on everyone's lips, '26, why 26?' He looked at his father intently. Burnum shrugged his shoulders, wiping the sweat from under the rim of his Akubra, 'We never learnt why, son.'

Ross put both hands to his face, trying to get his head around it. 'So, what happens if you take, say, 26 years off someone's life, who only has 25 years to live?'

The look on Burnum's face answered the question. They would be instantly – dead.

Ross shook his head to make sure he was processing this

159

correctly. It was then the picture came into full view. The Seventh List was the ultimate killing machine. Anyone who had less than 26 years to live – could be killed instantly, without even touching them.

0:00:36

Chris took a glass from the fridge. 'Beer...?'

'Does a bear shit in the woods?' Ross smirked.

Without looking, Chris poured the beer, angling the glass to minimise froth, it was poetry in motion. He plonked the picture-perfect beer in front of Ross, turning to Brett who was sitting in complete silence. 'How about you – Junior?' he smirked.

Brett gritted his teeth. Fff-uck ... how he hated Chris calling him Junior! One thing was for certain, Chris knew how much Brett hated it and Brett knew that Chris knew how much he hated it. He also knew now was not the time to make trouble, especially in the heart of arsehole village: Chris's hotel... 'Thanks, yes.' Brett pulled off the impossible, abstaining from giving Chris any visible sign of sarcasm. Brett was starting to think a little smarter for a change... As soon as Brett had taken his first swig, Chris got right down to business. Jimmy had made Chris executor of his will, many moons ago.

Brett seemed agitated by the news, losing the control he demonstrated a few seconds ago. 'Well,' he sneered. 'I guess there is nothin' to talk about, huh?'

Ross wondered where the little fuck got off. He obviously believed he was not even in the will. 'I gather you think you get nothing?'

Well, you hit the nail on the head, Skinny ... Correct! A distant voice deep in Ross' consciousness whispered.

Chris did not wait for an answer. 'Your dad re-jigged his will – a week ago. It will take a couple of weeks to come up from Sydney. I'll contact you then and let you know.' Someone called Chris's name from the other bar. 'Be back in ten to talk about the funeral arrangements, okay?'

'No problem, Oxy.' Shit, ten minutes alone with Brett, Ross thought. He thanked the Lord above he was at least at a bar, to numb the pain.

The bar was busy, the air full of shit-talking and the television in the corner bellowing out results from the fifth at Randwick... Plenty going on made it slightly easier for Ross to endure the pain of being alone with a brother he barely knew.

Then Brett said something profoundly out of character. 'I've missed a lot of your birthdays.'

'No big deal, Brett, trust me, it's okay.' Ross went back to his beer and caught a glimpse of the clock above the bar. Jesus, another eight minutes of torture to go.

Brett tapped him on the arm. 'No, I need to make up for that.'

Ross screwed up his face. Where was this coming from? He did not give a rat's ass about Brett not giving him presents for nearly all of his life. God knows he wouldn't want the crap gifts anyway...

Not deterred, Brett leant down into his backpack and while Ross was looking at the TV, put the small gift-wrapped box on the bar in front of his older brother. After about thirty seconds, Brett had to clear his throat to get Ross's attention. The older Taylor nearly spat his mouthful of beer across the bar.

'What is this?' Ross asked, quickly wiping his mouth.

Brett grinned.

Phew, those teeth ... and they say Coke rots your teeth, try

162

the powdered version.

'It's a birthday present.' He smiled. 'As I said: to make up for all those that I've missed.'

Ross saw the Tag Heuer brand on the watch face. 'Did you steal it?'

Brett managed to look offended, 'Been working for months, saving most of me bloody wages.'

'All right then, settle down.'

What was even more bizarre was that Brett got all giddy. 'Come on then, let's see how it looks on ya.'

Chris returned right on cue, as promised and Ross felt a wave of relief. Then – lo and behold – Brett offered to shout him a beer. Ross wondered if Brett might have turned a corner...

Chris ushered the Taylors into his private office, a tiny room out the rear of the hotel with barely enough room to swing a golf club, let alone a cat. He squeezed his way around his desk and as soon as his ass hit his chair, ran through the plans for Jimmy's funeral and wake. Jimmy was an organised bastard, even in death; he must have had an inkling of his sudden demise, for he'd plotted out the plans methodically, only last week. Chris ran through them point by point; it didn't take long. The wake would take place in the front bar of the hotel, which everyone in Old Yulara would have expected. The whole township knew Jimmy and Chris were like brothers and the only place worthy of such an auspicious occasion would be the one place Jimmy generally called his second home. 'Now we have all that straightened out,' Chris rose from his chair, 'I'm going to have to leave you both to enjoy the rest of your day; I have other things which need my attention.'

Ross saw Stuart sitting in the rented four-wheel drive when he followed Brett out front. 'Nice wheels,' he said, scanning over the Toyota Land Cruiser, thinking it seemed a little excessive.

Ross gave Stuart a subtle nod and headed to his own favourite scrap of metal on wheels.

'Enjoy the watch,' Brett grinned, 'I hope you like it.'

Brett had such a cocky look on his face. Nice watch and all, Ross thought, but it's not a bloody Rolex. 'Thanks, I will,' He muttered.

Ross felt the weight of the watch on his wrist. He certainly was a fan of a watch with some meat on it, bending his arm up and down a couple of times, it felt good.

Beep ... Beep ... Beep... The tracking device – activated.

0:00:37

Ross's mood was sombre. You'd expect it to be – smack bang in the middle of a crowded bar at his father's wake.

Like his old man, Ross loved nothing more than a beer, especially on a sunny Saturday afternoon. He surprised many attendees at the gathering by sticking to the annoying beverage of lemonade, annoying because it sent him to the bathroom constantly. And there was something annoying about going to the bathroom constantly – every time he did, he bumped into someone else who wanted to lay on the condolences thick and fast. Ross just wanted to stay in the corner with his close friends around him and see the night through sober, and in control.

The speech he'd made at the funeral was low-key and heartfelt, the room was devoid of dry eyes, even the tough bastards from the airport fought with their emotions. The tightly packed bar was a testament to Jimmy's popularity; the entire population of Old Yulara, just about every employee from Connellan Airport and many of the working residents of the Resort mingled in each other's personal space, happy to have paid their respects to Jimmy, in the way he would have insisted they do – at Oxy's Public Bar.

Oxy cut his way through the crowd to Ross. 'You look like you could use some fresh air.'

Ross agreed, following Chris out to the veranda. There they met up with John Kelsey, owner of Kelsey's Charter Services Yulara, the biggest helicopter charter service in that little corner of the Northern Territory. He doubled as Ross and Jimmy's boss, as well as one of Jimmy's closest mates. Having met flying the Hueys in Vietnam, it was John who'd happily accepted Jimmy's offer to be his first employee over thirty years ago.

John's previously taut and trim package had given way to thinning hair, large round glasses a permanent part of his face since turning the big five-oh. A love of home brew showed generously across his torso. With deep grey eyes in a dark-brown face, thanks to years in the sun, John possessed a friendly demeanour which attracted people to him with ease – since beginning his business over three decades ago, flying people from all over the world around Uluru and the Olgas, the tourists had loved him by the thousands.

The three men stood staring out across the desert. Uluru to their right, the horizon stretching as far across as their vision could stretch. 'How are you holding up?' John asked quietly.

'Not too bad, boss.' Ross shrugged his shoulders. 'What about you, bit over it?

John nodded, it was clear this week had been hard on him. Jimmy was to John as good as a brother, as well as being the most reliable and professional pilot he could have ever wanted. Fortunately for John, Ross had learned his own expert skills in the pilot's seat from Jimmy, and was one of the best helicopter pilots in the Northern Territory.

Chris raised his schooner into the air. 'Jimmy, we are going to bloody miss you brother.' Ross and John, nodding solemnly, raised their glasses and took a sip.

'What the?–' Ross felt a strong gust of wind on the back of his neck. Inky-black storm clouds had whipped up in seconds and were rushing towards Uluru and Old Yulara at a freakishly alarming rate, as if Armageddon itself was approaching. With gasps of amazement and profanities, people came out to stare at the storm coming towards them. Ross smelt the scent of fresh rain as the wind picked up harshly and blew across the veranda with attitude. With it came the desert sand, cutting into anyone who stood in its way and they retreated inside.

As Chris pushed the door closed he jumped at the crack of an almighty explosion of thunder, louder than he had ever heard before. It sounded as if the sky were splitting open and the world might spill into space with everything and everyone going with it, shaking the hotel as if there was an earthquake right behind it.

The rain came pouring down, hard and loud. John, Chris and Ross pushed their way through to the window and a collective thought came to all three...

Déjà vu.

Some hours later, Chris breathed a heavy sigh of relief. His pub had survived the storm ... just. The downpipes sounded as if they were going to fall apart from the torrent of rain, the roof, hell – how it had not caved in he had no idea ... but his hotel had emerged from the downpour unscathed. He had been looking forward to the wake ending, and now all the guests had finally left. Ross and John were last two in the bar.

The day weighed heavily on Chris's emotions; he was tired, his body ached, and bed was looking better than ever. The initial storm had died down, though the rain continued to fall in buckets – this had cleared his hotel like nothing else, most people concerned the longer they stayed, the less chance there was of them making it back home through the mud easily. The downpour had turned the dry patch of desert for 100 kilometres around into a quagmire of thick, red mud. In the following days, the plants would relish the rain and lap up its every drop, and the surrounding deserts would turn a rich shade of green.

'One more drink ... for him,' Chris announced, pouring them all two fingers of scotch. As they savoured their drinks, and Ross's first for the day, the rain, now lighter, continued to fall on the tin roof, providing a low, subtle hum. John was about to indulge the other two men in another 'Jimmy' story when a four-wheel drive pulled up out front.

Chris sighed. 'Jesus Christ ... who the hell is this?' He was in no mood for a local who wanted a nightcap. But it was Ian Petersen, back again. Ian was not a big drinker; a nightcap would be unusual for him to say the least.

The first thing Ross realised was the pulverised look on Ian's face. He had either seen a ghost, or someone had strung him up by his gonads for the last hour. He walked straight to the bar, avoiding Ross and making eye contact with Oxy. The two stared at each other for a few seconds before Oxy said, 'What's up with you, champ?'

'I need a drink. Bourbon. Straight.'

Chris reached for the shot glass, then a bottle of bourbon, without taking his eyes off Ian.

Ian's eyes had fallen to the bar, the look of shock not changing. Only when the shot glass was empty did some sort of coherence and colour return to his face. He put both elbows on the bar, dipping his head and running his hands across his face and into his hair.

Ross stepped closer and put a hand on his shoulder. 'What's wrong, Ian?' He glanced over to John and Chris. 'You look like you've seen a bloody ghost!'

Chris nudged him. 'What is going on Ian? Talk to us.'

'It's Jimmy,' he said before correcting himself, 'er, Jimmy's body.'

Ross leaned forward. 'What about it?' His heart began to thump violently.

Ian closed his eyes and whispered, 'It's gone.'

0:00:38

The tour guides sat around the fire, with their two, quite un-usual, Russian tourists. And when the sun went down in the outback, the jokes followed ... if that is what you could call them...

'And then he said, "now we can all get some sleep!" '

Justin was good at many things, Steve thought. Telling jokes was not one of them. Justin roared with laughter. Steve looked on, turning bright red.

Siamko and Mikita, in their first and only moment of unity, met each other's eyes and shrugged; they had not realised the Australian had been telling a joke in the first place.

Steve placed a log on the fire, turning to his lifelong business partner. 'Good joke mate, though I don't think our friends got it.' He smiled over at Mikita.

Mikita returned the smile. Justin, she thought, looked a little embarrassed. 'Don't worry; I am taking a while to understand your sense of humour,' she said.

Mikita looked up towards the stars and reflected on the beautiful night sky; a mesmerising blanket of pinpricked bright lights hung far above her. She had never seen this many stars before. The Australian guides had brought her and Siamko to a secluded camping spot below a large cliff face, one of the safest places to camp in Kakadu, they said. Surrounded by large ghost gums, it reminded Mikita of a sort of oasis. Save for the night sounds of various animals that occasionally came and went, it was peaceful and serene. Even in deep cover, Mikita could relax, tune out and enjoy such a moment when it presented itself.

Siamko, well, he was enjoying the view too, though he was not looking up, he was looking sideways – at her. He was secretly undressing her while Justin and Steve debated with vigour who was the better joke teller.

A familiar sound snapped everyone back to attention. The satellite phone. Siamko picked up the bulky handset and walked away from the campfire.

'Greetings, Comrade.'

Vadislav.

The guides made themselves scarce, one heading off into the bush, nature obviously calling him, and the other to his tent. Mikita crept closer to the fire, turning and warming up the back of her legs. She was listening intently to Siamko's conversation although it seemed it was all coming from the other end of the line. A few moments later, Siamko walked back, offering the phone. 'Yes, Vadislav, I will. Now you wanted to speak to Mikita, yes?' There was something about his grin she did not like at all...

'Hello, Vadislav, it's good to hear your voice,' she said confidently.

'How is the mission progressing, Mikita?'

'We've been at this location for a day now, still nothing to report.'

'Right.' A long pause from the other side of the world. 'Keep looking. I want this damn book – now.'

'Yes, we will continue the—' But he had already cut the line. She looked at the screen for a second, as if it would tell her something, before she caught in the corner of her eye; that darn look on Siamko's face again. It was a cross between a sneer and a smirk.

Something was up, shit.

'I am tired,' Mikita said, letting out a overstretched yawn, 'I think I may retire for the night.'

Justin stuck his head out of his tent. 'But I was just getting started with my jokes,' he shouted.

Steve cut in, looking at Mikita, 'You're better off in that case.'

'Goodnight gentlemen.'

All three watched Mikita head off to her tent. All marvelled at the white, skin-tight, three-quarter cargo pants she'd been wearing. Small wonder she led at the front of the line for the better part of the entire day.

Mikita snuggled into her sleeping bag. With years of training and experience, she remained alert to them sitting around the campfire, talking quietly. No one would come near her tent without her knowing about it.

Mikita slipped out her foundation and mirror pack. The small communications device powered to life and before the minute was out, she had sent a coded message to Dania. The message was as simple as succinct – there was a strong chance her cover was blown. She needed urgent directions from Achban.

Mikita slipped her head out to check everything was in order. The ambient glow of the fire reflected off all three men, they had not moved an inch. She waited for the state-of-the-art device to deliver a response. After recognising her fingerprint on the tiny mirror, the message appeared across the reflective screen, thanks to a wafer thin LED board set behind the transparent mirror. Mikita's heart sank. Achban was obviously not as concerned as she was about her fears for her cover being compromised. She snapped back into focus – she was one of the best Mossad agents the agency had ever seen. If the shit hit the fan, she would take evasive action and exit the assignment.

Mikita took one more look at the message to make sure she had read it correctly before tapping the tiny icon which deleted the message, and then turned off the device. With her head on the pillow, she began mentally preparing for the task Achban had instructed her to do.

'*Stay where you are and keep Siamko distracted.*'

* * *

Ross's head was in a spin; make that a spiral, heading downwards to hell. 'How can he just disappear?' He pushed the bar stool out from under him.

'Calm down son, sit down,' John said in an authoritative tone, loud enough for Ross to take notice and act accordingly.

Ian was despondent. Chris had given him another shot and it had evaporated quicker than the last. 'I don't know, Ross. The undertakers from Alice arrived to take him,' he buried his face in his hands, 'and he was gone.'

Ross headed for the door.

'Where are you going?' Chris shouted after him.

The rain was down to a light shower as Ross ran through the shallow puddles to his car. He powered down Giles Road, locked up the brakes and slid through the gates of Merrigang, pulling up centimetres from the front veranda. He almost busted down the front door, shouting 'Dad?'

After a few seconds of silence, his shoulders slumped. He looked down and realised he had dredged mud into his Jimmy's house.

'Ross.'

Mud nearly appeared inside his expensive jeans. Jesus. Ross ran back to the front door and flung it open, skidding to a stop in the middle of the veranda. 'Jimmy?' he bellowed through the sound of the rain on the tin roof above.

'He's not here.'

The voice came from the shadows from the opposite side. Ross nearly broke his neck as he spun around.

Burnum; a black canvas poncho covered his body from the knees up, the cape covering his head. In the darkness Ross could only barely see the tip of his nose.

'Where is he?' Ross shouted.

Burnum didn't move an inch. 'He's gone.'

The rain stopped.

Burnum slipped the poncho off his head and shook it out. 'He's no longer on the earth.'

The words ricocheted around Ross's confused mind. It had been a long and difficult day, and now … this. 'Is he down—' he flicked his head in the direction of Uluru, 'there?'

'No, Ross, he's not.'

'Are you bullshitting me, elder?'

'He is not … down there.'

'I want to go back, hold the book and call his name. Are you coming, or do I go it alone?'

Burnum had the uncanny ability to hold someone's stare until the other person's eyeballs practically popped out of the sockets. Ross stepped down from the confrontation.

The question of checking Jimmy's name in the book had Burnum intrigued, although he had done this a while ago and the Elders had found out then that somehow, he was not in the book. Burnum did want to check again … just to be sure. Something, deep inside him, told him he should. He looked out across the night sky towards Uluru. The clouds were clearing quickly, blotches of darkness dotted with stars. 'When do you want to go?'

Ross pulled his left hand up and checked his new watch.

173

Burnum leant forward. 'Nice watch.'

'Thanks,' Ross said. 'A present from Brett.'

Burnum smirked.

'What?'

Burnum's left eyebrow curled into an arc. 'Well, the thing is – he gave Adam an identical watch.' Burnum shook his head. 'How's that for generous?'

* * *

Brett let them know. 'The eagle has landed! He's on the move.'

'Where now?'

'How would I know? I haven't seen him in years...'

Dania and Achban exchanged a look of death. A sound from one of the laptops took Achban's attention away from Smacky and back to the screen.

Dania hovered behind.

'He's just passed the Resort.' Achban scurried to the dining table and looked closely at a couple of the maps. He came back to the desk and sat back in the chair, watching the dot move across the map on the screen. 'Hold on,' he said, scratching the thought out of his head. 'Maybe he's heading for the settlement over there.' He turned to Brett. 'What is that place?'

Brett cleared his throat. He liked the beer in Achban's room, it was free. 'Mootee-joo-tal-oo, Boss, that's what they call it.'

Dania could not wait for him to finish his beer; it wouldn't take long, that she knew for sure. As soon as the can was empty, the room would be empty of a skinny little Aussie runt.

Achban brought a map up from another file, Mutitjulu was the Aboriginal settlement Brett had tried to enunciate. He checked the time. Ross, or the blinking red dot, had remained in the same place for the last twenty minutes.

'Yes, he's gone to the settlement,' Brett told Dania as she ushered him out the door. 'He probably hangs out there all the time.'

174

Achban adjusted the cushion on the desk chair, preparing for the long haul. Dania had agreed to take shifts; she would take over in a couple of hours.

'I love you, Tel Aviv Covert Systems,' Achban breathed a second later, raising his hands and clapping hard over his head. One beep had become two. The second watch – activated. And now they were both on the move, together. A little later, Achban clapped again. 'They are at the rock.'

'Are you sure?'

'One hundred per cent, there is no doubt.'

'Why would they be out at the rock at this time of the night?'

'That is the 64 million shekel question.'

0:00:39

'Nice watch ... bloody heavy.'

'Pansy.' Ross smirked. 'Do you want me to ask Brett if he could get it swapped for a ladies model?' He was still dumb-founded by Brett's supreme act of kindness, not only giving him a birthday present, but Adam one as well? It just was so unusual.

Adam held up his middle three fingers. 'Read between the lines.'

Burnum flicked his hand up in the air. 'Guys – shut up,' he whispered, holding his middle finger up to his lips. Ross and Adam obliged and cut out the talking.

They were halfway across the no man's land between the Mutitjulu settlement and the rock. The sky had cleared from the horrendous storm that had dumped months of average rain-fall on Uluru in a matter of hours. There were small lakes dotted around the monolith. Even after the rains cease, the water streaming off Uluru, through hundreds of channels in the rock face, continued to cascade for many, many hours. To see it is amazing, even at night – it had been years since Ross had wit-nessed the extraordinary sight.

The water had turned many paths to thick, red mud. Oh the joy, of walking through it ... not.

Burnum put his fingers to a little cascade. 'The Seventh leaks,' he said. 'Over the many generations, many elders have spoken of entering the Heart of Uluru and feeling the occasional splutter of water from high above. It's good luck to have the rain hit you when you walk across the cave.' Burnum believed there were many minute cracks dotted over the rock, connecting with the ceiling of the cave below.

Distracted, water seeped far too quickly into Ross's boot before he could yank it out of the slightly deeper hole in the path. He stopped to shake at least some of the red water out.

'Come on, *piranpa*,' Adam hissed with a smirk. 'Let's get down there.'

Ross gave a small groan before catching up to the others. They were only twenty metres from the fenced off area where the secret entrance was safely hidden away. 'One of these days,' Ross whispered to Burnum, 'You will have to show us how this trapdoor works – it's amazing.'

Burnum nodded as the wall silently fell away to reveal the secret entrance. 'One day you may get a key of your own,' he said.

Ross gave Adam a fair nudge with his elbow, gloating. 'Did you hear that brother?'

'Dickhead,' Adam hissed, grinning before asking his old man, 'Can anyone open the entrance, Dad?'

Burnum shook his head and turned on his larger torch. 'No Adam, only the chosen three.' He took a long deep breath, rolling his shoulders and adjusting his backpack. 'Well, now you know the route, we'll hopefully get down there sooner.'

* * *

'What is it, Achban? Where have the signals gone?'

Achban rested his chin in the palm of his left hand, staring at the screen. 'The batteries were checked before I handed them over.' He sat back and intertwined his hands behind his head. 'Unless they've damaged them?'

Achban sat staring at the screen for another minute or so. A light went on in his head. He pulled out a detailed map of Uluru itself and scoured it so closely, Dania thought he was going to sniff it.

'What is it? What are you thinking?'

The signals on the computer were still dead. He wiped his eyes and took a deep breath through his nose. Clicking his tongue, he looked up at Dania. 'Get the Aussies out of bed.' He smiled, checking his watch. 'We need to go on a little night excursion.'

0:00:40

Brett was waiting for the Israelis as instructed, sliding into the back seat of the four-wheel drive quietly, half asleep. In the National Park, they killed the lights. Driving in darkness with a set of NVG's was second nature to Dania, thanks to her years in the IDF border squad.

Brett directed them to the Mutitjulu waterhole Car Park, where Dania hid the car, a large tree giving them the privacy they desired. Achban pulled out a laptop, showing Brett where the signals had disappeared. Brett studied the screen for a few seconds before clicking his tongue, a grin creeping across his face. 'I think I know the spot, it's not too far from here.'

Achban closed the laptop, his eyes narrowed though his smile was bright. 'Please, Brett, I would like to see it.'

Dania scanned the area. There was no movement of the human kind as far as her night vision goggles could see. She nodded to Achban who stepped out of the car.

Brett led an excited Achban down the muddy path towards the Mutitjulu waterhole. The sound of the cascading water, gathering in a now full-to-the-brim waterhole less than a hundred metres away was loud. They made a sharp left where the path continued its circumnavigation of Uluru.

The path made a sharp left again. To the right, a waist-high fence abutted shrubs and trees. 'This is it,' Brett said, pointing up into the thick cluster of bushes.

Achban stood against the fence and looked down, noticing the rusted, business-card-sized, metal sign.

KEEP OUT

It looked as old as Uluru itself. Achban shook his head and let out a small laugh. 'Interesting,' he ran his forefinger across the top of the sign. Achban turned back to Brett. 'You sure this is the spot?'

'This is it Achban,' Brett said confidently, and pulled out the fence-cutters.

The unlikely duo fought their way through the thick scrub, branches scratching them across their arms and faces. When they had reached the other side, Brett led Achban on through the very narrow gaps between the massive boulders and Uluru itself. Brett slipped through them with ease; his thin, scrawny body was made for gaps like these. Achban, a little thicker, had to suck all the air out of his lungs, but made it through nonetheless.

Moments later, the two men reached the eerily dark, dead end. Achban looked over to Brett. 'This is it?'

The wall of Uluru stretching hundreds of metres above him was ominous, almost overbearing to him for a moment, as if looking down on Brett with contempt. 'This is the spot.' Brett stepped back into the crevice they had just squeezed through to allow Achban to study the en-suite-sized area a little easier.

Achban panned the torch around and leant against one of the boulders; he was thinking aloud. 'How could the signal just...?' He leant down to knee height, shining his torch up into all the cracks and large holes. One hole, he realised, was longer, deeper and slightly wider than all the rest.

'Wait here,' he said and slipped up into the shaft.

Achban's head reappeared a few moments later, his smile from ear to ear. 'Brett,' he said, shining the torch at him. 'Go back to the car and ask Dania for the GF.'

Brett had no idea what a GF was, 'Righty-o then,' he said.

Achban knew the round trip would take Brett about ten minutes. He waited patiently, his excitement palpable. If his hunch was correct, things could really start heating up. He crawled back to the end of the tunnel and had another look, wondering if it may have been the infrequent home of a native animal of some sort. Evidence pointed to it; dirt, small branches, activity. He ran his hands across the many cracks and crevices above him. Was there something in one of the larger cracks? Just as the tips of his fingers disappeared into the crevice...

'Achban?'

Brett sat at the end of the tunnel with a strange-looking device in his hand and an even stranger look on his face.

'I guess you are wondering what this is.' Achban held up the unit. 'And what GF stands for.'

Brett studied the contraption closely. It was like nothing he had ever seen before, and looked expensive. Het met Achban's eyes. 'I guess it's not called a *Get Fucked!*'

Achban rolled his eyes, smiling faintly. 'You Aussies have such a blunt sense of humour.'

The unit was no bigger than a loaf of bread and weighed no more than five kilograms. At one end of the box a lid opened to reveal a small LCD screen with five buttons to one side. On the other end was a small rod which, when Achban pulled on it gently, reached about twenty centimetres in length. The end of the rod split into two.

Brett was taken aback by the device; it looked like something from a spy movie.

183

Achban looked at the screen again whilst flicking a lever. The screen came to life, backlit with a light blue, the information in white. He pulled at a lever at the bottom of the box. It flipped out and clicked into position, like a gun-type handle.

Achban 'pointed' the unit outwards, grinning over to Brett. 'This is what we call a *Grail Finder*, one of the best innovations to come out of Germany.'

Brett looked down at the screen. 'What does it do?'

Achban started panning it around the rock. Brett's knowledge was as long as his middle leg, and cocktail-frankfurter came to mind. 'The Grail Finder finds hidden tunnels, caves. We've been using it back home for years, very handy.'

Achban adjusted the tiny dial on the side of the screen. Brett heard the commencement of a low, dull, hum and every few seconds a chime, like a heart monitor, though just barely noticeable, would override the background humming sound. Achban systematically panned the Grail Finder across every available piece of rock he could fit the device into.

At the dead end, the sudden change in the tone of the chime was unmistakable.

Achban swung his head down to Brett, his teeth clenched, his smile, childish. 'As you Aussies would say – Bingo!' He turned the unit off. 'There is a large cavity behind the wall at the end of the tunnel.' He retracted the rod. 'That could be why the signals on the watches went dead.' The Israeli patted Brett on the back firmly. 'You've done well, now hand me my backpack.'

Skinny did as instructed. The sweet smell of cash drifted past his nose, and disappeared – things were looking up. He watched through the crack as Achban pulled some tiny devices from his backpack, twisting one end of the objects before placing them in cracks on the other side of the small area –pointing down towards the entrance to the dead end tunnel.

Thirty minutes later, Dania slipped on her seat belt and pulled the Land Cruiser out of the car park at the Mutitjulu waterhole site.

Achban's excitement was obvious; he was rubbing his hands together and smiling openly. 'Call Chonen when we get back to the hotel and make the necessary arrangements – immediately.'

Dania glanced his way, 'you that confident, Achban?'

'Yes.' He stared through windscreen with confidence.

An unfamiliar sound suddenly came from the rear of the four wheel drive. Achban and Dania looked at each other and shook their heads.

Brett lay across the back seat asleep, now snoring .

0:00:41

Chonen swung his legs out of bed and rested his feet on the floor. His mind began to power-up for what he had to do. First, to make contact with the leader of the team and instruct him where the rendezvous point was – a top secret location, an hour out of Sydney – and secondly, to hand over the keys to a brand new, blue and white, Outback Range A1919 5SL Winnebago Mark V. The team were to travel to Alice Springs and resume their cover until further notice.

Achban had picked the Winnebago himself, and after some careful modifications, two large steel chests, hidden in the large undercarriage of the Winnebago carried just a few 'bits and pieces,' obviously Achban wanted the cache well hidden. Chonen scrolled through his Blackberry to check the comprehensive inventory list in these two chests:

- twelve 5.56 × .45 calibre NATO Tavor TAR-21 assault rifles, six with IWI manufactured M203 40mm grenade launcher attachment

- six 5.56 × .45 calibre NATO MTAR 21 AR's (micro version of the Tavor TAR-21s)

- six 9 × 19 .38 calibre Luger-Parabellum Uzi sub-machine guns

- six 9 × 19 .38 calibre Luger-Parabellum Micro Uzi sub-machine guns

- six 5.56 × .45 calibre NATO M4A1 carbines with additional 'SOPOD' packs

- twelve 9 × 19 .38 calibre 'Bul' M5 pistols, six commander and six Ultra X models

- twelve 9mm semi-automatic Glock pistols, six of them the '19' model and six of them the larger and predecessor '17' model

- six 20 × 42 Calibre Paw-20 'Neopup' semi-automatic grenade launchers, with custom made 20mm calibre rounds

- six 40 × 46mm calibre MM-1 40mm revolver grenade launchers

The second chest filled to capacity with accompanying ammunition. Along with this, more NVGs, another Grail Finder and a long list of associated items a covert assault team may find handy in times of need.

Achban took a long, hot shower. A fresh wave of optimism came over him as if it were mixed with the water. Things were looking good.

They had woken Brett from his much-needed beauty sleep in the back seat of the four-wheel drive, dropping him off at his hotel before returning to Achban's suite to activate the remote devices now hidden at Uluru. The infrared 'trip wire' devices positioned immediately inside the small, dead end tunnel, and across the boulders which led back out of the area, would engage the second anything passed between the two miniature parts of the one device. Both units concealed within cracks and would not be seen or found easily. Once activated, they would give accurate information about what passed through the beams and could even indicate what set off the device; human, or animal. Along with the infra-red trip wire devices, Achban had set nearby; two of the world's smallest, live-feed digital cameras.

Once the Bluetooth connection synced amongst these state-of-the-art gadgets, the trip wire devices would activate the cameras immediately the beams for the corresponding units were broken. Both devices, along with all of Achban's innovative hardware, came from Tel Aviv Covert Systems, an Israeli company world-renowned for being at the forefront of technological warfare. A director of the company just happened to be one of the TSA's major benefactors and a true believer in the legend of the Akashic.

However, there was one drawback to these ridiculously small objects the Mossad used regularly.

Battery life.

Both units had a standby time of eighteen hours; something that was always in the back of Achban's mind and he habitually checked the time on a count-down clock in his laptop.

* * *

Deep below the main deck, the luxurious Romanov housed the majority of Vadislav Pravica's $50 million of furtive modifications, sealed off through a network of corridors, private rooms and finger-print scan locked doorways.

Guests of Vadislav, who often spent time with the billionaire on the Romanov, some for days on end, never even knew the room existed. The 22- man crew of the Romanov could monitor events worldwide from what most of them had nicknamed 'The Floating Bunker'.

In the operations room, Ivon Krutek and his team could oversee covert operations from near or afar. The floating bunker was cutting-edge, with monitoring systems akin to the world's top espionage agencies. Vadislav would often personally oversee operations himself; sitting in his big chair at the rear of the room, known as the 'throne.'

Tonight, the room throbbed with activity doused with excitement. The entire crew knew of Mikita's true identity now, and most loathed the fact Vadislav's little starlet was an Israeli spy. They were all keen to see her pay for her betrayal to their employer.

One of the satellite monitoring systems had picked up the encrypted message sent to the coordinates of Siamko's location. All Siamko had to do was ensure regular phone calls were made from his satellite phone, and this would give the Romanov his exact location. The crew in charge of the monitoring had no doubt the signal had come from Mikita – though surprisingly, they could not yet decipher it, a laptop which had a program which could crack any code in the world was currently en route to the ship.

Ivon stood behind the crewmember huddled over his keyboard, punching in complicated commands. 'Tell me you can locate the origin, Ivashko.'

Ivashko grinned. 'Give me a few more minutes, sir.'

Ivon looked over to another soldier who was waving excitedly 'What do you have for me?'

'A woman called him, the one from the Israeli Embassy; I was able to pick up what they said to each other.'

Ivon wondered why an outfit with Mossad backed expertise would dare speak on an unsecured, unscrambled line. 'Do you have the location of this woman?' he said.

'We are still working on it.'

'She said, "Send everything" and something about a kitchen sink.'

The captain of the Romanov stood back and ran a hand over his furry chin. Obviously code words for something, he surmised. He stood there, deep in thought, as his crew continued to tap away at their keyboards.

Ivashko muttered ecstatic swear words. 'We have the coordinates of the signal to where Vadislav's little whore sent her message to.'

Ivon pointed to the phone. 'Get me the boss, now.'

Vadislav was eager, picking up his phone on the first ring, 'What do you have for me, Comrade?'

'We have the location of the Jews.' The main screen burst to life with an image of the coordinates.

'Well, where are they, Ivon?' Vadislav asked.

Ivon scratched his head. 'They appear to be in the middle of nowhere in the desert.' Ivon held his hand over the mouthpiece and turned to Ivashko, 'enlarge the image.'

'Right,' Vadislav was growing impatient, 'Is that all you can see?'

Something on the image began to stand out. Ivon cocked his head, as the object grew in size. 'Vadislav, there's nothing out there apart from a oversized, giant rock.'

0:00:42

'Did you hear something?' said Adam.

'No ... it must be your imagination ... again.'

'Pull your fat head in, Ross. I'm sure I just heard something – in the distance.'

'Boys,' Burnum said, slightly annoyed. 'Keep it down.'

As Burnum suspected, the trip was far quicker this time. Ross, he was in a hurry, for sure, Burnum could see it in his strides. The boys had only looked up and around the first big cave a couple of times at the most. They had found it fascinating though, feeling the water drops hitting their faces, debating how wide the point between the ceiling of the cave and the top of Uluru, actually was. Ross believed it could be even as low as one metre and said to Adam 'How would the water get through if it was any wider?'

Adam shrugged his shoulders, he wasn't that interested either way.

Burnum suddenly came to a halt in the middle of a puddle. His head snapped up and he shot his arm up to signal them to stop, now.

Ross and Adam glared at each other, concerned.

Burnum looked directly up. He had turned his big torch on to full power. The ray of light centred on one particular section of the ceiling. Ross could feel his anxiety rising, as did Adam. Thirty seconds passed and there was not an inch of movement from the elder.

'What is it, Burnum?' Ross whispered.

Burnum finally dropped the torch down, turning it back to the secondary globe. His concerned expression was evident in his narrow eyes. 'Something bad,' he muttered. He looked over to Adam before lowering his gaze to the floor. 'We need to go back to the surface; I can sense something really bad down here.'

Ross and Adam shared horrified looks.

Ross frowned. 'But Burnum, we need to—'

Burnum waved his hand. 'I am the Gatekeeper of the Seventh,' he barked, 'we need to leave – now.'

Adam looked more worried than Ross. 'Okay, okay. If these are Dad's wishes, we need to respect them,' he said.

Ross struggled to remain calm. He wanted to go to the book, damn it. He realised Burnum was staring at him. Burnum's eyes spoke volumes, he sympathised with him, though his conviction overrode it. Something had spooked him, that was for sure and now – they would return to the surface.

A short time later, Dania raced to join Achban at the screen.

Thwop ... Thwop ... Thwop

The trip wire alarm was going off.

0:00:43

Siamko was in a talkative mood. He had given in to the demands of the two Australians and shared a beer with them. He could not remember the last time he had drunk beer. Vodka was a friend at least two decades old, and three-quarters of the way through the beer, Siamko longed for the sharp taste of the clear liquid. A familiar vibration on his ankle broke his thoughts of alcohol.

Mikita was still asleep. If there were any updates coming from the Romanov or Moscow, he did not want her to be made aware of it. He whispered to the men, 'Excuse me for a moment,' and took the phone away from the fire.

He let some time pass before returning to the camp, though the duration of the call was less than sixty seconds. Siamko wanted the Australians to believe the conversation went for a lot longer than this – not to arouse any suspicion about his sudden change of plan.

Justin wasted no time telling Siamko what he thought of his abrupt change of itinerary. 'But I thought we had the plans already laid out?' The two Australians cared not for the logistics of the Russian's sudden request, it was their wallets, who were concerned the most. They would lose wages. This did not please them in the slightest. After a few minutes, the tone of the conversation was growing strained. Siamko was losing his patience, he had been given clear instructions – head immediately for Alice Springs. There they would rendezvous with Ivon Krutek and six crew members from the Romanov.

Siamko had a thought; a very dark thought. If these idiots did not settle down and agree, he would take matters into his own hands. Then, another interesting thought came to mind, an ingenious plan. He strode over to Mikita's tent and called out for her.

When Mikita appeared from her tent, Siamko took her out into the bush, away from the campsite, and explained the change of plans.

'But we had agreed they would stay with us for a week,' she muttered.

'These are the orders. Fuck them, Mikita,' Siamko hissed. He was so close; Mikita felt the heat of his breath on her face.

Siamko cared not for their guides' predicament, their problems were their own. Siamko then relayed his solution.

The look on Mikita's face was of genuine horror. 'Just pay them out, for God's sake.'

'Vadislav does not like loose ends and this is a great opportunity for you to show your loyalty to him.'

Mikita looked into Siamko's grey, squinty eyes. You little fuck, she thought, you want me to just turn around and murder them?

She had killed before – but all her kills were a necessity, and in most cases, in self defence. But the cocky look on this thug – he acted as if it were a fucking game, killing two innocent men, for what, a week's pay?

Mikita looked over to the two Australians and back to the eyes of the Russian caveman. 'No,' she said flatly. 'I will sort this out.' She left Siamko alone with his murderous fantasies and spoke to the others in quiet, hushed tones.

With Siamko's proposal to kill the Australian morons now in tatters, and the knowledge of her true identity confirmed, another thought came to mind:

Kill the three of them.

But Mikita was to remain alive – for now. The orders were very specific. And Mikita was right. If they killed the Australians, people would notice their absence within days. This would draw attention they could not afford. Siamko smiled as he stood there in the darkness watching her talk to them. He hadn't really meant it; he was just fucking with her, and wanted to see how far he could take it.

When he arrived at the fire Mikita said, 'We've agreed to split the difference; they will direct us to Alice Springs and accept a couple of days' severance pay.'

Mikita said goodnight to them, again. As she zipped up the sleeping bag, preparing to send another message to Dania, a horrific sound suddenly pierced her ears.

Gunshots.

0:00:44

'There are three of them.'

'I love Tel Aviv Covert Systems gadgets.'

'State of the Israeli-art, Dania.' Achban's fingers blazed a trail across the laptop keyboard. One of his many obsessions was the latest and greatest in technology, whatever the device. 'What you are seeing,' Achban's eyes flickered to Dania's and back to the screen, 'are images from the camera inside the small, dead-end tunnel. With any luck,' he clicked his tongue, 'we may get a glimpse of who set off the trip wires.'

'Hopefully.'

'Hello, there,' Achban said to the screen. Bright lights flashed from inside the tunnel. The trip wire on the outside of the tunnel had not gone off. They had not come from outside the small cave...

Interesting.

Then, another burst of sound from the laptop: the watches were transmitting their GPS signal once again.

Achban clapped his hands with delight. 'Welcome back.'

0:00:45

Senior Constable M. Price had known Ross for years. They'd played in the same footy team when they both were lanky, pimple faced, post-pubescent teenagers. Matt had just re-signed for his fifth tour of duty at the Uluru Resort police station but nothing in his life as an NT police officer had ever prepared him for a situation like this. 'I'm lost for words, mate,' was all he could muster when Ross had taken a seat on the other side of the desk.

The conversation was awkward, and disjointed. Matt had been frank with his old teammate, though it was difficult not to feel emotionally connected to the situation. No leads, nothing, had come to the police about the mysterious disappearance of Bernie Taylor's body. No one had seen anything, nor heard anything. But one thing was for certain, the rumours and outlandish conspiracy theories were flying thick, and fast.

'We have the entire Northern Territory police force keeping an eye out, Ross.' Matt peered out the window. 'You'll be the first to know of any update, I promise.'

Ross rose to his feet, thanking Matt for his efforts as he left.

* * *

Brett flung open the door of the four-wheel drive and climbed in. 'Did you hear?' Stuart said, curious as to how his friend would react to the bizarre news.

'Of course I heard ... who the hell would steal a body?'

'Who happens to be your father?' Stuart said.

Brett glanced out the passenger side window, missing the insinuation of Stuart's last comment. Brett was not the master of reading between the lines at the best of times. From their hidden vantage point, they watched Ross's Ute scurry off down the road,

Brett turned to Stuart. 'Jeez, I'm bloody hungry, let's eat.'

Stuart kicked over the four-wheel drive and pulled out onto Giles Road, their destination was one of the Restaurants at the Resort shopping centre. About twenty metres down the road, Stuart said, 'Do you believe all this bullshit Achban laid on us last night?'

Brett exploded into a fit of laughter. 'A bloody secret tunnel at Ayers Rock?' He shook his head. 'Is this prick on the same shit I was on all those years ago? I mean, after all these years, no one else has ever stumbled upon it?'

Stuart nodded, 'The blackfellas have been here for what, forty thousand years and white men for what, about a hundred and fifty?'

Brett agreed and waved his hand in the air, 'and this fucker discovers this tunnel within a couple of days of setting foot here?'

Both men roared with more laughter.

'You think Achban is all there?' Stuart then asked.

Brett shook his head with absolute confidence. 'Mate, I think our Israeli friend is a can short of a six-pack.'

Brett then burped so loud Stuart nearly ran off the road.

'You bloody pig, Taylor.' Stuart swung out and gave him a clip over the back of the head.

Brett gasped. 'Mate, watch where you are—'

Stuart quickly pulled the steering wheel to the left. Phew, he had literally just missed a shiny Winnebago which was driving far too close to the middle of the road.

'Bloody tourists,' Brett barked through his car window.

* * *

'Comrade – we have been in Alice Springs for a day now.'

'Siamko, I am not deaf,' Vadislav said. 'You don't have to shout.'

'Understood, Boss,' Siamko said, a little softer.

'How did you go with the pesky Australian tour guides, my friend?'

Siamko laughed from deep within his belly. 'Shotguns make so much noise in the middle of nowhere.'

'You killed them?' Vadislav said incredulously.

'A wild dog came running into the camp, not far from Mikita's tent. One of the guides saw it, aimed his shotgun and BOOM! Mikita came running out of the tent screaming "No!" Siamko put a sliver of air between the phone and his sweaty ear. 'Obviously, she thought I had shot them.'

'Now,' Vadislav spoke in a serious tone, 'continue with Plan B, Siamko. Find the Israelis and monitor their every move – you will have the full support of the assault team from the Romanov. Do not do anything to Mikita, or whatever the little whore's real name is. I want her alive. And remember, Siamko—' Vadislav leant closer into the speaker phone. 'She's very good at smelling a rat.'

0:00:46

'Are we still getting a signal from both devices?'

'Yes.' Dania refreshed the screen, making sure the signal was still active. 'Both watches are Go.'

'Where are they?'

Dania checked her note pad. 'Merrigang, if Brett's pronunciation is correct – their father's house.'

'Good. What about the signals from Stuart and Brett's devices – still online?'

'Yes – still active.' She smiled at Achban. 'And if they realise their watches are tracked, I've attached another device hidden inside the Land Cruiser.'

Achban patted Dania on both shoulders. 'Well done.' At the window, he put his hands behind his back. 'Any update from Abelia?'

'Abelia … no word,' she said, shaking her head, 'Though she can take care of herself.'

'I want the team to get over to the rock tomorrow. Ensure they take both Grail Finders.'

* * *

'What did you say?'

Ross sneered. 'I said – you are a pain in the ass sometimes. Though after all these years you'd think I'd be used to it.'

'Thanks.' Adam grinned. 'It's good to see I am consistent at one thing at least.' He clipped Ross on the back of his head. 'Make yourself useful.'

Ross threw the empty can of beer in the nearby bin. Adam passed him another.

Adam had no doubt Ross believed Jimmy was still alive. Maybe it was wishful thinking, but Ross was desperate to get back down to the book and to find out for himself.

The conversation was solid for another beer and a half while Adam gave Ross his requested update on Erin. After a pause, Ross said, 'Do you think your Dad would mind if we tried for another trip down to the Seventh ... tonight?

A seven-car procession meandered past Merrigang on the Lasseter Highway. The last, a familiar relic of four-wheel drives from the last millennium, bellowed out his air horn to say hello.

'Oxy,' Ross shouted, raising his beer though knowing there was not a chance in hell, Chris would have heard him.

Adam stared out towards Uluru. 'I'm going to call the old man now.' He rose to his feet and threw his empty beer can in the bin. 'May as well get it out of the way, huh?'

Surprising Ross, Adam reappeared far sooner than expected, falling back to the couch with a strange grin plastered on his face. 'Well,' he said jovially, 'Dad has given the all clear – but he won't be going.'

Ross sat forward. 'You mean we go alone?'

'Ganan will be taking us.' Adam shook his head comically before going slightly pink. 'Apparently, he wants to spend some time with me, to get to know me better.'

Ross broke into deafening laughter. 'Mate, you're in deep shit now!'

Adam wore the onslaught well, the colour of his face soon

206

returning to a more relaxed shade. 'He'll meet us here at eleven tonight.'

Ross patted his mate on the back. 'Great.' Patting him a little harder. 'We'd better get the place cleaned up for your father-in-law, then.'

Adam's eyes narrowed though the smirk remained. 'Have you been told, today?'

Ross held his stare. 'Not that I can recall ... big buddy.'

Adam grinned. 'Piss off, then.'

* * *

Ganan looked over at Adam. 'You awake yet?'

Adam wiped sleep from the corner of his left eye. 'I didn't sleep well last night,' he muttered.

'Don't worry, Adam.' Ganan grinned surreptitiously over to Ross. 'I'm sure we have plenty of time to talk about my daughter.'

Ross held up his hand smiling to Ganan. 'Hey, you leave my best mate alone, you bully.' He broke into laughter.

Ganan winked at Ross, turning the torch back over to Adam. As he did, he reached up, his hand disappearing into a crevice in a now slightly familiar tunnel...

This time, Ross and Adam kept their eyes glued to the rock face, the one they knew would in a matter of nanoseconds – disappear. And they were not disappointed – but even watching the rock face move, they still did not understand how it could do so, with virtually no sound, nor clear mechanical movement. It simply just ... fell away.

Ganan could see their eyes full of amazement. 'Burnum told you, yes? Only the three chosen elders can open it, right?'

'So who constructed it?'

'The Ancient Race.' Ganan flicked his hand to signify downwards. 'The original owners of the Seventh List.' He faced the centre of Uluru. 'They brought it here thousands of years ago and asked us to keep the book safe for them, after searching the world for somewhere to hide it.' The Elder walked on. 'Has Burnum not told you the story of book?'

'Not yet, Ganan.'

* * *

Whatever had gone down, it must have been significant if Achban was prepared to wake her.

'Come quickly, it is very important.'

It was nothing bad – Dania knew all of Achban's tones by now; happy, sad, angry, bored, sarcasm, jubilant. Knowing it was the last one from the list, made getting dressed a little easier. Still half asleep, she rubbed her eyes and longed for a cup of coffee. Fortunately, Achban had put the kettle on; she could hear it warming up. 'Lay it on me, Achban, what did you drag me out of my bed for?'

Achban tapped a couple of commands on the keyboard, flipping from one program to the other. She looked down at the screen, as he clicked his tongue joyfully. 'The GPS signals went off-line a short time ago.'

'Well, I never.' Dania smiled more honestly this time. 'What a coincidence.' The signals had gone dead in the precisely same position as they had done the first time. 'Trip wires?'

Achban leant back and turned his face to the ceiling, his eyes shut. 'They ran out.' He let his chin fall and opened his eyes. 'You would not believe it – only thirty-four minutes ago.'

Dania shuffled over to the couch where she sat down heavily, the news was good – she had that aching desire to crawl back into her bed. 'So what now?'

Achban stretched his back before his hands fell firmly to his hips. He pushed his chest out and stood before Dania as if he was about to start a war. 'Notify the crew at daylight.' Achban clenched his teeth. 'The time has come ... we're going in.'

Achban's men were ready at 06.00 hours sharp, eagerly awaiting the mission debrief. Gilam, the tallest of the four, stood at 6'4". A good-looking rooster, his broad shoulders and taut body was packed with a healthy cover of lean muscle. With hazel eyes, a strong jaw and a walnut-coloured crew-cut, he possessed a firm but friendly demeanour.

Sitting alongside him in the alcove of the Winnebago, was Chasid, a tough little bastard whose 5'8" of a machine had seen some of the worst of the Israeli/Palestinian conflict his platoon had ever come up against. He had long ago lost count of the scars that littered his dark-brown, leathery skin. He rarely wore hair, so to speak, preferring the shaved, low maintenance option. His small brown eyes hinted of a prankster, a wise-ass who loved to pull the odd practical joke.

Davon and Ranan, the other two members of the TSA covert team, were 'blood brothers,' in the truest form – mates since one had thrown an apple across the kindergarten table at the other, resulting in a bruise the size of a basketball. Davon was as ugly as a hat full of arseholes – but had a heart of gold. If Ranan did not groom his moustache every five minutes, something was wrong. The women back home loved it and him ... frequently. Both men were of average height and looked better suited to an office, pushing pens, but they possessed the kind of tenacity the IDF relished in their soldiers.

All had slept well in the comforts of the luxurious Winnebago in the Uluru camping ground, and now stood side-by-side against the kitchen bench and listened to Achban's plan of attack.

And while Dania remained in the suite, monitoring the laptop for any changes or updates, Achban ran through the whole operation from go to whoa. His first instruction for the team was to get to the rock and replace the batteries in the devices planted there. Achban made it very clear; they would continue their cover as backpackers and at all costs not attract any untoward attention.

* * *

Gilam sent through a photo. 'Is this the spot? Over.'

Achban flipped the screen on the laptop. 'Yes, you have found it.'

'Copy that, Achban.' Gilam nodded over to Chasid. 'Batteries on all devices will be replaced first – watch for their signal to come online.'

Davon and Ranan kept watch. There was a bench seat nearby, where they sat, ate candy bars and looked at their cameras as if they were checking previously taken photos; two relaxed tourists giving their legs rest from the nine kilometre walk around Uluru.

Achban directed Gilam to the devices located in the dead-end cave. Chasid's height was better suited to crawl up into the small tunnel where he replaced the trip wire and camera located there. When Chasid had completed these tasks, Achban requested that he power-up his Grail Finder so he could get a second opinion on his original finding. Chasid quickly fired up the GF and moments later Achban heard the low humming whistle, loud and clear. 'I can see it,' Chasid whispered through his mic. 'There is no doubt, Achban. There's a large cavity behind this wall.'

Chasid firmly pushed against the wall. No movement. He ran his hand over it, trying to find a hairline crack or any sign of, anything ... but found nothing. He was about to suggest to Achban that maybe it was just a cavity and nothing else, but lightning does not strike twice, GPS style. This was the exact place Achban said the tracking devices had gone blank, without a trace. It could mean only one thing.

Achban instructed Gilam and Chasid to find positions where they could hide out for the rest of the day, unseen. In addition, they were to stay there until at least nightfall, and as close as possible to the secret cave.

Thick bushes to the far left provided their cover. Chasid was even able to get a whisper thin view through the narrow opening that led to the small tunnel.

Ranan and Davon walked off, the Grail Finder securely stowed in Davon's backpack. Achban's instructions were succinct: get to the top of the rock and see what the Grail Finder comes up with.

* * *

'Ganan...?'

'Yes, Ross?'

'Which one is it?'

'You don't remember?'

Ross cocked his head. 'Come on.' He smiled. 'Could you recall which book the right one was after your second visit?'

'Yes.'

'Smarty-pants.'

Ganan sat next to Adam, at the 'table' in the cave. Ross stood a couple of metres away from the mesmerising wall of books. With all candles in the room lit, shadows flickered around the crevices; an eerie but addictive sight to see. 'I need a hint; they all look exactly the same.'

Ganan smiled, waving his hand in mock defeat. 'There are seven rows.' He looked beyond Ross to the wall. 'You need to find the second book from row four.'

Ross turned, a fresh wave of excitement glowed in his eyes. He counted aloud and, taking one last quick glimpse behind him at Ganan and Adam, slowly put both hands into a crevice. His insignia glowed brightly. He touched the book, the nerve endings underneath every single hair follicle on his neck, arms and head pinged ... it was a great feeling. He pulled the object out and moved carefully over to the table, catching the strange smell of the book. It wasn't an attractive smell, though it was addictive all the same. 'If this book fell into the wrong hands...'

Ganan frowned, 'the reason it is all the way down here, is to protect it, and all the people in it, from people who would use it for evil.'

Ross ran his hand over the cover of the book, shit; it was mind-numbing to him to comprehend what he was touching. 'What about those people we told you about – up there somewhere right now, who Brett happens to know. Aren't you guys worried about them?'

Ganan shrugged. 'Over the years we have heard of many people looking for something we often thought sounded like the book.' He leant over and rested his hand on the cover. 'But nothing has ever happened.'

After a few moments of silence and reflection, Ganan nudged Ross; it was time to do what he had come to do. Ross went through the motions, methodically. Ganan was impressed; Ross had listened to Burnum's instructions well.

'Bernie – Walter – Ron – Taylor,' Ross whispered. He leant back and looked down at the page. The image cleared, revealing a list of thirty-nine names. Ross studied the list for a few minutes. He knew the day Jimmy was born and Ganan had told him the hour.

His sullen face said it all.

'He's not in there.'

Ross left the cave in a sullen mood. With the book omitting his father's details, it was if Jimmy had died twice. It stung.

He followed Adam and Ganan back through to the mammoth Heart of Uluru. Ross, wasn't in the mood for being awed by the cave a second time, he just wanted to go home and now officially mourn the passing of his father.

Ganan sat them down and went through the instructions carefully, even though the two others had done this once before. Just as Ganan let the first word out, Ross opened his eyes. 'Hold on, Ganan.'

Ganan looked over to him, slightly annoyed. 'What is it, Ross?'

Ross flicked his wrist and looked down at his watch. 'It's daylight up there.'

'It's nearly dusk.' Ganan adjusted his backside on the ground to get more comfortable. 'It's okay. No one is usually near the waterhole at this time of the day. Don't worry.' Ross thought better of arguing with the Elder. He closed his eyes and rejoined his hands with the other men.

The chanting began ... and went on.

* * *

Achban had just left his desk to turn on the kettle when the laptop all of a sudden starting chirping sounds. 'Shit.' He pounced to the desk and ripped at his headset. 'Gilam, Chasid, come in ... Gilam, where did they come from?'

'Achban ... code blue.'

Achban cursed under his breath. The targets were within hearing range.

0:00:47

Vadislav loved a good-looking helicopter. His recent purchase, the design inspired by his luxury yacht, was testament to this. The Eurocopter EC175-SSS was one of the sleekest looking helicopters on the planet. Every panel was jet-black, every other available part chrome and glistening, all windows bullet-proof and heavily tinted, the nose long and sleek. The 4218 kilogram machine punched out 1916 horsepower and in full throttle would give even a car-enthusiast a woody.

The chopper descended to Alice Springs airport as if she were a supermodel – gatecrashing a retirement home's New Years Eve party.

Ivon slipped out of the cockpit, the heat of the afternoon a contrast to the icy-cold air-conditioning he'd savoured for the last couple of hours, marvelling at the stark desert landscape of the Northern Territory.

Siamko waved from the waiting van and walked over to greet his colleague. 'Comrade, great to see you again, welcome,' he said. They exchanged a firm handshake. 'As you can see, my friend, a van awaits to transport you and the crew to the hotel.'

Ivon smiled, noting Mikita sitting in the front seat, with her legs hanging out the door. 'How is your little friend treating you? No trouble, I assume.' He grinned.

Siamko rolled his eyes and snorted. 'Her time of usefulness will come to an end soon.' He reached out to help Ivon with his bags adding, 'And I intend to enjoy every moment of it.'

Ivon smirked. 'You are a lucky man, Comrade.'

'How far off is the truck with the rest of the supplies?' Siamko whispered, not wanting Mikita to hear.

'Maccek and Ivashko radioed in a few minutes ago; they just left Darwin,' Ivon said, mimicking Siamko's hushed tone. 'They will be here in nineteen hours, I'm told.'

'Excellent, Comrade,' Siamko dabbed the sweat from his face, 'now we get some rest, for when the truck arrives we head straight for this place they calls "Eeere's rock." '

Mikita turned to Siamko. 'We are going to there straight away?' she asked, trying to hide her surprise.

Siamko was getting tired of the charade.

'We should have gone there first,' he hissed. 'Why we wasted our time with those stupid idiots in Kakadu—' Siamko waved his hand to the north. 'Now get in the van and shut your mouth.'

Siamko had smashed his authority over the back of Mikita's pretty little head. Ivon's cold stare added fuel to the fire.

'Okay,' Mikita said quietly, making sure she gave Siamko the impression he had subdued her. She glanced down to her watch to avoid all eyes. She would have to warn Dania, as soon as possible.

The drive to the Desert Palms was short, and awkward. No one spoke, save for a few sly comments when crewmembers spotted a couple of scantily-clad female tourists skipping hand-in-hand down the main street of Alice Springs in nothing but red bikinis.

At the motel, they unloaded the bags and awaited further instructions from Ivon. Mikita smiled faintly, walking off to the reception area. 'I need to freshen up. I'll meet you back here at the van in thirty minutes.'

When she was out of sight, Ivon turned to one of his men. Nikifor grinned, holding up his hand respectfully. 'I am on it, Boss.' He flipped open his laptop.

Ivon leant into the van. 'Stay here, Niki. If my gut-feel is correct, our little Jewish whore will attempt to send a message to her people in the next few moments.'

Fewer than three minutes later, the computer's hard drive buzzed to life. Niki looked at the screen. 'Fucking Mossad, who do they think they are?' He punched commands into his favourite program. The Sentinel software was the most expensive program ever used, available only to the top espionage organisations around the world – acquired by Vadislav from a crooked bureaucrat in French Intelligence for a wad of cash and a night at the Ritz with three of Vadislav's 'friends,' from the Moulin Rouge. Niki grinned as the program chewed up the message and spat out the decoded message, in Russian, of course.

'*Red alert red alert target coming to your coordinates within half to full day Out.*'

* * *

'Check out the reading on the GF,' Davon muttered.

Ranan waited for the tourists nearby to walk off, though he knew it was highly unlikely they would speak Hebrew. He leant in and gazed at the screen, before shaking his head in genuine disbelief. 'The Grail Finder must be faulty, the reading is not possible.'

Davon clicked his tongue. 'I have checked and re-checked and recalibrated the unit twice.'

Ranan checked the readings again, as well as the settings. He looked up askance, there were no tourists nearby, the closest – a large group of Japanese, strangely all wearing white gloves were heading off to the Summit cairn about fifty metres away. He met Davon's eyes. 'Call it in,' he said, checking his watch. 'We'll take another two readings over there.' He pointed to an area well away from the beaten path. 'And then get out of here.'

'Achban, over.'

'Talk to me, Davon.'

Davon looked down to the screen one final time. 'Boss, I need to ask you a question.'

Achban rolled his eyes, a small tut followed. Davon was notorious for his clowning around. 'Out with it, Davon,' Achban said with a small hint of impatience.

'If the Grail Finder's current readings are correct, your theory of there being a cave inside this large rock has just been confirmed.'

'Dania get over here and pinch me, I need to ensure that I am not dreaming,' Achban shouted.

Ranan cut in on the secure comms. 'That's not the amazing part Achban.' He gave Davon the hand signal to put away the Grail Finder, another group of tourists approaching. 'How far down did you say the GF reads to?'

'Depth of at least two hundred-and-fifty metres, in the right conditions, and a hundred metres across, why do you ask?' Achban asked.

The two Israelis, perched high on the rock, gasped at the same time. 'Put it this way, Achban...' Davon smiled. 'Forget about Brazil hosting the World Cup in 2014 – there is enough room to hold it below where we are standing.'

0:00:48

Ross slumped on the couch, his feet sat up on an old tree-stump his old man had made into a footstool. As far as Ross was concerned, there was not a more physically comfortable spot on planet earth than this one. The soothing, balmy afternoon breeze flowed across the veranda, clashing for a moment with the ice-cold air that up until a second ago had been trapped inside the beer he'd just cracked open. It did not get any better than this, he thought. The only thing missing was his old man.

Ross had moved out of Merrigang fifteen years ago, though never really left – he slept at 'his place', hung out with Adam on the banana lounges and cooked the infrequent meal there, but Merrigang had always remained 'home'. Now, Merrigang was Ross's own, all to himself.

Jimmy had told him over hundreds of malt-sandwiches (beers), 'When I check out – Merrigang is yours. It's already as much yours as it is mine.'

With the half-drunk beer sitting between his hands, resting on his lap, Ross leant his head back and felt the slow grasp of sleep sliding over him. He welcomed it with open arms; the surroundings were perfect for a Central Australian siesta.

At 135 decibels of deafening sound, the air horns belched out 'La Bamba' as if the tune were a golf ball being sucked through a drinking straw. High pitched and painful.

Adam.

Ross, jerked from the heavenly sleep he had just fallen into, considered sticking one of the air horns in a similar place to the Seventh – where the sun never shone. Then came the dust. The twit had pulled into Merrigang with such gusto, half of the desert had come with him.

'G'day, mate!' Adam bellowed as he jumped out of the four-wheel drive. He noted the filthy look his best friend was giving him. 'How are you feeling, my friend?'

'Better ... now.'

'I'm glad my company has that effect on you.'

'It always has mate, since you are up and the bar is open, make yourself useful.'

'I see Oxy has visited.' Adam noted.

The esky was packed to the brim with Ross' favourite beer.

Ross cocked his head and smiled. 'He can't bear the thought of not coming around and keeping the esky stocked up, so who am I to argue?'

A large smirk crept across Adam's lips. 'Well, the fact that you now have to pay for the beer you drink?'

Ross waited patiently for Adam's roar of laughter to subside. 'And don't you forget smart-arse; I'm keeping tabs on how many you drink. Expect a bill at the end of the month!' Ross took a swing at Adam's head, missing by a country mile and joining in the laughter. A couple of minutes later the laughter ended as the cans grew lighter.

'So, what can you tell me?' Ross said, spotting one of the company helicopters passing far over head and looking forward to getting back up there. He loved flying. It was his second home and where he often felt most comfortable. Well, other than his old man's front veranda.

Adam made himself comfortable on the couch. 'The three elders are planning their next trip down to the Seventh – a supply trip.' As the name suggested, it was an expedition where they took as many supplies as they could carry to stock up their campsite far below the surface. They made the supply trip every couple of months and had done for decades.

'Sounds interesting.' Ross's tone suggested he did not think anything too mesmerising about the knowledge of the upcoming supply trip. 'Make sure they don't forget the beer nuts and DVDs.'

Adam drew out the laughter for far too long.

'What's so funny?'

'They want us to help,' Adam said.

Ross sat up straight. 'We have to go down again, so soon? Bloody hell, if we knew about this two days ago, we could have waited.'

As if on cue – the AAT bus meandered past Merrigang, heading towards the Resort. It gave them something else to stare at other than the odd helicopter, the desert, or Uluru, albeit only a few seconds. Ross watched it disappear over the sand dune.

'When?' Ross enquired.

'Tomorrow night.'

Ross lifted his feet from the footstool and sat on the edge of the couch. 'Do you think it is wise to go down so often when we have these friends of Brett's snooping around?'

Adam could only nod. 'The side effect of being one of the three oldest and most respected elders around these parts is that it makes them very stubborn,' he said. 'They are not concerned with these people; they reckon they'll leave soon enough.'

Ross could tell by the hollow expression on Adam's face, he did not agree whatsoever with the elders' relaxed attitude. It would be hard to argue the point with the Pitjantjatjara Elders, but Ross knew it had to be done. Something deep in his stomach was sending him a clear message: stay away from the Seventh. He put it aside for now. 'Well, at least we can have a night off tonight, huh.' Ross grinned, finishing the can and throwing it in the bin in one fluent action.

'Speak for yourself, slacker,' Adam grunted. 'When are you going back to work huh, man of leisure?'

Ross stood up lazily and rubbed his chest. 'John said another week if I wanted.' He walked over to the esky and held a can in the air, looking at Adam.

Adam nodded. 'Last one, some of us have to work tomorrow.'

'Speak for yourself girly-man.' Ross laughed, falling back into the couch, and flipping his feet back on the footstool. 'Besides, how are you going to come down to the Seventh when you are supposed to be working, have you thought about that, Einstein?'

The grin on Adam's face stretched from ear to ear. 'Well,' he said, toasting the air himself, 'it seems I won't be able to come.' He turned to Ross and laughed. 'Or lug that huge backpack all that way down to the campsite.'

Ross faced Uluru, picturing the long walk down, with a 30-kilogram backpack strapped to his back. 'Bastard!' he spat.

'Don't you forget it!' Adam laughed.

* * *

'Ranan ... come in.'

'Ranan in.'

'Report?'

'The two of them are sitting on the veranda.'

'Data?'

Ranan blew the sand out of his microphone. He was hidden from view under a large cluster of *tjanpi* – spinifex – on a small rise, a hundred metres from Merrigang. The floral scent of the

222

silver leaves, literally in his face, dared him to sneeze many times but he overcame the urge each time.

In Ranan's left hand was a set of Steiner Military C binoculars. They allowed him to see the fine print on the cans of beer they were drinking. In his right was an Orbitor listening device, one of his favourite toys. Capable of hearing voices at three hundred feet, Ranan felt as if he were sitting on the couch himself, every word as clear as the Northern Territory afternoon.

'Just got the tail end, the winds had picked up and distorted the receiver, slightly. They talked about the "others" wanting to venture to a place called the "Seventh Place", by tomorrow night.'

Achban said, 'The Seventh Place, hold on, let me check something.'

Ranan felt something crawl up the back of his right leg. The seconds seemed like minutes.

'There's nothing in the notes of this so called Seventh Place.'

Whatever had crawled up Ranan's leg was starting to nibble, he was aching to sit up and put an end to it – but couldn't. Not until Achban had given him the all clear.

'There are only six sacred sites around the...'

The line went silent once again. It felt as if the bug was about to burrow into Ranan's calf. He had about thirty seconds before he'd have to move. 'Achban, come in...'

'Apologies, Ranan,' Achban cut in loudly. 'I had to check something.'

Ranan started to squirm. It could be a small scorpion, shit. 'Achban ... orders'

'The Seventh Place, there is no reference for this anywhere on the maps or the notes we have obtained.' Achban suddenly clapped his hands so loud Ranan's ears nearly burst.

'This can mean only one thing,' Achban said more to himself than to his soldier. 'Ranan, back to base, immediately. We need to prepare to intercept them the next time they venture into that tunnel.'

'Copy that, Achban.'

Ranan wormed backwards on his stomach until he fell just below the ridge line. He dropped the devices and violently ripped at his left pant leg, pulling it up to expose his calf. A bull-ant, the size of his thumb, was well into its main course.

0:00:49

They split into two groups to avoid detection, Ganan and Derain about ten metres in front. Burnum walked the stretch of land between Uluru and the Mutitjulu settlement at his usual fast pace: a gear below running. Ross decided a light jog was easiest. The night, devoid of moonlight and covered by thick grey cloud, made Ross feel as if they were walking across one of the three impossibly large caves underneath Uluru.

Without moonlight, and torches being too dangerous, Burnum had to rely on his senses and memory to traverse the makeshift paths. A sharp gust of wind confronted Burnum, just as he stole a glance to the top of the rock. The wind was cold and strong, for Burnum it felt as if someone had slapped him in the face from the afterlife.

Burnum threw on the brakes. He almost skidded to a stop and crouched down in the native bushes, hidden from view.

Ross followed suit. 'Burnum, what's the problem?'

The elder seemed submerged in his thoughts. 'Something's not right,' he whispered.

'Can you be a little more specific?'

'Ever get the feeling you are been watched?'

Ross smirked. 'Not since that bunny-boiler from Alice Springs stalked me a couple of years ago.'

Burnum stared warily into the armada of black shapes, the *wanari* – mulga bushes – a couple of hundred metres away receiving particular attention. 'We are being followed, Go!' he hissed, his legs exploding to life, running towards the Mutitjulu waterhole at great speed.

In less than a second they were on top of Derain and Ganan. 'Go through the second entrance and meet us at the Heart,' Burnum said.

Ganan and Derain split off, their slim figures melting into the dark night.

Ross wondered why they were not running in the other direction, back home. He parked the thought as his brain told him to run as hard as he could after Burnum. 'Second entrance, you never told me about a second entrance?' Ross said, through shallow breaths.

'We rarely use the other one,' Burnum said curtly. 'Now keep up boy.'

Ross scrambled under the fence first. Burnum reached into his back pocket and took out a pencil thin torch. He looked around again before nodding to Ross to head towards the tunnel. 'Okay, let's go,' Burnum whispered, desperate to get inside.

The two men darted up the tunnel with the speed of ferrets, almost crashing into the dead end on top of each other. Ross reversed back to give Burnum enough room to manoeuvre himself. The elder reached into the crevice without delay.

Ross felt a cool breeze whisper across the nape of his neck. Two men were scurrying up the tunnel behind them.

Burnum was angry. 'I told you to go to the second entrance ... what are you doing here?'

A bright light exploded in the Australians' faces. In this confined space, it was blinding. 'Do not move an inch,' a sterile voice barked from behind the tip of a shiny, 9x19 calibre, Uzi-Micro sub-machine gun.

Ross squinted at Burnum. The elder had either found Buddha, or that red dot centred in the middle of his forehead, just above his nose … was…

'Achban, come in – Over.'

'Report – Over.'

'We have two of them; the entrance to the cave system is open.'

The Israelis ordered the two Australians to sit and they had no choice but to comply. Within minutes, Achban stood between his two men, itching to venture further into the tunnel and see what lay beyond. 'Gentlemen,' he said in English. 'Please introduce yourselves.'

'Fuck you, that's my name,' Ross spat.

'Ach! Such profanity to a stranger?'

'When you have guns pointed in my face, I will use profanity.'

Achban was far too excited, ignoring this, in his eyes, pathetic attempt at aggression. He grinned. 'I will go first then. My name is Achban Honi. I am the leader of the group known as the TSA or The Society Akashic, for those not good with acronyms.'

Ross and Burnum showed no sign of recognition. They had no idea who this guy was and wished this were a nightmare they were sharing.

'These are two of my team.' Achban nodded to his men. 'Gilam and this is Davon.'

The soldiers nodded, continuing to point both torch and guns at the two Australians. Achban relaxed against the cave wall and went on to tell his two new friends of the TSA's worldwide search for the Akashic Record. Achban checked his watch. 'Now, my new friends, care to take us on a tour of this place?'

Before Ross could think of a smart-arse answer, one of the big soldiers was dragging him to his feet.

'Move.'

Ross and Burnum had to walk at the front, followed by the two gun-toting Israeli soldiers. Achban tapped Burnum on the shoulder. 'So tell me about this place, Burnum?'

Burnum held Achban's stare. 'This: sacred place.'

Achban cocked his head. 'What a lovely story, my new, Indigenous friend.' Achban put his hand lightly on Burnum's shoulder, that slow, deep laugh rising up once again. 'Well, you'd better show us this sacred place Burnum, for we are very interested in seeing much, much, more of it. And, Burnum ... we have your friends.'

The elder felt a nauseating pang in his stomach. He wished he could have wound back the clock and just stayed in bed. He was only now beginning to fathom the enormous, earth-shattering consequences, of what he had allowed to happen. He would go down in history as the first elder to fail the Heart of Uluru. He shuddered with the thought of the consequences of his actions in the afterlife.

Achban stepped slightly closer. 'Tell me, do all these tunnels lead to the same place?'

'Yes,' Burnum muttered, as if the word was a large piece of wood stuck between his teeth. He could only hope the uninvited guests would not notice the cave and walk straight over the edge.

But the TSA leader quickly gauged that the edge of the path ended only a metre in front of him. He panned the torch around the massive cave, still not believing what his eyes were seeing. He caught his soldiers' eyes; they were as gob-smacked as he was. 'Chasid,' Achban barked into his mic. 'We have entered a gigantic cave...' Something way over the other side of the massive expanse caught his eye.

'Achban,' Chasid broke in. 'We see you.'

The Israelis signalled with their torches from opposite sides of the giant cavern.

Achban grinned. 'Confirmed.' He turned to Burnum. 'Elder, does the track over there join with this one?'

Burnum nodded, not daring to look into Ross's eyes.

Ross ground his teeth. These guys were professionals and the opportunity to do something were at best – slim.

'Chasid, the track you are on joins with ours, we need to get our new friends all together.'

Achban drew a long, satisfied breath through his nose. 'Please,' he gestured to the wall behind Burnum and Ross. 'Sit down.' His comms crackled. 'Talk to me, Dania.'

Dania took a deep breath. 'The Russians are coming.'

* * *

Ganan met Burnum's eyes for only a second, as he passed him and sat down next to Ross. Most people had not known each other for 90+ years. Their mothers had been close friends. Burnum was only four years old when he had first laid eyes on Ganan, when Ganan was only just born. They'd grown up as close as two best friends ever could.

In that solitary second, the two confirmed what they knew had been coming their entire lives.

Achban muttered something in his native tongue to his four soldiers. They adjusted their footing, to remain standing and comfortable, all four nozzles of their guns remaining steadfastly pointed at their guests sitting on the ledge.

Achban picked up Burnum's 'Big Daddy' and shone it out into the abyss, his left hand casually falling to rest on his Glock. 'We are here to find a very ancient, very special artefact.'

Burnum stared into the darkness, knowing he would be there, soon enough. Ross yawned as if he was due for a week's sleep.

Achban thought how nice it would be at that moment to put a bullet in the back of Ross's throat, just above the tonsils. He leant down to Derain, who the whole time had been staring into the nothingness, and when their eyes met, Achban realised he had just found what he was looking for.

Pay dirt.

Achban crouched down in front of the third Elder. He leaned in closer to him and whispered, 'The Akashic Record.'

Ross's temper snapped, 'We don't know what the fuck you are talking about arsehole.' He shot a killer look towards the soldiers. 'Now get these fucking guns out of our fucking faces.'

The venomous words echoed out into the massive chamber, allowing the last f-word to dissipate into the far wall, a few hundred metres away.

Achban clicked his tongue, rolled his eyes and shook his head at the same time. 'Ross, we believe your father knew of the artefact.' His eyes now bore into Ross's. 'Your brother informed me his heart literally stopped beating at the mere mention of it.'

Ross closed his eyes and took a measured breath.

'Speak of my father again,' his eyes flew open to meet Achban's, 'and I promise you, I will rip your throat out with my bare hands.'

In a swift, harsh motion, Ranan flicked his Uzi up, connecting the butt of the gun with the side of Ross's head, just below the right ear. 'Shut it – asshole.'

Ross certainly had no trouble doing that. The searing pain of the quick jab shot right through his skull before reverberating down into his body. He fell forward and groaned under his breath.

'Ranan – enough,' Achban held up his hand. 'We are wasting valuable time. Who is going to cooperate with us, and take us to the *book*?' Achban tapped on his Glock. 'And save themselves from a premature death?'

He pulled the Glock from his holster, touching the tip of it with his lips. 'Gentlemen.' Achban spoke as if he were on a podium. 'I will give you sixty seconds to decide—' he waved the Glock out into the abyss, 'who will take me to the Akashic Record.'

Silence.

Ross thought of lunging at the prick and sending him over the edge into the abyss, but he had never taken a man's life, and to add to this, he would be dead before Achban was.

Achban turned and looked over the edge. He said something, almost in a whisper, in his native tongue.

Chasid then stepped forward and crouched down over Derain. 'You are going to show us where the book is, or else these others are going to die.'

Derain held his hands up over his head and cringed. 'I don't know about the book; trust me, I tell the truth.'

Achban's face showed a slight hint of bemusement. 'I am an expert in body language, *mate*,' Achban said, mockingly. 'And you are lying to me.'

Derain curled into the foetal position.

Achban kicked him in the shin. 'Show some dignity, man,' he roared.

Burnum knew the moment was just about on him.

Ganan leant back, at the same time Burnum did, both sitting on either side of Derain, who was whimpering as if a child.

The two elders looked at each other and wished it wasn't going to end this way. They both hoped it would be painless.

'Now,' Achban snarled to his men.

Ranan and Davon stepped forward, lunged at Ganan and threw a hand underneath his armpits, dragging him towards the ledge.

'No,' Ross shouted, his attempt to jump to his feet foiled by another harsh hit with the butt of the machine gun, this time harder and at the base of his neck. He fell back, the agony so intense he thought he would black out.

Achban flicked the safety latch on the Glock off, and placed the gun on the bridge of Derain's nose. 'Tell me where the book is, now,' he hissed through gritted teeth. 'Or the old man goes over the edge.'

'I don't know what you are talking about,' Derain said feebly.

Achban cocked his head and signalled to Chasid and Davon. Burnum closed his eyes and whispered an old chant. Ross rolled over to his side and held his neck. It throbbed so hard he thought he was going to vomit. He stared helplessly over to the edge. The world had slowed to a speed he could not fathom.

Ganan managed to lock his own eyes on Burnum's – for one, maybe two seconds.

Then – he was gone.

0:00:50

Although there was plenty of ventilation in the restroom, the air, for Abelia, seemed thinner than normal. 'The helicopter was heading in your direction until they learned Vadislav was on his way. The word is – no one even knew he was coming.' Abelia shook her head in frustration. 'Vadislav is full of surprises.'

'Okay, get out of here.' Dania flicked her head in the direction of the door.

Abelia shook her hands over the basin and left.

Dania chose the end cubicle and commenced the long wait. When it was safe enough, she hurried back to Achban's suite, confident no one had followed her.

Closing and locking the door, she turned on the lights.

To find Siamko sitting on the couch.

The Russian grinned, sitting forward. 'Shalom. You would be the one they call Day-na.'

As she kept her eyes trained on the little Russian ape, Dania's ears registered the cold, harsh sound of two MP 446 Viking automatic pistols having their safety latches flicked off. Two massive shapes in the periphery of her vision told her she had more company than she wished for.

One of the shadows let off a long wolf-whistle that sent a shudder throughout Dania's body.

'Behave for the woman,' the other Russian said, in a sarcastic tone. What he said next sent a cold chill down her spine. 'You can have her once the mission is over, Comrade.'

Siamko rose to his feet and flicked through the maps laid out across the dining table. He sauntered to the desk and ran his hands across the laptop's keyboard. 'Nice comp-uta,' he drawled in rotten English. 'What is all this for, Dania?'

Dania had twice been in hostage situations in her time with the IDF. Her instincts, and her training, slipped her into a transient state, calm but alert, ready for the nanosecond of opportunity to escape, or turn the tables on these Russian thugs. She stared at Siamko as if his ears were made of plasticine, which looked quite possible.

Siamko wasn't fussed that she had not answered him. In time, she would do more than just talk. He brought his face inches from hers. This took a little effort, as he was a good few inches shorter than she was.

Even with the height disparity, Dania caught her first clear smell of the ugly, small man. If she made it out of this situation alive, she would prefer to sip her own spew out of a cocktail glass, hell, even through a straw, than spend another second smelling this guy's putrid breath.

'Cat got your tongue, Jew?'

Dania blinked as the full force of the wretched stench hit her face. Fortunately for her lungs (only), he bent down and placed both hands on each side of her ankles. He ran them up her legs and frisked her. He made sure, much to her disgust, to touch her breasts.

The whites of Dania's eyes transmuted to a dull ashen grey, waiting for the smelly Russian thug to finish touching her up. As he retracted his large hands, she spat in his face.

234

Ivashko and Ivon chuckled quietly, knowing she had just fucked up.

Siamko smacked her in the face so hard, she fell to the floor. He pulled a handkerchief from his pocket and wiped the spit off his face. Little Siamko would have preferred sucking it from her tongue. 'I will chop every finger, one by one,' Siamko hissed, kicking her. He leaned forward and looked her in the eye, 'you Jewish pig'.

Handcuffing her, Ivashko dragged her to a chair.

'Thank you, Ivashko.' Siamko nodded. 'Now, come and sit next to your new girlfriend.'

Ivashko pulled up right next to her. Dania could almost smell the testosterone permeating from his pores. She caught a whiff of stale Vodka, and told herself not to panic. Yet.

Ivon patted Ivashko on the shoulder. 'If she makes one move,' winking at him as he smiled, 'put a bullet in her – wherever you want.'

Siamko added, 'Just be quiet about it, we wouldn't want to wake the tourists, right?'

Ivashko could only muster a grunt; he had not taken his eyes off Dania's crotch the whole time.

Siamko stood above the table, throwing maps on the floor. He ran his thick fingers over the laptop. 'What is it you are looking for out here?'

'We are looking for the tomb,' Dania muttered.

'Well, it seems we have comedian in our midst,' Siamko said coldly. 'Ivashko, show our friend here what we do to women who do not obey and respect us.'

Ivashko leant over and ran his tongue down the side of her neck. She cringed at the long warm snake which slithered out of his mouth and left a trail of sticky saliva on her neck. He then gave her a harsh backhander across the left ear.

'If you want to spend some time alone with Ivashko, keep

going down the path you are going,' Siamko said.

'Fuck you,' she moaned, 'you Russian thug,' blood trickling from her mouth.

Siamko sighed. 'Well it seems she is no hurry to help us, Comrade, let us go and have Vodka and leave her with Ivashko. He can help her change her mind.'

Ivashko ran his hands through his hair and straightened up his shirt, as if he were about to take her on a dinner date.

'Don't kill her; we come back very soon, understood?'

Ivashko nodded.

Dania made a concerted effort to open her eyes and remove the fogginess from her senses.

Ivashko rose from his seat and stood in front of her.

He casually slipped off his jacket.

Then, he reached for his belt.

Oh no.

He unclipped it.

'I like a woman who plays hard to get.'

There was a knock at the door, and then an enthusiastic female voice, 'Room service!'

Ivashko took his hand away from his zipper, quickly re-securing his belt. 'If this is dinner, you will be my dessert.'

Three, then four quick knocks, evenly spaced. 'Room Service.'

A piercing light lit up in Dania's head. IDF training manual page thirty-five, section nine, paragraph four, line two... With her hands handcuffed behind the chair and her legs tied together, there was only one thing she could do. She shoved herself heavily to her right and went crashing to the floor.

Ivashko had barely registered what she had done when he saw a super-quick flash and the Bul M5 Ultra X semi-automatic dispensed two bullets into his upper chest.

Alas, Ivashko. No dessert for you.

The big Russian hit the floor only centimetres away from Dania. She came face-to-face with him for one final time, his eyes wide open, the life behind snuffed out forever.

Abelia was already pushing the Russian's lifeless legs out of the way. She fell to her knees and put her hand under Dania's head. 'Let's get you out of here, my friend.'

* * *

Ross's throat had shrunk to the size of his aorta. Desperately, he tried to erase the sound of Ganan's body hitting the cave floor, hundreds of metres below. Burnum sat frozen, staring out into the darkness.

Burnum had known today was the day he would lose his friend. They had made a pact, decades ago, to know who went first. But there was one excruciating fact the Seventh List withheld. The knowledge of *how*. Burnum swallowed hard. Ganan was a gentle, kind man. He did not deserve to die in such a terrible way. He hoped Ganan had passed out way before he—

That was the hope.

The old man's death was nothing more to Achban than bird shit on a windscreen ... an idle inconvenience that would wipe away. He pulled the Glock from its holster once again, barking in Hebrew to his men.

The Israelis lunged at Derain, picking him up like a bag of garbage, dragging him to the edge. 'Stop, stop, I beg you,' Derain squealed. 'I will do anything.'

Using his hair as a handle, Achban pulled Derain's head over the lip of the abyss, pushing the nozzle of the Glock directly into the soft skin just below the bone of his chin. 'Tell me,' Achban hissed, 'why I should not send you to the same place I just sent your friend?'

'I will lead you to it,' Derain cried. 'Just promise me you will not kill me here.'

237

'You stupid bastard, what are you doing?' Ross shouted.

Achban slipped the Glock back into its holster and secured the latch. 'Now this is what I call cooperation,' he gloated.

'Damn you to hell,' Ross hissed. 'You killed an un-armed, defenceless, old man – you complete and utter arsehole. De-rain, you can't–'

Gilam swung the Uzi and smacked Ross across the face, just hard enough to shut Ross right up.

Burnum put a restraining hand on Ross's chest. 'Ross, no,' he whispered. 'I have lost one friend today; I don't want to lose another.'

Derain, for the first time in his life, led a group down into the bowels of the Heart of Uluru; the follower now the leader. Achban was at the rear of the pack, savouring fantasies of what lay ahead. Casualties were a part of any mission, so far the plan was going extremely well.

They reached the end of the *Werma Wartin* (Long Track) tunnel and stared out into the infinite, inky darkness. He felt ill; he had betrayed everyone.

'*Harah*,' Achban muttered when torchlight revealed the gargantuan cave.

Ross's gut churned to listen to the soldiers basking in the amazing sight of the giant cave. That the time would come to turn the tide was his only shred of hope, and Ross barely hung onto it.

'How much further is it?' Achban lifted a water bottle to his lips. 'Be specific, my friend.'

Derain shook as the four words reverberated around him. 'About two more hours.'

Achban seemed to consider the elder's response, before offering the old man a drink from his untouched bottle. 'How rude of me. You must be thirsty and I think you have earned a drink for your hard work so far.'

Derain looked at the water sloshing around in the bottle. His throat was dryer than the desert high above him, and by God, he was desperate for anything to wet his throat. He caught a glimpse of Ross's eyes in the shadows, as he reached for the bottle offered to him by the Israeli. He wondered what was worse, being trapped in the Seventh for eternity, or the young Taylor boy getting his hands on him.

Achban stared down into the Deep Hole cave. If his eyesight served him correctly, the cave was about seventy metres across with a long, narrow ledge running along one wall, as far as his torch could show him. He took another look, yes; she was a deep, deep cave. Deep enough to cause the odd ache and pain if you were stupid enough to step over the edge and pretend to be Superman.

'Whoa, very deep huh?' The Israeli gave Derain a solid nudge. 'And this path I assume is the only way through?'

Derain took his time making eye contact, though when he did, the whites of his eyes shone brightly. 'Yes, very deep, very dangerous,' he muttered almost in a whisper.

Achban took one last look at the ledge, flicking his head in a show of bravado. 'Secure your equipment,' he barked at his men. 'This will be a little tricky.' The soldiers secured their Uzis and utilised their Glocks while Achban gave final instructions for the order of their travel. First was our friend, the betrayer (Derain), then two soldiers followed by Burnum, Ross and the other soldiers. The TSA leader brought up the rear.

Burnum knew this particular ledge, in this particular section of the cave, better than any living human being alive. Every square, narrow inch of the ledge was second nature to him. He knew where it was most dangerous, and where you could take your finger off the panic-button. Burnum owned this ledge. Ganan's face appeared in his mind. The look he gave him seemed to be one of permission.

Initially, his plan seemed too daring but from here on in, it was all downhill, towards the book. He was the senior elder of the Seventh, he owed it to the Heart of Uluru and the hundreds of Elders who had served the Seventh before him and kept the book safe.

And he owed it to his best friend.

Burnum's brown lips curled surreptitiously, for the first time in many hours. The weight of the world felt momentarily lifted from his shoulders.

It was time to even the odds.

'Now watch your step, closely and the Australians,' Achban urged his men as they commenced. 'This looks more dangerous by the second.' He adjusted his backpack again, worried that the weight may play havoc with his balance.

'Shit,' a soldier up the front of the group hissed.

'Gilam, are you all right?'

'I am okay,' Gilam muttered. 'Just too much edge under my left boot.'

'Derain, are we nearly at the end?' Achban shouted impatiently from the rear.

The Elder peered downwards, if only for a second. 'Almost there, only a short distance to go,' he shouted back.

Burnum, inhaled slowly, methodically, inhaling every possible drop of oxygen.

The time had come.

It was now, or never.

'For you, my friend,' he muttered under his breath.

0:00:51

'Knock again.'

'I have knocked three times shithead, no answer.' Stuart referred to the small card hanging off the door-handle. 'Do not disturb.'

'Let's look through the window.'

'Brett you are a Peeping Tom from way back, you can't help yourself, can you?'

'I'm sure if you caught a glimpse of Dania in the raw, you wouldn't complain.'

Brett was the first to arrive at the window, looking into sheets of black. There were no lights on. He turned to Stuart. 'Do you have that torch they gave you?' he whispered.

'Right here.' Stuart passed it over.

'Bloody hell!'

'What is it?'

'Take a look for yourself.'

Stuart peered through the narrow slit in the curtains with the torch hard up against the glass. He turned it off. 'Shit, that wasn't Dania, was it?'

'Not unless she's turned into a very big man,' Brett said confidently. The first thing he'd noticed was the dead guy's massive shoes. 'To the Batmobile, Robin,' Brett whispered and scurried off through the garden.

'Where are you going?' Stuart snapped, running after him.

'The Winnebago, moron, hopefully the Israelis are there, safe and sound.'

* * *

'Open this door,' Siamko whispered to Ivon through gritted teeth.

Ivon picked the lock and a few seconds later, slipped his Viking from underneath his jacket and clicked the safety switch off. He swung the door open, ensuring it did not bang against the wall.

So far so good.

The two Russians spotted Ivashko's body lying neatly on the floor and met each other's glance.

'He may have been big, but he was always a pussy,' Ivon said, slipping his Viking back into its holster.

'Do you think he got one more in before he bought it?' Siamko said with a smirk on his face.

Ivon shook his head. 'Not likely. Now let's move his body into the bed and make out as if he's asleep. The last thing we need right now is unwanted attention.'

0:00:52

Burnum was not a murderer; the thought of what he planned to do weighed heavy on his conscience. He rehearsed the move a number of times in his mind. He had to be careful not to hit his head on the ceiling, and possibly knock himself out in the process. It would defeat the purpose of what may end up being a suicide move anyway. But he had to take the chance, for his secret weapon was now directly below him.

Something no one else on the ledge knew about.

Burnum raised both arms and jumped forward. His target was not only the soldier in front of him, but the one in front of that soldier too. Ranan and Davon, the men who had thrown Ganan off the edge. Burnum now had within his grasp, literally, two of the Israeli soldiers. There was now only one thing to do.

Fall.

Burnum threw himself sharply to his left. The move had its desired effect on him and his two new friends. The cries of shock and despair from the two soldiers were loud and frighteningly desperate. They had no way of saving themselves.

Their screams grew faint as they fell helplessly into the darkness.

* * *

'Quick,' Dania hissed, spotting the Glock, 'the gun.'

Abelia passed the gun and Dania tiptoed to the door. She peeled the curtain back just enough to get a glimpse of who was outside. She let the curtain go, letting out a small, childish giggle. 'Are you in for a treat,' she said. 'You are about to meet the King of Sleaze.'

Abelia gave her an inquisitive look, 'worse than Siamko?' she smiled.

'Not far off, oh, and the King of Sleaze's friend, who is actually quite the gentleman, nothing like his friend.'

Dania unlocked the Winnebago's reinforced bullet proof door and peered down the steps to the two Australians.

'Dania,' Brett gasped, 'we hoped you would be here.'

It was Dania's first glimpse of the caring side of Smacky.

'We went to your room and when you didn't answer, we looked through the window. There's a dead guy lying on the floor,' Stuart said, a little freaked out.

Dania held up her hand. 'Get in here, quick,' she barked in a whisper. 'Wow, nice Winne—' Brett instantly laid eyes on Abelia. He couldn't remember the last time he had seen such a beautiful little woman in the flesh, who wasn't gyrating around a stainless steel pole in the skimpiest of underwear. Little Brett nearly exploded there and then.

Abelia sized him up. This was quite easy, he was not that tall. If she and this awful looking man were the last two people on earth, she would sooner jump into a volcano (and thereby ensure even dead he could not get his hands on her) than bump uglies with him.

What amused Dania was the look on Brett's face. He looked like he was about to get down on one knee. 'Brett, Stuart, this is Abelia.'

The 'Abelia' effect quickly went to work. Both straightened their backs, both touched their heads in seconds, trying to neaten their hair, and their eyes glowed uncontrollably, Brett far more than Stuart.

Stuart was blown away by her beauty; though he held it all in good stead, which won him instant respect from the gorgeous Israeli bombshell.

'Nice to meet,' Brett stuck out his left hand for Abelia to shake, 'to meet you.'

Abelia did not move an inch.

Dania waved them to a seat.

Stuart smiled. 'Nice to meet you, Abelia.'

Abelia liked something in Stuart's eyes. He was the first Australian she had met who was genuinely handsome.

'Nice, to meet you too, Stuart.' Abelia rose to her feet with the poise of a beauty queen and offered her hand.

The move surprised Stuart. His cheeks turned an instant, crimson pink and he shook her hand lightly, hoping it was not the last time he touched her beautiful skin.

She retreated to the couch.

Fucken arsehole, Little Brett shouted to big Brett internally. 'Before we talk about that body in the Hotel suite,' Dania announced, moving over to the kitchenette, 'we have some significant news.' Dania pulled out a jug of iced tea and offered all of them a glass. 'So tell me, at school, when you learnt about the rock Stuart, did they tell you about the subterranean tunnel system with caves the size of football fields, hidden deep within its walls?'

Stuart could not help but share a curious glance with Brett, though he did it in such a way as to not offend the beautiful Israeli women.

Not that it mattered to Brett; he had more chance of shagging Stuart, than the two stunners sitting nearby. Brett could not help himself; he let out a scoff.

Stuart couldn't help a small grin. 'You're joking, right?'

245

'Achban is down in it as we speak.' She glanced at Brett. 'And one of his guests is your older brother.'

Brett's face turned to a scowl.

Abelia was amazed that he could make himself look even more uglier.

'I knew it.' Brett tried to look important. 'I knew that arsehole brother of mine knew about this secret cave system, and never let me in on it.'

Dania sat forward, though no closer to Brett. 'And your father knew too, right?'

'Or so it seems. Thank fuck he's dead.'

Stuart blushed.

* * *

Ross was nearly caught in Burnum's move, and scrambled to grip the rock face. It had happened so damn quickly.

Chasid and Gilam, behind Ross, stood rigid. Like any highly trained soldier, they focused on safety first, securing themselves while their falling comrades screamed sounds they knew they'd recall in their nightmares – for years to come.

Derain – he ran like the wind, nearly falling into the deep cave himself. He made it to safety a few moments later. His whimpers continued to confirm his title as the weakest Elder ever allowed into the Seventh.

Achban was furious. Two of his men were down and both had been carrying explosives. 'Run, run, get off the ledge as fast as you can!' he screamed.

Hand grenades, even with the safety pin still inside, do not take kindly to hitting harsh surfaces at more than five kilometres an hour...

'Run, run, *run!*' Achban cried.

Ross hoped he would reach safety and be the only one to survive. In a few moments he would find out.

B-O-O-M!

The reverberation wave from the explosion took less than a second to make it to the top of the cave.

Achban wavered, with only one metre to go. He lunged for balance. Chasid spun and as best as he could, reached for Achban, balancing precariously over the edge himself, hands grappled and Chasid dragged Achban to safety.

It was over.

Burnum had achieved his goal.

Two more souls would now live with the others, in Spirit Land.

* * *

'Oh well,' Vadislav sighed, as if in losing Ivashko, he had just lost an insignificant bet. 'What else do you have to report, Siamko?'

'Looks like it was all about this big rock out here, Comrade.'

'Ayers Rock.' The Russian billionaire pronounced the outdated name perfectly.

'Yes, Vadislav,' Siamko said. 'Ears Rock.'

'Ayers Rock, Siamko, practice your bloody English, Comrade!'

Siamko's left ear was fast turning into a sweaty appendage; he could feel the heat of the phone and was keen to ring off. 'Yes, Vadislav,' Siamko repeated, 'I will.'

'How is my personal secretary going?'

Siamko laughed in a way that would make Abelia's blood run cold. 'She disappeared a few hours ago.' He clenched his teeth. 'Don't worry, we will find the little whore.'

'I hope for your sake, you do … my friend.'

And the line went dead.

0:00:53

Chasid and Gilam exchanged glances. Achban, walking a few metres ahead, heard the sounds too. He grabbed Derain by the scruff of his neck. 'Is there another way down here, old man? We can hear people, don't lie to me.'

Derain stared into Achban's eyes and did not waver. 'Anyone who dies here, Uluru, their spirit stays trapped down here.' He raised his hand and waved into the infinite darkness of Spirit Land.

Chasid laughed. A secular Jew, he did not believe in any sort of spiritual hogwash. When you're dead, you're dead, as far as he was concerned.

Achban held up his hand to Chasid, telling him to pipe down.

Achban shone his torch into the myriad of tunnels and open caves. 'Come on Derain, ghosts?' He shook his head dismissively. 'Do you honestly believe we are walking through the cave of the dead?'

'Woo-oo,' Chasid mocked before the group, on Achban's command, moved on.

Chasid, better watch your step.

'Shhhhit,' the Israeli soldier gasped a second later as he tripped and fell flat on his face.

Achban pulled out his Glock and pointed it at Ross. He was the only threat now.

Gilam helped Chasid to his feet. 'Keep an eye on where you're walking, you klutz.'

A cross between a shrill, a moan, and an opera singer holding a high note far too long came from deep within the rock, as if it were coming from every direction.

Achban slipped his Glock into the holster and pulled up his Uzi.

'Shit, Achban, did you hear that?' Chasid shouted.

Gilam was one tough bastard, but the hairs on the back of his neck told him – be alarmed, be very alarmed. He held the Uzi as if it were a handgun, wrapping the strap around his wrists and forearm. He pointed it in every direction, ready for whatever came next.

'I can hear them,' Chasid squealed, holding his wrist and shaking his head madly. 'It's Davon and Ranan, I can hear their voices.'

The three Israelis were pointing their guns and torches in all directions. The tension was mounting, and quick. Ross stood dead still, unwilling to provoke any panicked movement from one of his captors.

Achban grabbed Chasid by the collar. 'Soldier,' he hissed, 'that's enough.'

Help us.

Chasid.

Come please.

Ross heard the voices as if he were in an IMAX cinema with speakers set up in every available nook and cranny. 'Shit,' he muttered under his breath. He had a sudden desire to crouch down to his knees.

'Get over there with Ross,' Achban said to Derain.

He didn't need convincing. Derain was on his arse next

to Ross a second later. Ross shuffled a foot away. He would not make eye-contact with the Elder. As far as he was concerned, he would never speak to him again. Ganan and Burnum's deaths were on his shoulders; their blood was on his hands.

Derain spoke with unmistakeable authority. 'Your men are with the others now, the spirits of the Seventh.'

Chasid wouldn't have a bar of spirits and afterlife. He pounced on Derain, grabbing him by his hair. It happened so quickly, it caught everyone by surprise. 'Where are they?' Chasid hissed. 'You stupid old man.'

'They are dead; their spirits are trapped with all the others.'

Achban was out of patience. 'Enough,' he shouted, so loud it reverberated through the caves and tunnels, the echo washing back over them.

Derain muttered to himself, moaning in pain.

Achban barked like a hyena. 'No talking.'

Then it happened.

'What the fuck?' Chasid snarled.

Blackness.

Hundreds of metres underground. Every single torch, stone cold dead. The terrifying noises, growing louder by the second. Movement all around them.

'Something is grabbing my leg.' Chasid screamed.

'Chasid, put on your NVGs. Now.'

Derain felt around in the darkness and found Ross's arm. He shuffled over to him and whispered in his ear. 'Lie on the ground and block your ears, quickly.'

Ross followed instructions. He was quietly shitting himself.

Achban could not get his backpack open; his frustration was getting the better of him. Then something pushed passed him, almost knocking him off his feet. 'I have had enough of these games, whoever you are.' His Uzi, as if controlled by his

251

mind, swung back over his arm, the trigger coming to rest in his hand. He slipped his finger through and turned the safety latch off. 'Dodge this.'

Gunfire bounced off the walls and bullets whirled in every direction.

Gilam was flat on his stomach, his training told him to get as close to the ground as possible the second the lights went off. But Chasid, well, he was panicked.

Gilam called out to Achban, 'Cease fire! Someone will get hit.'

Then – two bullets landed squarely in Chasid's chest. A shriek of horror fell from his mouth.

Ross had rolled onto his side, his hands hard up against his ears. A hand gripped his shoulder, as if the person could see in the dark and wanted to calm him down. 'Ross, don't panic.' The voice was low-pitched, reassuring, and as Ross realised whose voice it actually was, he wasn't sure if he was relieved, or ready to freak out some more.

Burnum.

Ross waved his hand into the darkness, wanting to believe Burnum was still alive and not a corpse back at the bottom of the Deep Cave. He threw his hand around in the darkness, hoping to confirm that it was actually Burnum, and not his spirit. But he felt nothing. He had started to wonder, before he felt two small objects pushed up against his stomach.

'These may help,' his old friend whispered.

He ran his hand over them, a torch and a small handgun.

'Lead them to the final place, I will take the quick way up and get help,' Burnum whispered.

Burnum placed a firm hand on Ross's shoulder, if only for a second and said, 'Stay alive my friend, I will see you soon.'

And then he was gone.

Ross slipped the pistol into his left sock and the torch into his right.

The torches suddenly started working again. Light filled the area.

Chasid was lying in a pool of his own blood.

Achban cursed and ran the few steps to the fallen soldier. Another wayward bullet had pierced Chasid's neck. Achban tried in vain to stem the flow of blood from the wound. It was futile.

Gilam slipped his hand underneath Chasid's neck and lifted his head. The two met each other's eyes. Chasid, the whites of his eyes fading, smiled at his friend. 'Davon and Ranan...' he whispered through curdles of his own blood. 'I can see them—'

Gilam held his hand. 'Chasid, no, wait.'

Chasid's chest lifted as he took his last breath. His head tilted to the right and went limp.

Gilam looked over the body of his friend of many, many years. The anger started to rise from the pit of his stomach. He looked up to Achban with disgust.

'I'm sorry Gilam,' Achban whispered. 'I did not mean for this to happen.' Achban turned to Derain, 'now take me to the book Elder.'

A few minutes later, Derain led the now considerably smaller group across the Lair of the Devil Dingo.

Gilam kept a close eye on Ross's every move, walking a metre behind with the Uzi permanently pointed at Ross's back.

The loss of three of his men had killed Achban's enthusiasm for the wonders of the cave system, and replaced it with an impatient, volatile mood.

Eventually, the group reached the last stretch of the journey, where the small ledge stretched across the bottomless heart of Uluru.

'Another deep cave, I see. How deep is it?' Achban asked, not keen to get too close.

Derain shook his head. 'We don't know, we think it's so deep it has no bottom.'

Achban clicked his tongue, scoffing at the Elder's comment. He shone the torch across the narrow ledge. 'You two,' flicking his handgun at Ross and Derain.

Derain held his breath. This was the last pathway before these men reached the Seventh List. He wondered if he would make it to the other side, or if they were going to push him over the ledge to join the other elders in Spirit Land.

Achban stood at the entrance to the small cave. His powerful torch lit the room in a stark, unattractive, white light. He noted the candles and barked at Derain to light them. When the elder had done so, Achban slipped off his backpack and nodded for Gilam to keep a vigilant eye on Ross and Derain.

He carefully scanned the wall at the rear, with the myriad of indentations, each housing a flat, dusty object which, stepping closer, he saw were books. The last few years' work had paid off. He had reached the climax, the top of Everest, and if there were a more momentous occasion in his life, he struggled to remember it.

After a time, he slowly turned and laid eyes on Derain.

Derain caught his breath; those narrow eyes told him: he would not leave this room alive.

'Derain,' Achban said coolly. 'Please show it to me.'

Only when Ross realised Derain had not moved a square inch, did he allow his eyes to wander over to Derain's direction. When Ross finally met the Elder's eyes, he could see the sadness and regret deep within them.

'I'm sorry,' Derain whispered. The elder rose to his feet and walked carefully past Achban to the far wall of the cave. Derain had to count the holes across and then down, he had never easily remembered which of the actual crevices contained the actual one. Once he had located what he thought was right book, he reached in. 'The Seventh List,' he whispered, each word as painful as passing a kidney stone.

He faced the other men with the book resting against his stomach, held with both hands. Derain could see the captivation in Achban's eyes and remembered it was the same look he had, when he first laid eyes on the ancient book.

Achban placed his hand lightly on the top of the book, letting his index finger run along to the edge, before reaching underneath and feeling the weight of the book in his own hand. Achban turned and looked to his last remaining soldier, as if for absolution. 'The Akashic Record,' he said reverently, 'is in our hands.'

His grin was damn well annoying, Ross thought. Any wider, he could fit the bloody thing sideways in his mouth.

Achban placed the book down on the makeshift table, like the many elders had done many, many times before.

You see, for the Seventh List to continue working, it had to come in contact with at least two living souls within every lunar cycle. The reason the elders would come to the book every month. Under Burnum's watch, they had never missed a cycle, ever.

Achban then saw it: the insignia on his wrist. He stood agape, if only for a moment.

Gilam saw his own wrist. 'What is it?' he asked.

Derain leant forward. 'Every soul has one, every one different to any other. It only becomes visible when you are within reach of the book.'

Achban rubbed his wrist, the habit of anyone who, for the first time, saw it on their skin. 'It is amazing.' Achban showed that grin again. 'Is that all it does?'

'It is connected to the book, yes – it directs you to your name in it.'

Ross closed his eyes. He had an inclination of what would

255

happen next.

Achban's eyes narrowed. 'Show me,' he ordered.

As Gilam kept his Uzi trained on Ross, Derain shuffled to the table and sat down in front of the book. Achban noted that his insignia now shone brightly, noting the colour identical and the inner patterns clearly different to his own.

Derain carefully opened the front cover of the book and lifted the first three pages. While Achban watched his every move, he placed his hand across the fourth page, his hand hovering half a centimetre from touching the page itself. Derain methodically turned back the three pages and the front cover, and looked to Achban. He closed his eyes for a few moments, and peered down to the glass circle in the middle of the front cover of the Seventh List.

Achban leant in a little closer after seeing movement in the circle, which had previously been dark and lifeless. 'It is amazing.'

Derain removed his hand from the page. He shook his head as if making sure his eyes were seeing correctly.

He would soon join the others.

Spirit Land.

He sat back and looked over to the main wall, unable to meet Ross's eyes.

Achban looked down to the page and could see a small line of writing, next to a tiny image of Derain's insignia:

He had to look closer to guess it was Derain's date of birth, and date of death. 'This is unbelievable,' Achban said, looking up to meet Gilam's eyes, too excited to register the dirty look Gilam was giving him.

Gilam was still reeling from his friend's death. Achban had not batted an eyelid and appeared to have already moved on from the event, and this cut hard into Gilam's core.

Achban reached into his breast pocket and pulled out a small notepad and pen. In the semi-darkness, he fumbled and the pen slipped from his hand and landed directly on the open page of the ancient book.

Seated back over near Ross, Derain gasped.

Achban scooped up the pen and peered down to the page, frightened he had damaged the book. 'Damn it,' he muttered, pulled out his handkerchief and delicately wiped the page. 'Sweet Jehovah,' he muttered. 'I will give you one chance to tell the truth, Taylor.' He took another look at the page, as if confirming his thoughts, nodding to himself. 'You can change the date of death?' Ross closed his eyes. The facts were simple. Achban had the book. He and Derain were now obsolete. But he had the gun in his left sock. If he could just wait for the right moment, they may make it out of the cave alive, maybe.

Pigs fly backwards on Sundays, his dad always said.

Achban pointed his Glock at Derain's head. 'Well?'

Ross ground his teeth. 'Yes.'

'Thank you.' Achban slipped the Glock back in its holster. 'Your cooperation is much appreciated.'

He leant closer to the book and touched the screen. Tap, tap, tap. He shook his head. 'Once you have changed the date of death for a person, how does it come into effect?'

Derain pushed his hand up against the younger Australian, holding it for a few seconds before letting it go. It was his way of saying goodbye. 'I'm so sorry for what I have done, Ross,' he whispered.

Derain began to chant in his own tongue and Ross recognized it as the same as the one he heard from Burnum, when Ganan was about to die. Ross' blood instantly ran cold.

'No.' Ross growled, attempting to quickly stand up.

Gilam stepped forward and pushed Ross back onto his backside. Ross stifled a moan as he knew he could not stop the inevitable.

Achban slid his hand under the front cover of the open book and without preamble – slammed it shut.

0:00:54

'So what's the score?'

The Israelis had no idea what Brett meant.

'What do we do now?' he added, in response to their blank looks.

'We need to hide this bus, somewhere completely out of view,' Dania said.

'I know a good spot.' Brett grinned, looking over to Dania and stealing a surreptitious glance at Abelia.

Dania joined him at the table, looking down at the place on the map where his finger was pointing.

'It's the local garbage dump,' Brett said. 'If my memory serves me correctly, there is a large shed there too, we can park behind it. It's only open once a week.'

Dania wanted to pat him on the back, but thought better of it. 'Good. Show me the way, let's go.' She turned to Abelia. 'Get on the phone to Chonen and let him know what we are doing. We'll send the coordinates as soon as we get there.'

* * *

Derain had only just made eye contact with Ross, when the front cover of the Seventh List closed abruptly. The effect was instant. His eyeballs suddenly tilted up until Ross could only see the whites. It was very unnerving. His only consolation: there appeared to be no pain, no anguish. Derain had fucked up, but Ross still felt that his death completely unnecessary, and devoid of any dignity.

The deceased Elder's head slumped forward, where it then fell into Ross's lap. 'I'm sorry, friend,' Ross whispered in the Elder's ear, struggling to fight back his emotions.

Achban scoffed at Ross's little moment, picking up the book and slipping it under his arm, his look of sick satisfaction, abhorrent. He grabbed Ross roughly by the hair and pushed his head back until it hit the wall with a thud.

Achban bent down and checked Derain's pulse, or lack thereof. He grinned over to Gilam. 'It works, Gilam. It actually worked!'

Achban had dropped his guard and that was all Ross needed. He slipped his hand down into his sock. The small gun came into his hand easily. He lunged as he punched Achban as hard as he could in the limited space. Squealing, Achban fell back, the Akashic Record flying out of his grip and sliding along the floor towards the wall where he had lived for the last fifty-two thousand years. Ross, his pent up anger now coming free and easy, laid into the Israeli with a fury of lightning quick clenched fists.

Achban cried out to his last remaining soldier for help. Ross looked askance – and caught his breath.

Gilam was standing still against the far wall.

His Uzi? – hanging off his left shoulder.

Only when Achban cried out a second time, did Gilam finally act, grabbing Ross by the shoulder, easily lifting him off the TSA leader and throwing him against the wall of books. He swung his Uzi around to Ross. 'Don't move an inch.'

Achban nursing his aching face pulled out his bottle to wash the blood from his cheek. 'What the fuck were you doing, you stupid pig?' he snarled. If he had ever wanted to turn Gilam against him, for good: he just did.

'Focus on the job at hand,' Achban muttered, 'not on what happened to your friend, who died a hero.' He rose unsteadily to his feet, walking over to the book and picking it up, muttering words in Hebrew.

Gilam tied Ross's hands behind his back. 'Don't move an inch,' he repeated.

Ross knew it would be wise at this point, not to.

Achban placed the Akashic Record in his backpack and turned on his torch. He systematically blew out every candle. When he was done, he nodded for Gilam and pointed his torch in Ross's direction. 'Enjoy the eternal darkness, Ross. Say hello to your father and his old friends.' Achban grinned, though the side of his face still stung. He nodded to Gilam. 'Kill him.'

Ross closed his eyes and felt a sickening pain deep in his stomach. He was going to join the Elders, along with the other souls in Spirit Land. The bile of adrenaline flooded his throat.

This was it.

Time to die.

Ross felt a metallic object thrown near his feet. He fought back the tears. They were going to blow him up!

And then, the thought, was interrupted: by the sound of a Glock; firing three loud, back-to-back shots.

So death was painless, after all.

Then Ross wondered, how can you wonder, when you are dead? And he could hear the receding voices of the two remaining Israelis. He wasn't dead?

Ross freed his hands after only a few twists and turns. He shuffled to the entrance of the cave. There he saw on the other side and about to completely disappear from view – Achban and Gilam.

He navigated his way back to the cave of books.

Right where he had been sitting, waiting to die, a small torch sat in the middle of the floor.

Gilam.

The Israeli soldier had thrown him a torch, not a grenade. Ross looked down to Derain's body; Gilam had fired the three shots into his body, this was the only way.

The man had saved his life.

Ross leant down and closed the Elder's eyes.

He realised he had a problem. He believed the route he intended to take back to the surface, would not be possible for the deceased Elder. Carrying him all the way up was not an option either. He picked up the body of Derain and took him out to the ledge of the abyss. It was the only dignified thing he could do. Ross whispered some words to Derain and lifted him up, before letting him go into the inky darkness.

He returned to the small cave and gathered all his possessions into his backpack, along with two other items from the cave he knew would have to come with him.

A few moments later, Ross made his way across the ledge, not daring to look down. Moving swiftly and with purpose, he knew every second counted. If his plan worked, he would have many hours' head start on Achban.

Ross made it through the narrow tunnel and crouching by some enormous boulders, shone the torch close to the ground. Confident he had his bearings, he turned off the torch, before climbing up and sneaking a look out into the massive cave. In the far distance, he easily spotted the Israelis making their way to the other side. The relief he felt was enormous.

Now – all he had to do was pull off the impossible.

Chant his way back to the surface.

On his own.

Would it work?

He was going to roll the dice and hope so.

After changing his position a few times on the ground behind the boulders, he believed he was in the same position he was – the first time he had done it with Adam and Burnum. He closed his eyes and began to chant. He hesitated, wondering if he was doing it correctly, trying to remember how many times he had to repeat the same, rather difficult words.

Then – suddenly – Ross felt the presence of another, right beside him. He was about to curse his luck – the Israelis had obviously doubled back and found him – when big, leathery, familiar hands closed over the top of his own.

Burnum.

'Don't stop Ross, keep going,' The Elder whispered.

* * *

The brightness burned through Ross' eyelids. The temperature around him: much, much hotter. The wind, warm and stronger – he was back on *terra firma*.

Ross put a reassuring hand on his old friend's shoulder. 'You lost men close to you today.' Ross bowed his head before meeting Burnum's wet eyes. 'I can't tell you how sorry I am, Burnum.'

'We need to get back to Merrigang, re-group, and think of a plan.'

Ross had never seen such intent in the man's eyes.

'Him.' Burnum's eyes fell, indicating the Israeli still deep below the inside of the rock. 'We have to stop him.'

Ross adjusted the small pistol, wedged in his belt, making sure his shirt covered it well. He nodded to Burnum with the same determined look. As he began to move toward the wafer-thin opening to the outside world, the elder grabbed Ross by the arm. 'It's never been to the surface. Leave the books here, I will explain why later.'

* * *

Blink ... blink ... blink...

'What's that?' Abelia said, the sudden sound of something going off catching her by surprise. For a second she thought it was a bomb.

Dania, behind the driver's wheel, fixed her gaze into the rear view mirror. 'Shit,' she said pulling the Winnebago over to the side of the road. 'I know what it is.'

The laptop was securely fastened to a side bench. She fumbled with the mouse. Blink ... blink ... bl–

The signal went dead.

'What the?' Dania gasped.

'What happened?'

'One of the tracking devices had re-activated.' Dania shook her head. 'And what's more, Achban's signal and communication has not returned.'

Brett said, 'Was that my arsehole brother?'

Dania nodded silently. 'I think so.'

Abelia realised what it implied. 'So he may have escaped from Achban?'

Dania slammed her fist on the bench top. It was rare for her to show such raw emotion. 'Most probably.' She knew the serial number of Ross's GPS unit, all of them were tagged on the screen, but it had gone dead too soon.

'Maybe it was a phantom signal?' Abelia had heard of them before, though they were as rare as Halley's Comet.

* * *

'Piece of shit.' Ross smashed the watch so many times with the brick-sized rock, the rock itself disintegrated. 'Birthday gift – my ass.' He stood up and spat at the small heap of metal which a few moments ago had been a expensive looking watch.

Burnum ducked and pulled Ross down with him. A large, gleaming Winnebago was moving down the Lasseter Highway and the Elder was not prepared to take any more chances – the stakes were now very high.

'When I get my hands on my brother, he's going to wish he was killed at Mum's wake,' Ross hissed.

* * *

Burnum had not minced his words.

'No, this can't be happening,' Adam muttered, in tears. Gan-an was like an uncle to Adam, he'd known him his whole life, and now, he was gone. He also had a heavy heart for the woman he adored, and had done for as long as he could remember.

Erin.

She deserved to know.

Ross, freshly showered, caught the tail end of the conversation Burnum was having with his son. He wore the towel as if he were Rocky. Knowing he had many hours' head start on that murderous arsehole still deep within the Seventh, he felt a little like the fictitious boxer. Ross made a bee-line for the esky. If there had ever been a time in his life he needed a cold one, it was right now.

Burnum turned to him as he snapped the top of the can open. 'Now is not the time for drinking.'

Ross met his eyes for a second before shaking his head, doing it subtly as to not offend him. 'After what I have seen in the last few hours, I think I can at least have one,' Ross said, his tone cool and devoid of any antics.

Burnum's eyes fell. 'That, I can't argue with.'

It was at that moment that Burnum knew, Ross had stepped into the fold and was now standing alongside him as a leader, and soon, he would be the true leader.

Adam, as if the quick discussion between his friend and his father had given him permission for one, gave Ross the signal.

Ross flipped open the esky and passed one over to his mate. 'You'll be all right?'

Adam, a veneer of anger slowly appearing on his face, met Ross's eyes. 'Yes,' he said, louder than he intended. 'Just tell me the plan, brother.'

Ross threw the towel onto the veranda railing and took a couple of swigs, the alcohol taking its effect and calming him down. He rested against the railing. 'We blow the entrances to the Seventh.' Ross's bottom lip curled into a snarl. 'And trap that prick inside.'

Adam raised his beer into the air, toasting the idea, his approval obvious. Burnum held up his hand with two fingers outstretched. 'One,' he said, 'we must blow it from the inside and wait for them; we must get back the book.'

Burnum looked out over to the source of his problems – Uluru. 'And two, unless you have explosives and know how to use them, and the last time I checked you don't have either, who's going to do all the blowing up?'

Ross grinned from ear to ear. 'I think it's about time we pulled Oxy into the team. Oxy's profession before running remote, dusty pubs,' he smiled for the first time in twenty-four hours, 'was blowing shit up for the Army.'

* * *

Jimmy had once told him, if you want to get Oxy's attention, place your hand on top of his. He would then either take notice of what you were saying, or knock your lights out.

Oxy fobbed him off. 'Mate, I'm flat out at the moment, can it wait?'

Ross could feel the need to protect the Seventh List pulsing through his veins. He'd always had a soft spot for responsibility, though up until now, only had short windows of opportunity to embrace it. Although the billions of other people on the

266

planet would never know, for these few moments, he was the most important person on Earth.

Ross leant over the bar and laid his left hand on top of Oxy's. There was not an ounce of fear possessing Ross at that exact moment. Well, maybe just a little bit. 'Trust me, it cannot.'

Chris met his gaze. 'Upstairs.'

Ross followed him up.

'Talk to me son,' Chris said in a fatherly tone.

Ross shook his head. 'You'd better take a seat. Even the short version is bloody long.'

* * *

'Copy that, Dania. En route to the new coordinates. We will rendezvous with you shortly.'

'Thank you, Chonen, over.' Dania put the handset down on the table.

Abelia tapped her on the arm. 'How long before they get here?'

'Thirty minutes or so.'

Brett and Stuart sat on the leather couch in the plush interior of the Winnebago. They had stayed out of the way of the women and were keeping their conversation to a low hum. 'What'ya gonna do with the money, brother?' Brett snickered.

Stuart let one of his big grins envelop his face. When he did this, his eyes appeared shut. 'Maybe take an overseas trip to the Middle-East,' he whispered, just loud enough for Abelia to hear. Stuart met her eyes and they smiled at each other.

Smacky ground his teeth, he was beyond jealous. He buried the feeling as deep as he could. 'A trip – good idea.' He ignored the fact Stuart had not turned back to him yet. 'I reckon somewhere like Rio de Janeiro, where the parties and women never end.'

'Let's get the book on home soil first, before you get carried away with spending the money,' said Dania without looking up from the laptop.

Brett let out a childish huff.

Dania gasped. 'You have got to be—'

Abelia looked for herself. 'Mother of God,' Abelia muttered.

Stuart leant forward. 'What's going on?'

Abelia looked up from the screen and met Stuart's eyes. She whispered in Dania's ear. Dania nodded.

'A year ago, Achban uploaded a unique program to his Blackberry, one that contains hundreds of politicians, industry leaders, famous and infamous dignitaries' names, and their dates of birth. Where applicable, and the information obtainable, the details also include the hour and minute they were born. Names from every country in the Middle East.' She pointed to the screen. 'The Palestinian Prime Minister, the President of Iran, and the leader of Hezbollah have all died, mysteriously, within twenty-three minutes of each other. Achban is in possession of the Akashic Record. He has to be.'

Brett put his hand up. 'I hope he doesn't have my date of birth.'

Dania smiled. 'Of course he does.'

0:00:55

'We have searched the entire resort, Siamko. There is no trace of them.'

'They must be somewhere, expand the search to the outlying areas.'

'I am on it.'

'Be ready in five minutes to leave for the rock, I want to check out those two marked points we saw on the Israelis' map.'

'Understood, Siamko.'

The Romanov crewmember left the room and Siamko turned his attention to his long lost, best friend.

The Mini-Bar.

Checking his Rolex, a classic fake, the logical side of his brain asked: was it right to have Vodka at this time of the morning? The other side of his brain answered as it always did: There's a bar open somewhere in the world right now, it may as well be here!

He bloody well needed the calming effects only Vodka could bestow on his senses. The stupid book was nowhere to be found. One of the crew was already dead. Mikita, the little whore ... gone. Oh and then the real heart of the shit casserole: his Boss was en route.

The Russian loved the feeling of twisting the cap off a brand new bottle. He licked his lips as he poured the clear liquid into a small wine glass. As the last drop came from the bottle, he put the glass to his lips, savouring the unique smell, before the entire contents disappeared down his throat. Siamko savoured the immediate rush it gave his nervous system, a wave of enlightened relief coursing through his body, if only for a second.

An abrupt knock on his door ended his moment of alcoholic solitude. Siamko moved silently, checking the peephole. He pulled the door open. Niki just stood there, frozen.

'What the hell is it?'

'Maccek just received a call from the Romanov.' The man shook. 'The most terrible news was just announced on the RIA Novosti's website.'

Siamko shrugged his thick, square shoulders, the Vodka wearing off. 'Well, spit it out, Comrade.'

Niki's eyes fell and he ceremoniously slipped the baseball cap off his enormous head. 'Vadislav is dead.'

* * *

Chris took one more look at Ross before floating over to the double glass doors of the Pub's second floor balcony. Once outside, he held onto the railing as if it was holding him upright. He looked over to her and knew, as did the others who learned of her enormous secrets, that he would never look at her they same way again, ever.

Uluru.

'Whoa,' he gasped. 'Now that's what I call a secret.'

Ross knew how Chris felt. 'And it has to remain that way, huh.'

'Jimmy was my best friend. Any secret of his will remain a secret of mine. Forever.' Chris took a last look at the turquoise sky, nimbus clouds high above. He turned to Ross, his face akin to a soldier ready to go into battle. 'Give me five minutes. I'll meet you at your truck.' He smiled as he walked off. 'All the stuff I need is in Jimmy's shed.'

Ross's heart skipped an uneasy beat. All this time, there were explosives in the old man's shed? Shit!

The Ute flew through the gates of Merrigang not six minutes later. The red dust engulfed Merrigang as Ross ripped up the handbrake, and threw open the door, nearly booting the dogs out of the way.

Burnum and Adam sat on the veranda holding their hats across their faces. 'Dust sandwich, my favourite,' Adam mocked, as Ross raced up to the veranda, Chris only a few feet behind.

Burnum stood to his feet. Chris was already raising his hand and the two men shook hands firmly. 'You've had an interesting twenty-four hours my friend.' Chris's gaze fell. 'I am sorry to hear of the loss of your two close friends.'

Burnum nodded, his eyes spoke for him.

'The time has come,' Ross said, at that moment becoming the unofficial leader of the resistance, of sorts. 'This arsehole will be within reach of the first cave in around three hours. Remember,' Ross pointed his finger into the air for effect, 'the soldier with him, Gilam, chose not to kill me. I think he turned when Archbarn, or whatever the bastard's name is, killed his close friend, one of the other soldiers. Now, Chris tells me all he needs is in Dad's shed.'

As Chris headed off to the shed, Ross locked eyes with Adam. 'Mate, get all the guns from Dad's cabinet plus every available piece of ammo in there, and get it into duffle bags and into the Ute, all right?'

Adam scurried inside.

'Now Burnum, before we go any further, how did you survive that little stunt down there?'

Burnum raised his eyebrows, a faint hint of delight drifting over his frown. 'Another ledge, five feet below. It's only about four feet long and a foot wide.'

Ross's respect for the Elder, which had always been at DE-FCON 5, now rose to a new level. The guy had balls. What a move.

'You done Adam?' Ross called, seeing no sign of guns or ammunition.

'You've got to see this, come,' Adam called back. Inside, Ross and Burnum found him staring at the TV.

'Can't you go one day without your soapie fix, brother?' Ross smirked.

Adam turned up the volume. The news anchor's face was grave. 'Repeating today's top story: the world is in shock at the mysterious passing of seven prominent international figures, across the globe.'

Ross sat down.

'The Palestinian Prime Minister died without warning, followed only minutes later by the President of Iran. The leader of Hezbollah collapsed some ten minutes after that.'

Ross met Adam's wide eyes.

'Fifteen minutes later, the President of Syria collapsed while making a speech in front of hundreds of people, and minutes later, was pronounced dead at the scene.' The anchor took a long, deep breath. 'Across the globe, the Secretary General of the United Nations collapsed whilst dining with other UN delegates in New York. Shortly after, news came in from Egypt, where Mr Fahalluh, ranked as the sixty-second richest person in the world, with a personal wealth of 18 billion US dollars, died while sipping champagne aboard his luxury yacht with his family.'

Burnum stood, a look of horror chiselled on his weathered face. He swayed from side to side.

'The seventh reported mysterious death is another billionaire, this time from Russia. Listed as the thirty-sixth richest man in the world, Steel magnate Mazen Marcos was found by his personal secretary slumped in his office chair, deceased. Lastly, there are reports of the death of another Russian billionaire, Vadislav Pravica, though this is still awaiting official confirmation.'

'Turn it off!' Burnum barked.

His face contorted with anger, the elder shut his eyes and swallowed hard. Achban was killing them one by one. There would be more. They had to stop him.

Ross met the old man's eyes, with fire in his own.

He was ready.

Chris broke the uneasy moment. 'I'm good to go,' he shouted from outside.

0:00:56

'Come on, Achban.' Gilam felt sick. 'That will do for now.' The tall Israeli soldier, once a killing machine with absolutely no conscience, had come full circle.

It had started with a small twinge when he watched his two fellow soldiers throw that poor elder off the ledge. The deeper he went into the cave system; the twinge became a gnaw, which became stronger as they went deeper. Then, when he watched his best friend, Chasid, die unnecessarily at the hands of the TSA leader; his conscience reset itself entirely. The man he had for many years looked up to, like a father figure – had become a vicious, cold-hearted murderer.

Achban snapped at him, as if he were a pit-bull. 'The more we do now,' he hissed, 'the sooner our country's freedom.'

'Can we just get out of here first?' Gilam fired back.

'Soldier!' Achban spoke in a sharp, condescending tone. 'Patience ... we will get back to the first cave soon.'

Gilam lunged for Achban, grabbing him by the shoulder.

Achban spun around and shone the torch directly into Gilam's face. 'What now?' he shouted, ready to go for his Glock.

Gilam raised his hand. 'I just heard something.'

Achban shook his head before walking off. 'You have not been the same since...'

Gilam grabbed Achban by the back of the neck.

Achban knocked Gilam's arm away. 'Stand down, soldier.'

'Go on, finish the sentence.' Gilam's nostrils flared in anger.

'I will apologise one more time for what happened to Chasid.' Achban spoke with no emotion. 'It was an accident.'

Gilam did not waver; he was never going to forgive Achban for what had happened.

Violent sounds from on high, like thunder, or small explosions, caught them by surprise.

'Let's go,' Achban muttered, breaking into a run.

* * *

'Bloody hell!' Ross whacked his explosives expert on the arm. 'You call that a small explosion?'

'What?' Chris shrugged his shoulders. As far as he was concerned, it *was* a small explosion.

Burnum waited for the dust to settle and peered into the tunnel with the aid of his Big-Daddy torch. Nothing would get through this tunnel now. Satisfied, he nodded his approval. 'Now for the other one.'

As the Elder led them to the other side of the Deep Valley cave, Chris caught his breath. 'Well, I'll be damned,' he said as the enormous expanse materialised from the darkness.

Ross patted him on the shoulder. 'Ah, you'll get used to it.' He looked out over into the abyss, knowing his comment was far from the truth.

* * *

'ETA, ten minutes.'

'Copy that, Chonen.'

'Have you heard from Achban, over?'

'Not yet – we lost radio communication at a certain distance below ground.'

'Copy that, Dania, see you shortly.'

* * *

'Call him again.'

'I just tried for the fifth time, Siamko.'

'A retired politician who lived in Murmansk, on the Barents Sea,' Siamko muttered. 'There's a chance he is the Vadislav Pravica who died. Ivon, pass me the satellite phone, I will sort this out.'

Siamko had not even dialled the numbers when the phone suddenly rang; he answered it without delay.

'I hear I am dead, Comrade.'

Siamko's lips curled into an expansive grin as the familiar voice filtered through the earpiece. He gave Ivon the thumbs up. 'That is what the world is saying,' Siamko said.

'Have you heard the other news, comrade? It seems far too big a coincidence, considering most of the dead are, or were, enemies of Israel.'

'Yes, it appears so Vadislav. Achban must have the book.'

Vadislav agreed. 'The time has come to take what is ours, Siamko. We arrive in one hour, meet me at the Airport.' He rang off.

As soon as Siamko put the sat-phone down, Ivon called him over. 'I think we may have found the Israelis. I have been searching the area, ten miles in all directions from the rock. These satellite images are refreshed every hour.' He pointed to a small compound. 'This large Bus or Van was not there last time I checked.' He clicked on the mouse as the image grew larger. 'Looks like the local garbage dump.'

Siamko shared a joyous glance with Ivan. The day was getting better by the second. Soon, Vadislav would have the damn ancient artefact straight from the bookshelf of God himself.

And Siamko would have Mikita.

* * *

'Watch where you're walking. It's the body of the one we threw off the ledge above.' Gilam had seen enough bodies in his time to fill a 737, but seeing the body of a defenceless, innocent, old man, strengthened his new resolve even more.

Achban sidestepped the pool of blood around Ganan's crumpled body. 'What did you expect?' He looked up, knowing that some eight hundred or so metres above him, was the surface of Uluru itself. 'What do you think is the distance between the surface of this rock and the cave ceiling?'

'Grail Finder readings stated that in some areas, it was less than six feet.'

'Right,' Achban said, peeling off his backpack and reaching for his comms radio. He flicked it on and smiled over to Gilam.

Gilam did not smile back.

'Dania, I have in my possession – the Akashic Record.'

It has only cost five people their lives, three of them, our own men, thought Gilam.

Achban relished Dania's excitement. 'We are on our way out, meet us at the exit point marked on the map.'

'Copy that, Achban. Chonen and the second crew have just arrived; they'll be waiting for you when you come out.'

'Copy that, Dania, out.'

The TSA leader took a long, deep, satisfying breath. Soon, Israel would repay the years of heartache and pain it had suffered at the hands of so many, all around them. And Achban would lead the charge. 'Well, my friend, we are nearly there, but we have much work to do.'

I am not your friend, Gilam's sub-conscious hissed.

Achban headed to the tunnels leading up to the exit point. Gilam looked hard at the back of Achban's head. He could not get the vision of Ganan's disfigured body out of his mind.

And then he saw his best friend.

Chasid.

* * *

'Is that the asshole?' Chris peered through the gloom.

'Yes, the one just talking on the walkie-talkie.'

'And he is the one who killed our elders?'

'Yes, and accidently killed one of his own men, simply because he panicked.' Ross turned to meet Chris's surprised reaction. 'And I have to tell you, he didn't seem to bat an eyelid about it either.'

Chris's mouth was now a snarl. 'Well, it's quite obvious he cares for only one thing.'

Ross nodded; there was no doubt this man cared for nothing but the Seventh List and its powers. 'Remember,' he said, tapping Chris on the arm to make sure he had his full attention. 'The soldier with him saved my life.' Burnum and Chris nodded and all three took one more surreptitious look over the ledge.

* * *

'You want to steal this book,' Stuart said incredulously, 'from the Jews?'

'Keep it down you Moron!' Brett scowled childishly. 'Why not? Do you know how much money that thing would fetch on the black market?' He rubbed his thumb and index finger. 'Mate, tens of millions, hell, maybe more.'

Stuart looked at his friend with narrowed eyes. 'And you think you will over-power a group of soldiers, by what, farting on them?' He pushed his arse sideways, for added theatrics. 'Oh, and how do you plan to escape, Houdini?'

'If you weren't a foot taller than me and two feet wider at the shoulders, I would smack some sense into you.'

Stuart rolled his eyes.

Brett took an extra long drag from his cigarette and as he blew out the smoke said, 'Have you ever heard,' looking over to Uluru, 'of anyone base-jumping off that pile of shit?'

'Forget about your fantasies of stealing the book,' Stuart whispered. 'They will kill you in a heartbeat. Unless the damn thing falls into our lap, which I am sure it won't, let's just settle for the nice wad of cash the Israelis offered to pay us.'

Stuart – you have a good heart, but aren't big on intuition. You are never going to see the money.

0:00:57

The Russian skyscraper stooped in order to step through the Learjet doorway, sliding his Cutter & Bucks from his top pocket and slipping the sunglasses across his eyes. The afternoon sun was brighter than it had appeared through the tinted windows.

Siamko and Ivon stood on the tarmac, just out from the terminal building at Connellan Airport. The afternoon wind was mild; it blew a subtle gale to the north, and cooled the sheer excitement of seeing their boss right before their eyes.

'My friends,' Vadislav greeted both men with his strong handshake, 'It is good to see you both.'

As Vadislav walked to the four-wheel drive, Siamko informed him where the Israelis were hiding out. Vadislav laughed. 'In the garbage dump huh – where they truly belong.'

As Ivon drove from the airport, Uluru came into full view and for the first time Vadislav saw it from ground level for himself. 'So this is the home of the Akashic Record, it is quite an amazing sight Comrades.'

'How far off is Romanov-1 from arriving?' asked Ivon.

Vadislav pictured the sleek helicopter and grinned. 'Less than an hour. When it arrives, we will check out the new home of our Jewish friends.' He gritted his perfectly white teeth. 'I look forward to catching up with my personal assistant, we have much to discuss.'

Vadislav requested information on the security of the area. Ivon confirmed that only two policemen were stationed nearby. In addition to this, there was a small group of un-armed Park Rangers. Siamko confirmed all necessary arrangements to immobilise them were already in place. The Russians would avoid human casualties unless absolutely necessary.

Unless they were Israelis.

* * *

'Achban, a private jet just landed at Connellan Airport,' Dania reported. 'We believe it had Vadislav Pravica on board.'

'That's impossible,' Achban snorted. 'I just erased...' He fell silent. 'Shit, I must have chosen the wrong Vadislav Pravica. Fuck it. I will take care of it in a—'

The piercing sound of a high-powered rifle, letting off a round, ricocheted off the gigantic cave walls, the bullet striking just centimetres above the TSA leader's head.

'Down,' Gilam hissed, diving over and pulling him to the ground. 'We have company.'

Another crack pierced the silence and a small chunk of rock a couple of feet above them broke free from the wall.

'Torches off!' Achban commanded. He grappled with his back pack. 'Where are my fucking NVGs?'

Achban, seconds before killing one of his own men, had fumbled with his own set of NVG's, dropping them on the cave floor, where they still sat, deep in the darkness of Spirit Land.

'Here,' Gilam threw his own pair over to Achban. 'Take mine.'

A third crack of the gun sounded out across the darkness. They were under siege. 'Shit,' Gilam hissed, trying to keep his voice down. 'I'm hit.'

282

Some distance away, another man shouted the exact same profanity.

'What is it?' Chris said, lying next to Ross on the ledge and wondering what had gone wrong.

'I think I just hit the good guy.'

'Good one, you so-called state champion sharpshooter. Try aiming the bloody thing,' Chris snorted.

Ross cocked his gun. Just as his eye snuggled the infrared telescopic sight, the ledge centimetres away from his face was hit with return fire, sending dust and chunks of cave wall over Ross.

'Damn it,' Ross choked. 'Burnum, down quick.'

Achban slid his Glock back into the holster. 'Let's make a run for it; the tunnel which takes us out of here is just around the corner.'

Gilam gritted his teeth and held his hand over the wound. He had been shot a few times before and knew by the feel that he would survive, as long as he didn't lose too much blood. He followed Achban down into the tunnel.

'Those damn Australians,' Achban roared.

'What's the problem?'

Achban aimed his torch. 'Take a look for yourself.'

What was once a tunnel was now a crumpled wall of debris completely sealed off, a dead-end.

Gilam winced. 'What do we do now?'

Achban pulled out his comms, panting, his chest heaving with frustration. 'Dania, come in.' He wiped the grit from his sweaty forehead. 'We're sealed in. Get the second crew mobilised. Tell them to get the C.E.D's (Concealed Explosive Device) up to the top of the rock. If we can't get out through the tunnels, we'll make our own exit point.'

* * *

'Four men have just left the van. Two carrying large black duffle bags, over.' Dmitri reported.

'Okay Comrade, how many are left, are the two women still in there?'

'I haven't seen them come out, over.'

Ivon thought for a second. 'Stay where you are and send Maccek to follow the men who just left, got it?'

Dmitri nodded to Maccek who shuffled off in the direction of the group heading towards the big rock on foot. Dmitri continued to spy on the beautiful looking Winnebago, quite out of place in its surroundings.

* * *

'So,' Dania waited until Abelia met her eyes. 'Vadislav is here. How do you feel about that?'

Abelia turned towards the mirror. If fear were pulsating through her body – she was not showing it. She ran her index finger across both eyebrows before meeting Dania's eyes in the reflection. 'I do not fear him,' Abelia said. 'My training and experience – I can take care of myself. If Vadislav thinks he is going to kill me, he may get a very rude awakening.'

0:00:58

The Israeli soldiers, disguised as a camera crew, scampered up the rock with their extra baggage, telling angry tourists they had special permission to film the sunset from the top of the rock. With no rangers in sight, the con ... was on.

Brett and Stuart had decided to tag along. Dania had been glad to be rid of them; she could now focus on the mission at hand to get Achban out of Uluru.

Ascending Uluru is a challenge within itself. The climb up is a bitch, unless you love a horribly steep climb on an open rock face. Half a century earlier someone had installed a small chain fence to hold on to. The soldiers treated the climb as if they were in a training camp. Even with the heavy bags, they made light work of it. Stuart saved face also; he was generally fit and lagged not too far behind.

Smacky? Well, he was in his own league. The minor league. His lack of weight did not assist him, he was grossly un-fit.

'Where are they now?' Siamko spoke into the microphone.

Maccek watched them through his large, high-powered binoculars. 'Nearly at the top.'

'What are they doing?'

'That, I cannot tell you. Two are carrying large, rectangular bags. One carrying a camera tripod.'

'Watch them as long as you can, Maccek. Even when you lose sight of them, watch the surface for any further activity.'

Maccek resumed the watch.

'There is more to that big rock than meets the eye,' Vadislav said to his two most trusted men. 'Ivon, I suggest we prepare to take Romanov-1 on a trip and crash the Jews' little picnic on top.'

Ivon was on the phone before Vadislav had finished his sentence. 'Romanov-bird-zero-alpha-one, this is Ivon, when are you due at the rock? Over.'

'Copy that Ivon, this is CB0A1 – five to seven minutes before arrival, Comrade. Over.'

Vadislav took the phone. 'Romanov-bird, this is Vadislav. Take the airport helicopters out immediately on arrival. We'll guide you to the car park where you'll pick us up. Over.' Vadislav handed back the radio phone and smiled at Ivon. 'Take a couple of the men over to the police station and ensure they will not interfere with us.'

Ivon headed off. Vadislav rubbed his hands together, grinning over to Siamko. 'I think the time is upon us, Siamko.'

The two Russians epitomised the cliché – 'fish out of water' – one wearing Armani, the other considerably more crumpled, both aliens in the middle of the vast desert of the Red Centre.

The young driver of the second four-wheel drive lifted the back door of the truck and smiled at his boss. 'Boss,' he said. 'Maybe when we meet up with your Israeli friends in the garbage dump, you can greet them with this?'

Vadislav let out a small, deep chuckle. 'Very good choice, Boris.' The Russian billionaire picked up the South African Neopup 20 × 42 calibre semi-automatic grenade launcher as if it were a rifle.

It didn't make bullet holes.

It made black holes.

286

'Achban, Dania, this is Ari, we have found a shallow point.'

'Excellent work, Ari.' Achban's patience was starting to run low. 'How long before you detonate?'

'Five minutes. I will let you know when we are ready, over.'

Achban looked to the ceiling of the cave; shortly, he would see daylight, or what was left of it, and then in the foreseeable future, Israel's enemies would bow to Achban. The phone distracted him from his delusions of grandeur. 'Dania, what is it?'

'We ... we just saw Vadislav's helicopter heading from the airport.'

Ari could also see the lone black helicopter circling. He swallowed hard and reported. 'Fuck ... it's heading in this direction!'

'The Russians, damn them!' Achban shouted into the mic. 'Get a move on up there, we are out of time.'

'The sequence is automatic, Achban,' Ari pleaded. 'You know how they work – we can't short-circuit the countdown.'

Achban rolled his eyes and cursed. In order to make the bombs safe to ship and store, they could only be detonated through timing mechanisms. If you tried to short-circuit them, they simply shut down. Even shooting at the bombs would not work.

Dania and Abelia could hear the conversation between Ari and Achban. The tension was quickly rising. Then, it got a whole lot worse for the women in the Winnebago.

Abelia rushed to the window. 'Dania,' she said, 'we have company, over on that ridge.' She pointed.

Dania stole a peek through the slit in the curtain. 'Achban, we have a marker, on the van.' Dania met Abelia's eyes. 'We have to get out of here. Now.'

* * *

'Siamko, come in?'

'Niki, what have you got?' Siamko was hidden on the blind side of the large maintenance shed, fewer than thirty metres away, the long rectangular workshop, along with a large pits of garbage, was all that separated him from the Israeli women in their plush Winnebago.

Soon, it would be a thousand pieces of plush.

Vadislav curled his lips into a deep, satisfying smile. He winked at Siamko. 'Shoot them.'

Niki was not one to hesitate. He stood up and held steady, flicking the safety off on his PP-2000 Russian-made sub-machine gun, and let loose. The bullets ripped into the Winnebago, shattering the windows and punching holes all across its sleek, gleaming body; making confetti of the Israelis' expensive portable digs.

* * *

Ross, Chris, and Burnum had lain low since they themselves had become the target. Ross had only dared a surreptitious peak over the ridge, to where he had last seen the Israelis. Burnum barely moved, as if he were recharging his batteries, ready for what was to happen next. Chris did what half the human race seemed to do every fifty-nine seconds. He checked his cell phone.

Not that he was waiting for a call. His watch had not worked for months, even though he still wore it religiously. His phone was the only way he could check the time. 'They'll have to come this way soon.' The big man grinned, hoping to have the arsehole who had killed the two elders in cold blood, by the neck. 'Or come up with some ingenious plan to escape through solid rock.' He tapped Burnum affectionately on the arm. 'How are you holding up, old man?'

'I'll be etter when we get the book back,' he whispered.

'Don't worry. Ross over here is going to save the day, aren't you, mate?'

Ross smiled. 'I'll give it everything I've got and go down fighting if I have to.'

* * *

Achban settled his back against the wall. 'Well, while I'm waiting, I may as well take care of some loose ends.'

'What are you talking about?'

'Our Australian guides have outlived their usefulness.' Achban spoke coldly. 'It's time to check if my new book can assist me in disposing of them.' Achban tapped on the keys of his Blackberry. He flashed his teeth like a bulldog about to devour his prey. 'Ah yes, now let me see...'

Gilam looked up to the darkness and felt as if someone had stolen his reason for living. Everything had changed when they killed the first innocent man. Only yesterday, Chasid had let Gilam in on a little secret; his girlfriend was 13 weeks pregnant and when he returned, he was going to ask her to marry him. Now – thanks to trigger-happy Achban – Chasid was dead.

'Stuart Andre Moore,' Achban whispered. The Israeli kept his eye on the page, cross referencing the information from his Blackberry. 'Well, well.'

Now this was new.

Stuart Andre Moore was due to die; Achban checked the date on his watch and let out a little wolf whistle, within a couple of hours, 26 years from today's actual date.

Achban raised his eyebrows, discarding the interesting point of what he discovered about the big Australian, before closing the book and slipping his Blackberry back into his pocket.

'Goodbye Stuart Moore, enjoy your last few hours alive, and thanks for nothing.'

The worried cries of Dania crackled through the comms-radio.

'Achban, help!' Dania moaned, 'we are in trouble. The Russians are here... Shit, Vadislav himself. We're on foot. Achban, we need back up, now!'

'Ari, are you getting this, what is your status up there?'

Ari wasted no time responding. 'Two minutes from detonation Achban, over.'

'Send men, quickly!' Achban hissed, his spit hitting the mouthpiece of the radio and deflecting back in his face

'Copy that, Achban.' Ari flicked his hand and two soldiers bolted off in the direction of the track back to ground level.

Vadislav couldn't believe his eyes. The women crawled from under the van, and ran. He hoisted the Neo-pup in the air as if it were a rifle. Weighing nearly six kilograms, only a man of Vadislav's strength could pull off this little charade. 'Mikita!' Vadislav shouted, his voice carrying across the garbage dump as if he had swallowed a megaphone. 'Or who ever the hell you are, I suggest you and your friend give yourself up, or meet the same fate, as your beautiful new toy.'

The Russian billionaire smiled at Siamko and whispered, 'Get me one of these when I get home, they look very nice...'

As the first grenade left the Neo-pup, Vadislav quickly recocked the gun and let off another, just for good measure. He grabbed Siamko by the scruff of the neck and dropped below the ridge line of the sand dune they had been standing on.

Ka-boom.

The Winnebago disintegrated. Debris was thrown fifty metres into the air and the garbage dump rained chunks of metal in all different shapes and sizes. Vadislav had a sneaky look over the ridge. All that was left of it were two large storage compartments caught in the twisted undercarriage of the unit.

Dania had fallen to the ground when the grenades detonated, Abelia alongside her, both trying in vain to shelter behind a large mound of car parts and junk. Abelia muffled a scream. 'Shit, a rat the size of my poodle.'

They fell backwards, trying to get some distance between them and the vermin, which was nearly as big as a domestic cat. It hissed at her, showing a mouthful of sharp teeth. Their new pet leaped for the nearest piece of tasty, fresh meat.

Abelia's big toe.

The Russian billionaire spotted his personal secretary. A surge of adrenaline rushed through his body as he watched her struggling and cowing behind a pile of junk and garbage. He looked down at his shoes: Berlutis. 'Niki, get them. I want them alive.'

The soldier ran.

Abelia ignored the pain that exploded in her left foot, and beside Dania, ran like the wind. The women were super-fit, and when you are running for your life, you find energy from a secret source. They jumped the large mound of garbage as they drew to the exit of the dump. All that was left between them and the next township was about two thousand kilometres. Abelia barely made it over and stumbled, groaning in pain. 'Damn, I'm bleeding.' Her dirty left foot was covered in blood.

Abelia screamed in agony a second time. The blood flowing from her foot had attracted a second rat. This one was the size of a small dog! The bigger rat lunged and sank its foul teeth deep into her ankle.

Dania ran back to her friend.

'No, Dania, go,' Abelia shouted, her tone broken but defiant.

Dania hesitated, the Russian soldier closing in fast.

'Achban help, Abelia is down. Russians closing,' Dania shouted into the radio.

Ari cut in. 'Russian helicopter just landed near the rock.'

'For fuck's sake Ari, get us out of here,' Achban growled.

Ari checked the detonator one final time, giving his fellow soldier the signal. 'Ten seconds,' he said.

0:00:59

Niki dropped Abelia on the ground in front of a pair of very expensive Berluti shoes. Dirt covered a reddy-brown smear over her entire left foot, blood still coming from various cuts. The Russians caught a whiff of rotting garbage and thought it was a worthy scent for this sack of Israeli shit sitting on her arse in front of him.

Even with her in this state – little Siamko stirred...

'Well, hello my fine little friend.' Vadislav smiled, teeth clenched, his lips barely moving.

Nine...

Vadislav picked her up by the larynx, his enormous hand nearly wrapping itself completely around her throat and neck.

Eight...

Abelia looked into his eyes; she had never wanted to pee more than right now.

Seven...

'It appears the local rats have a taste for our little Jewish friend, Siamko. What shall we do, tie her up and leave her to them?'

Six...

Siamko laughed like a hyena. God, he had looked forward to this very moment. As Vadislav held her head out towards

293

him, he landed the back of his hand across her face with the pleasure of a world's number one hitting the winning shot on centre court at Wimbledon.

Five...

Vadislav saw her eyes roll back into her head and knew the chances of her running off – were zero. He released his killer grip and she fell to the ground without any resistance.

'Rope.' Siamko smiled over to Nikifor, placing his foot on Abelia's wounded ankle and pushing hard. 'And hurry, Comrade.'

Four...

Siamko leant down to within centimetres of her face. Even in a garbage dump and almost unconscious, Abelia could clearly smell his foul breath. She dry-retched when he kissed her roughly on her bruising cheek. 'Yes,' he said, tempted to make the next one on the lips. 'Leave her here with the rats, where this bitch belongs...'

Three...

He pulled out his Viking, flicking off the safety switch. 'Now,' Siamko grinned, as he lowered his gun in her direction. 'You are going to regret—'

Two...

Abelia vomited all over the Berlutis. So this is how I die, she thought.

One...

KABOOM!

Ari's cataclysmic explosion sent a shock wave through the centre of the rock where it met the earth and sprayed out hundreds of metres in all directions. A flock of geese flying in formation over two kilometres away stopped abruptly as if they hit an invisible force field and in a panicked, unorganised state flew off in the opposite direction. The bang was louder than five sonic booms. The ears of anyone within a hundred metres of the rock would be ringing for hours. Seconds after the explosion, a small mushroom cloud formed as what sounded like an earthquake, high on top of the rock, began to rumble.

The Israelis on the surface of the rock were protected from the ear splitting sound by ear muffs specially designed for close combat explosions. Tel Aviv Covert Systems of Israel, of course.

Ari was first to spot the hole he'd blown. It was no bigger than the size of a large car, unmistakable against the orange hue of the rock.

Excellent, he thought. Achban will be pleased.

A thunderous crack from within the rock signified that the plan may not have been a good one. The sound grew louder, and before his very eyes, a vast area of the top of Uluru – not five metres from his feet – simply broke up and disappeared into the black abyss below. And the destruction was immense: a gargantuan hole, now the size of four football fields – had exposed the Heart of Uluru to the outside world.

Vadislav forgot his shoes at the sound of the massive explosion. 'Fuck, what was that?' he shouted to Siamko.

The three men stared at the rock, still recoiling from the magnitude of the explosion.

Abelia took the opportunity to run, but she could only limp, her bruised and battered body aching with every step she gained.

Vadislav gave Siamko a boyish slap across the back of the head. 'Dummkopf,' he joked in his best German accent. 'Get that desert rat back.'

Siamko was a pretty good shot, most of the time. He proved it again today. He smiled as Abelia collapsed in a screaming heap into the desert sand.

* * *

From within the rock itself, the massive explosion was terrifying. The unexpected shrill of the bomb detonating only a few hundred metres above nearly blew their ear drums to smithereens.

'What the fuck?' Chris shouted as he struggled against shards of rock, and dust assaulting his eyes, ears, and throat. An enormous part of the cave ceiling was coming down. Chunks of Uluru the size of his apartment fell past the ledge the three men were now on, positioning themselves to avoid being crushed by the collapsing ceiling of the cave.

Ross was having the mother of all coughing fits, trying to spit out the mouthful of debris he had swallowed amidst the chaos. Through the thick mist of red cloud, Uluru was collapsing around him. The parts of the rock blown out hit the bottom of the Deep Cave and disintegrated, sending a thick, heavy plume of reddish dust back up in the air.

Pre-dawn light flooded the cave. Burnum took off his Akubra and relieved it of the thick layer of red dust. Ross shared the ghostly stare with him, as the light grew brighter and they looked out across the Deep Valley of the Liru.

* * *

Dania knew Abelia's capture had given her a lifeline. She'd been running as hard as she could to the rock when the explosion hit. Now, she could not stop staring at the dust rising high above the rock.

When Stuart heard the Israeli women were under attack, he knew he had to help Abelia. The soldiers had ventured off to commandeer a vehicle but Stuart had other ideas. He ran like the wind to the garbage dump, literally falling to his knees when the bomb went off, rolling into a ball and back up as if he were back on the Rugby field. He spotted Dania from some distance, a wave of relief coursing through his veins. As the distance between them grew less, Stuart's excitement evaporated into despair.

Dania was alone.

She collapsed into his arms and let out a small cry. 'They have Abelia, Stuart. They have her...'

Stuart kicked the ground. 'Damn it!' He ripped off his sweaty T-shirt, revealing a ripped muscular upper body, tucking the shirt under his belt. 'Wait for me.'

'Where are you going?' Dania asked, surprised not only by his bravado, but by his well-kept body. She grabbed him by the arm. 'They have guns, she's probably already dead.'

'I have to try!'

* * *

Vadislav took in the view of Uluru, dust billowing from the top of her, a fresh wave of confidence re-igniting his core. 'Let's go and find out what the Jews are up to,' he said to Siamko. He peered down at Abelia's small, motionless body. 'We can take our new pet for a ride.'

'Boris, come in. We need you over here, Comrade, south of the rock. Vadislav wants to take a closer look on top.'

'Copy that, Nikifor.' The chopper pilot pushed the cyclic stick of the multi-million dollar Eurocopter forward, left pedal down and turning southward.

Boris brought the chopper down into the garbage dump. The billionaire slipped on the headset and turned to him. 'Everything go to plan at the airport?'

Boris flicked a switch, nodding. 'Yes, Comrade. All three choppers immobilised.'

The Eurocopter rose off the ground, much slower than normal, as per Vadislav's explicit instructions. Once Boris was sure all was in order, he banked left and headed to Uluru.

Stuart heard and spotted the chopper, like some fierce-looking bird; black, sleek, with military modifications to its sides and underbelly. As the chopper drew closer, his heart sank. He had been running like a man possessed, as if Abelia were the last woman on earth, but now he skidded to a stop. There she was, dangling underneath the chopper, helpless.

Barely conscious, she could not see her knight in shirtless armour sprinting back to the rock to find Dania.

0:00:60

Vadislav had radioed the rest of the Romanov-1 team. As the chopper exceeded the ridge line, the Russians inside the cockpit collectively gasped. 'Well, well, well,' Vadislav muttered into his headset. 'When the Jews really want something, nothing, even the world's oldest rock – gets in their way.'

Millions of years worth of arkose sand was now a smouldering cataclysm of dust seeping from the gaping hole the Israeli bombs had created. The bottom of the deep cave was now awash with fragments of Uluru, the largest, a massive chunk big enough to land two helicopters on side by side.

'Boris, take me down through the hole, let's see what we can find.'

Boris was undoubtedly Vadislav's best helicopter pilot, a regular on the Romanov for the past two years. He could take a chopper into places only pilots with no brains or big balls did, and some that only pilots with no brains and big balls dared. It was safe to say that even for Boris, venturing into this mammoth hole was no child's play.

'If I am not a chopper pilot's asshole,' Ross looked intently through the haze of dust, 'that's a Eurocopter. They have the most distinctive sounding turbines.'

Chris saw the red dot dancing around the middle of Burnum's chest and hit the panic button. He dived for Burnum and took him down below a small, newly created ledge just as a bullet whirled centimetres from the top of his skull and smashed into the wall directly behind him. 'Farck, that was damn close,' he said.

'Any luck?' The TSA leader had prepared well for the explosion. A tunnel that tapered off through a series of tight bends provided the cover he needed to survive.

Gilam picked up his binoculars to survey his aim. He did not want to be responsible for any further innocent deaths. He wanted to be done with killing, for good. His heart almost stopped beating when he registered who he was looking at through the binoculars. Shit. If Achban sees him, I die.

'I missed.' Gilam remained calm, though his mind was racing to come up with a plan.

Achban spat on the ground. 'Shit. Give me the binoculars.'

Gilam steeled himself. He would wait for Achban to put the lenses to his eyes, and then send him over the edge. It was the only way, to save his own life and to avenge his best friend's untimely departure.

A two for one deal...

Achban gave him a dirty look, muttering something derogatory. Gilam repositioned his feet into a karate stance; for better grip and take off, the lenses now millimetres from meeting Achban's eyes.

The noise of the Eurocopter was deafening. Achban cursed, groping for his Uzi. The Eurocopter dropped further into Uluru, Boris manoeuvring until the cockpit was less than fifteen metres away from the stunned Israelis standing on the ledge, and two mounted sub-machine guns nestled directly underneath the cockpit. They then saw something – dangling below. Even Achban caught his breath.

Abelia.

Gilam's eyes met hers. Fear. Anguish. Her body was wrapped tight with the rope, her clothes dirty and bloodied.

Boris switched the chopper into hover mode, considerably lowering the decibel level of the rotors. Vadislav thanked him, before leaning forward and flicking a switch. A loud screech indicated the loudspeaker was now on.

'Shalom,' Vadislav said, facetiously. 'You must be the famous Achban Honi,' the Russian mocked, 'the decorated IDF leader.'

Achban reached to his belt and pulled out his radio-unit, holding it up to the cockpit. 'Stay on current channel, team,' Achban said into the mic, holding up two fingers for channel two, looking as if he were waiting for the Russians.

Vadislav nodded. 'Patch that son of a bitch in, channel two.'

Achban heard the purring sound of the activation. 'And you would be the super-rich and super-famous Vadislav Pravica.' Achban bowed in an exaggerated move. 'How nice to finally meet you.'

'Well Achban, my friend,' Vadislav spoke slowly, 'we have a slight problem.'

Achban shook his head, waggling his finger like a school teacher scolding a student. 'You Russians always talk in riddles! Get to the point.'

'Gilam this is Ari; I know you can't talk right now.'

Gilam resisted a mad urge to look up to Ari's vantage point, high above the ledge.

'I can take the chopper out right now. Orders?'

Gilam gulped the acidic fluid trickling down the back of his throat.

Abelia.

'Gilam, orders.'

Gilam turned his head to minimise the view the Russians had of his face. 'Ari has shot at the chopper. Orders?'

'Hold,' the TSA leader whispered and took off his backpack.

'Move again, Jew and you're dead!' Vadislav hissed through the loudspeaker, his patience waning.

As Gilam subtly tapped out instructions to Ari in Morse code, Achban laughed, holding up the Akashic Record.

'Is this what you want?'

'So, I see you have the book, Comrade. Would you consider a swap?'

Achban screwed up his face. 'What could you have that I would consider swapping for something as valuable as the Akashic Record?'

Was this guy for real? Gilam's respect for Achban, what was left of it, disappeared for ever at that moment.

'How about I sell it to you?'

Vadislav roared with laughter. He took his finger off the microphone button and turned to his men. 'Typical Jew, it's all about money.' Vadislav pressed the button again. 'Name your price, Achban.'

Achban bent down to the book, running his hand across the top as if it were the bonnet of a new car and he the salesperson. 'A priceless artefact like this – which has the power to play God...' he shouted. The move was so quick – he impressed even himself.

'How much ... Jew?' Vadislav was getting impatient.

Achban flicked his head as if his shit smelled of roses. 'It's yours,' he grinned, 'for a hundred billion shekels.'

Vadislav laughed again. 'I've had enough of this stupid Jew,' he said. 'I think it is time we disposed of him.'

Siamko, nestling the control pad for the twin sub-machine guns on his lap, flicked off the safety switch and grunted to Vadislav. He was ready.

'Understood, Comrade.' Siamko smiled.

Vadislav smiled through the cockpit window, his mouth so large and his teeth so white, Achban could see it as clear as day.

'Sounds like a plan Achban,' Vadislav said. 'Do we get a discount for cash?'

'Travellers cheque will do – then I know the cheque can't bounce...' Achban took a deep breath, shaking his head, before laughing at the top of his lungs. He was not laughing at the joke.

'Gilam – I can take the shot – just give me the signal,' Ari whispered.

'Negative, Abelia is on that chopper,' Gilam grunted into his radio, angry Achban had not even acknowledged Abelia, or her safety.

'So tell me Vadislav...' Achban straightened his back and wiped his forehead as if the whole event was a chore. 'What is the point of owning the book – when you are –' He dropped to a crouching position, his hand already under the front cover ... his insignia burning brightly on his wrist. Achban took one more look at the helicopter, and grinned childishly.

Vadislav's patience had run dry. 'Do it.'

Achban slammed the front page shut.

Siamko's fat little fingers fell down onto the button. Bullets rained down on the ledge. Achban was already rolling behind a section of wall. Gilam dived in the other direction.

Something was horribly wrong in the cockpit of the Euro-copter. 'Siamko, stop,' Boris howled.

The billionaire's body had turned to jelly. Well, jelly with a backbone. He lurched heavily to the right, causing Boris to fumble with the controls of the chopper.

Gilam flattened his body as the spinning rotor blades of the now out-of-control chopper narrowly missed his head by inches. The aircraft lurched violently forward and made contact with the ledge before the spinning blades made contact with something slightly unforgiving.

The rock face.

Shards of exploding metal blade shot out in every direction, as the two Israelis scrambled for their lives. As the motor continued to spin the stubs of what was left of the rotor blades, the cockpit of the chopper then crashed hard onto the ledge.

Achban met Gilam's eyes, pointing frantically. Gilam was relieved; he must have seen Abelia too.

No.

Achban was pointing at something else.

The book, teetering on the edge. The Akashic Record.

Gilam's heart sank to a depth he thought not possible. Had Chasid's death taught Achban nothing? He spotted the rope, still attached to the chopper. On the other end was Abelia. To the right, was the book. Any closer to the edge and it would slip over and disappear.

The cockpit of the chopper lurched backwards. The doors jammed, the surviving Russians were unsuccessfully trying to escape, their frantic movements only doing more harm.

Gilam punched the ledge in frustration – Achban had a clear shot of the rope from his side. If Gilam attempted to grab it from his side, he would risk being squashed between the cockpit and the ledge. The seconds were ticking.

The chopper lurched backwards yet again.

Achban went for the rope. He'd save Abelia. Gilam's relief washed over him.

Wrong.

Achban had certainly dived, risking his life, though as the chopper lurched back a final time, commencing the slow motion fall into oblivion – Gilam had a clear view of the other side of the ledge.

Achban. The Akashic Record safely in his arms.

The sounds of grown men screaming distracted Gilam as the cockpit and the ledge finally parted way and the chopper disappeared from view.

Achban stumbled to his knees, close to the edge, a sly grin on his face.

The chopper bounced down the cave wall. A few seconds later, it hit the bottom of the open cave and exploded in a massive fireball.

Gilam rose to his feet reeling from the shock, feeling he might vomit. The thought of Abelia's last moments on earth made his mind spin. It had not had to end that way.

The TSA leader watched the fireball erupt, his face expressionless.

0:00:61

'Try again, comrade,' Maccek said flatly.

Ivashko did as recommended.

Still nothing.

'What has happened to them?' Ivashko said after another failed attempt at raising Romanov-1.

Adam was in his element. 'Gentlemen,' he hissed, shotgun in hand. 'I believe you may be trespassing.'

Maccek swung around to reach for his pistol. The butt of another shotgun smacked his hand hard. 'Don't even think about it, cock,' Erin snapped, thrusting the pistol out of Maccek's belt before pushing him forward with the barrel of the shotgun. 'I'm not in the mood.'

Adam was impressed. Erin had the moves. Those years of working behind Chris's bar to save up to go overseas paid off when it came to tackling meatheads. 'Up against the light pole, fellas.'

Ivashko spat at Adam's feet. 'Who the fuck are you two?'

Adam was busy disarming the Russians and handcuffing them to the pole while Erin kept her shotgun ready.

Adam looked like a man possessed. 'We are Anangu. Owners of this place. Before you get any ideas, think about that hill over there,' he pointed to a sand dune peppered with shrubs about a hundred metres away. 'Our man with the high powered rifle and the telescopic sight will put plenty of bullets in both your legs.' Adam clicked his tongue. A sly grin came over his face. 'Dingoes love nothing more than the smell of blood. They will eat you for dinner, my friends.'

He hoped to hell the small white lie would do the trick...

* * *

'Ari, come in.'

'Achban ... are you okay, Boss?'

'Yes, Gilam and I are fine.'

'Abelia?' Dania cut in.

Gilam looked to the bottom of the cave, hundreds of metres below. The helicopter wreckage was still burning, thick, toxic smoke obscured his view. Not that he wanted to see. He stepped back and bowed his head, speaking a prayer for another member of his team dead at the hands of his leader.

Collateral damage.

Gilam raised the radio to his mouth, taking a deep breath before pushing the button. 'Dania, I'm sorry. Abelia is gone.' He wondered how Dania would take the news that the TSA leader had chosen the book over her friend – if he chose to tell her.

'Dania,' Achban said firmly. 'We have the Akashic Record! We must remain focused, and get home.'

Dania did not respond.

With the Russians all but snuffed out, their leader now roasting at the bottom of the cave below, Achban turned his focus to the other task at hand, the threat on the other side of the ravine. 'Ari, can you see the shooters?'

'Negative. Will continue the search. Over.'

'Let's go, this way.' Ari signalled to Brett. 'And you, stay close.'

Brett stole another look into the bowels of Uluru, where he could see the wreckage of the black helicopter. He caught up to Ari and tapped him on the shoulder. 'Anyone seen Stuart?'

Ari spoke into the microphone. 'Dania, have you seen Stuart? Over.' He nodded, pointing to the Mutitjulu waterhole. 'Stuart is with Dania at the base of the rock, over there.' Ari looked over the edge and shook his head. 'She's really upset.'

'What happened, brother?' Brett asked.

'Abelia was on that helicopter.'

A fresh wave of optimism came over the Australian ex-con. He caught a glimpse of the setting sun and smiled, clenching his fist in excitement. Stuart may be just pissed off enough to consider helping him steal the book, now with his little woman dead.

* * *

Achban headed to the coordinates Ari had given him, where the TSA leader and Gilam could be winched out of the cave. Soon, he would be a ghost, and this darned place a distant memory. 'We are nearly there soldier. I'm sure you are looking forward to a hot bath and a good meal before we celebrate?'

All Gilam could see was Abelia's face, upside down, her body wriggling in a vain attempt to break free. 'You could say that.'

'This is it.' Achban held the rope out to Gilam. 'Perhaps you think you should go first, my friend?'

'No sir, you should go first.'

Achban smiled, turning to the rock face to commence the ascent.

Only then did the soldier's face go limp. Trust me; you are no friend of mine, not now, not ever, he thought bitterly.

'Can you see them now?' Chris whispered.

Ross cocked his rifle and wiped the telescopic sight with his shirt. 'Jeez, clear as day, not. What do you think?'

'Well, it's a fair distance but what do we have to lose?

'You're right. We have to stop this bastard once and for—' Ross stopped mid-sentence. 'My God, is that Brett on top of the rock?' He passed Chris the rifle so he could look into the sight to get a better view.

'Shit,' Chris hissed. 'You little bugger, it is too.'

Ross took back the gun. A new level of anger swept over him. It was the first time he'd seen Brett since it had all gone down. He stared at the arseholes on the other side of the open cave. The clock was ticking.

'It's now or never mate,' Chris said, giving him a friendly nudge.

Ross found a comfortable position, his left eye lined up behind the telescopic sight, focused on the axis. The lighting was shit; he'd just have to do the best he could. His finger rested against the trigger as he held the gun steady, ready to take the shot.

Chris whispered, 'Miss, and you'll be banned from my pub – for life,' his comment followed by a small snicker.

Achban was halfway between the ledge and the top of the rock. With the Akashic Record in his backpack, his time of greatness would soon come, he thought. He looked down, just barely being able to see Gilam. 'Come soldier, let's go.'

'Now or never, Ross.' Chris was not fucking around.

Ross blinked instinctively as his finger pulled the trigger.

Crack.

Contact.

Achban squealed in agony as the bullet entered his left calf. The searing pain shot all the way up his leg and into his torso. 'Ari, help,' he groaned.

Ross reloaded, aimed and let off the next shot.

Bang.

A distant plume of rock face burst into the air.

'Shit – No!' Gilam muttered.

Ross's second shot had split the rope clean in two. The problem was, Gilam was on the wrong side of the cut, free-falling off the rock face.

'Gilam!' Achban shouted, Ari shouting the same into his radio-comms.

Silence.

Achban swallowed. Well, he had the Akashic Record. The men were unfortunate losses, but soldiers die every day. The mission remained up until now, a success.

Ari shook his head. Gilam was a good man; he had worked with him many times. 'Achban, what do we do?' he shouted grappling to help Achban up the last two metres and pull him to safety.

'Is he dead?'

Ross berated himself. By the looks of it, he'd killed the soldier who'd saved his life. 'I can't see,' Ross snapped. 'Lift me up onto this ledge.'

Chris hoisted Ross onto a bump on the rock face.

Ross stretched his neck, shielding his eyes from the sun. 'Okay, let me down, quick,' Ross said.

'Well?'

Ross allowed himself, a small, snickering grin.

Gilam took a deep breath.

The three metre fall flat on his back had winded him. He preferred this to falling an additional seven hundred... As he lay there, on the ledge, in a bit of a daze, with the radio squawking, a peaceful calm passed over him. He knew what had just happened was his way out of this mess. He reached for his radio and flicked it to mute.

'Take another shot.'

'They're too far away now,' Ross protested.

'Just for the hell of it mate.' Chris stood as tall as he could to get a better glimpse of them. 'You may get lucky; you have nothing to lose, huh?'

Ross met Chris's fiery eyes. Man-mountain had a point. Achban's pace was slow thanks to a bit of a sore calf. 'All right.' He reloaded, clearing grit from his eyes before pitching the gun back up to his shoulder. 'For Dad, you pricks.'

Crack.

Brett and Ari were the first to react. Brett pulled a sudden act of chivalry out of his arse; lunging for Achban, he awkwardly knocked him down, falling on top of him and probably saving his life. Instinctively, Ari lunged for Brett.

Bad move.

Blood burst from Ari's chest, his body shuddered as his heart ceased beating – thanks to the bullet that had entered through his upper back and clipped his ticker on its way through.

Another Israeli casualty.

Achban was well on his way to becoming the last man standing.

Brett was fascinated by the volume of blood exiting the dead soldier, until the Glock in Achban's hand came into full view.

'Thank you, Brett,' Achban said, the pain of his calf still searing. 'Now, unfortunately, your time is up.'

Smacky was many things – dumb as a plank of wood was one of them. But like his older brother, he had a fuse, and when it broke – look out. Spending half his life in some of New South Wales' roughest prisons, the younger Taylor had learnt how to take care of himself – taking on and beating the suitcase out of men twice his size. His secret to success?

Speed.

Brett sprang and was on Achban in a second. He clawed at his eyes and sunk his left boot into the TSA leader's calf – the one with the bullet. The effect was as immediate – as it was painful. Achban stumbled. Brett rained punches down on him. When he hit the deck, Brett jumped on his chest, making sure his bony little knees landed hard on his ribs. He was sure he cracked one.

Make that two.

As the pain from his calf, met the pain from Achban's chest, he knew he was in a world of trouble.

Brett punched harder than ever before.

Achban was out.

Cold.

'Fucking asshole.' Brett spat on him as he rose unsteadily to his feet. He rolled the Israeli onto his side and rifled through his backpack. When his hands landed on the object of his desire, an explosion of excitement pulsated through his body. He lifted it out of the backpack and held it high up into the air

His excitement was short-lived. He saw the shadow before he heard the man approach. The party was over – already.

'Fuck, it,' Brett cursed. Achban's Glock was at his foot. He grabbed it, spun and pointed the gun menacingly in the direction of the shadow.

'Well fuck me!' Brett let the Glock drop.

Stuart Moore.

23rd December 2038 5.48:00 PM, minus 26 years.

'Wow – you are one tough bastard, Taylor.' Stu nodded over to the Israeli. 'I was watching, waiting to see if you'd need help, but hey – you took care of business.' Stuart smiled and added, 'I see you have your little book, brother.'

23rd December 2038 5.48:20 PM, minus 26 years.

'Fucken ay.' Brett spat on the rock face. 'And that arschole was going to kill me. I knew he would double cross us. But like most arseholes with guns, they underestimate my speed.' Brett ran his fingers through his hair proudly. 'And freaking agility.'

23rd December 2038 5.48:35 PM, minus 26 years.

Stuart held his hand up for a high-five, meeting Brett's fiery eyes. Brett obliged, smacking his hand hard. Stuart looked intently at the book. 'What do we do now?'

23rd December 2038 5.50:45 PM, minus 26 years.

'Before we go any further,' Brett said, kicking Achban in the arse, 'we need to send our friend here home in a body bag.' He pulled the Glock from the top of his jeans and checked the safety switch. 'Go back to what is left of the team and tell them you lost Achban and the book.'

'I'll give it my best shot,' Stuart said.

23rd December 2038 5.50:50 PM, minus 26 years.

Stuart had just turned his back when Brett called out. 'Meet me behind the old man's house – in two hours, right?'

Stuart agreed, giving Brett a faux military salute for good measure. The ex-rugby player smiled as he met Brett's eyes. 'Done,' he said, 'I look forward to—'

23rd December 2038 5.51:00 PM, minus 26 years, precisely.

Time.

Stuart froze, as if he had just become a statue made out of concrete. Brett looked at him for a second and wondered what the fuck he was doing. And then in slow motion, Stuart, his eyes still open, fell sideways and over the edge. Brett, aghast at what had just happened, ran.

0:00:62

Gilam rose from behind a rock ledge. The tall Israeli walked to where his superior lay and leant down to check for a pulse. Faint – but still there, all the same. He pulled the backpack from the TSA leader's shoulders and shoved in a familiar item. In a matter of seconds, he was done, and the backpack was where he had found it. He surveyed the man he had once admired. He patted the top of the pack and whispered, 'For Chasid and Abelia, you cold-hearted bastard.'

Within seconds he was gone, running back through the gaping hole, into the bowels of Uluru. What ever happened, he'd done the right thing. He hadn't run far when he paused to stow the Akashic Record into his own pack. He clicked the latch on his backpack shut, the book now safe. Unless there was an echo, he knew that second click, damn it. The safety latch of your everyday shotgun. Gilam turned slowly, instinctively; he slowly dropped his right hand for his Glock.

'Not a good idea, bro,' snapped a voice in the shadows.

Gilam raised both hands, until they were above his head. As the two double-barrel shotguns came into view, he was relieved beyond imagination. It wasn't Achban, after all. The TSA leader did not wear a baseball cap. 'I am on your side, now,' Gilam said in English.

The shotguns did not lower. Although Adam knew the story Ross had told him of this soldier, he was not ready to drop his weapon – yet.

With two fingers, Gilam carefully and slowly pulled out his Glock from the holster and threw it to the ground.

'I have seen the death this book has caused today,' he whispered. 'Even before Achban starting knocking people off from within it. The soldier he killed down below,' Gilam looked into the shadows, 'was one of my best friends. He was going to go home and propose to his pregnant girlfriend. He died because of Achban.' His voice grew angry. 'Who didn't care when he killed him.'

Adam lowered his gun.

Erin's shotgun remained trained on the Israeli soldier. 'You killed my father,' she said.

A man, beyond the two men, spoke from the shadows. 'No,' he said.

Burnum.

'Erin,' he said. 'This isn't the one.'

Trembling, she lowered the weapon to her side.

Burnum came close to Gilam. A faint grin appeared for a moment. 'I see you put a replica book in your boss's backpack,' he said.

'Yes. But he's not my boss. Not anymore.'

Burnum looked over the edge into the Deep Cave, savouring the very little time left before the world descended on the Seventh place.

'I am sorry for your loss, Burn-nam,' Gilam said solemnly. He glanced over at Erin. 'I'm sorry.'

The elder raised his hand to the Israeli's shoulder and met Gilam's eyes. 'I am sorry you lost your friend down in Spirit Land,' Burnum said. 'You have done well by us today. Thank you.'

'What do we do now, Dad?' said Adam.

Burnum slipped the Akubra on to his head, adjusting it, before looking up towards the sky. 'Let's get out of here.'

Adam looked incredulous. 'What about the arsehole still knocked out, on top of the rock? What if he wakes up – you're going to let him walk off the rock and escape?'

Burnum looked long and hard into his son's eyes, before doing something he did rarely. He winked at him. The corners of his lips curled. 'He won't get off the rock.' The elder nodded for them to get their things together to make a move.

Erin gave Adam a puzzled glance. The elder's son rolled his eyes. 'Hold on.' Adam called to his father. 'Where's Ross?'

Burnum pointed up to the summit-cairn of Uluru. 'He went after Brett. I need you two to go down, find Chris and make sure he's all right. If Brett gets away from the summit, you're gonna need to stop him.'

* * *

A small pool of blood was the only thing indicating Achban's last known position.

'He was always one tough bastard,' Gilam cursed. 'I should have thrown him over the edge when I had the chance.'

Burnum shrugged. 'Well, it will end soon, one way or the other.' He patted him on the shoulder. 'You can escape now, if you wish.'

Gilam saw someone else looking at him through Burnum's eyes.

Chasid.

'When I know Achban's dead. Until then – I stay.'

Burnum did not waver. He unhooked the hessian bag from his shoulder. The one that contained the true Seventh List that he had taken from Gilam. Now, he gave it back. 'Take care of this for me,' he said.

317

Gilam was taken aback. The elder was trusting him to guard the very thing he, up until a few hours ago, was desperate to acquire for what he had thought was the good of his country. 'I don't know what to say Burn-nam.'

'I looked into your eyes, fella, I can see you will do what is right.'

Gilam took the book.

'Now,' Burnum stared into the distance. 'You wait. I need to find Ross before he kills his little brother. Bad boy, that Brett. Very bad.'

0:00:63

Ross saw him from some distance. The little fucker sitting with his back turned, enjoying a cigarette. Ross managed to bridge the gap between them without detection. He stopped about ten feet away. 'So, my little brother has helped a bunch of arseholes murder innocent people, and then desecrate our rock, you stupid fucking wombat.'

Brett jumped to his feet and struck a pose. Sometimes he liked to think he was a rapper. 'And you, my brotherrr ... knew of the cave system all along, and did not tell me.'

'As if I could trust you, you bloody murderous prick.'

'Oh, go and fuck yourself, Ross.' Brett's voice grew angrier. 'I always lived in your shadow, always the loser.' His lips twisted into a snarl.

'While you were the golden child.'

'And this is how you right wrongs?'

'I did it for the money. If you were in my shoes, you'd have done the same.'

'Brett, they killed innocent people.'

'Fucking blackfellas. Who gives a fuck about them, anyway?'

That was it. Ross jumped. Brett dropped his backpack and threw a wild volley of punches, hoping one would make contact.

Ross was substantially bigger than his puny brother, but he had not spent years of his life in prison, defending himself from larger, angrier men who – literally – wanted his arse.

Ross blocked and threw a quick left that connected with Brett's face. He heard the sound of bone crunching.

It seemed to have little effect, except to make Brett angrier, which filled him with adrenalin. Fingernails, longer than normal on a male, slashed across Ross's face, connecting with the soft tissue of the eyelid and peeling it open like a tomato. Ross stumbled back in searing pain and the shock of the blood spurting into his eye.

Brett, seeing the opportunity, lunged with more aggression. He grabbed his opponent's shoulders – going for his signature Liverpool Kiss, but Ross saw it coming and threw his head back. Ross's bottom lip smashed against his teeth as Brett's forehead connected. For a second, he thought his lip had been ripped off his face. The flash of white pain took his resilience to a new level. And Brett's nose was calling for his big brother's fist.

As the fist connected, the junior Taylor felt the cartilage in his nose, snap; the massive jolt of pain reverberating back deep into his brain. He fell backwards, rolling over once, landing a few feet away.

Ross tore his shirt, bundling the cloth to his bloodied eye and lip. It was over. He'd knocked the arsehole out.

Wishful thinking, Rosco.

Brett opened his eyes. His face an inch from his backpack. The one with the world's smallest, lightest and most compact parachute. The one with the Akashic Record – now in his possession. His ticket to freedom and wealth. A better life.

And the Glock! The silver, loaded Glock. Pulling out the handgun, he rolled over and managed a smile. 'So,' he said, pointing the pistol. 'I guess this is where this ends.'

Ross stumbled to his feet.

Shit.

'Do what you gotta do, arsehole,' he shouted, spitting blood at him. 'Just make sure it's the money shot.'

Brett Taylor looked him over, reaching down for his backpack. He clutched the book, and slipped the backpack around his shoulders. 'I know I should kill you,' he said with disdain. 'And you deserve to die with far more pain than this,' he hissed. 'But remember this moment,' Brett grinned, 'For I spared your life.'

He suddenly spun around and ran hard towards the ledge. A second later, he leapt.

Brett would add Uluru to his list of BASE jumps.

But not for long.

Ross ran to the cliff's edge.

A hand fell on his shoulder a few moments later. His heart jumped. 'Shit,' he gasped, 'you could've said something.'

20 metres from the edge of Uluru, in mid air.

Burnum shrugged. 'Sorry,' he muttered, watching Brett's parachute burst to life.

The old man shook his head. 'Ross, there was something else I never told you about the other 25 books.'

40 metres from Uluru, 30 metres off the ground.

Ross met Burnum's eyes, his expression asking the Elder to – please explain?

'The fake books are not meant to leave Uluru,' he muttered.

Ross shrugged his shoulders, 'What happens if they do?

60 metres from Uluru, 15 metres off the ground.

Ross heard his brother let out a joyous hyena sound, as far as Brett was concerned, he was already in Rio De Janeiro.

'I don't think I want to find out,' Burnum grabbed Ross by his sleeve and added, 'we do not want to see this,' turning and hustling them both off in the opposite direction.

75 metres from Uluru, Brett met the ground with a 10 out of 10 perfect landing. He quickly discarded his parachute and looked back up the top of Uluru, expecting to see his asshole of a brother looking down at him.

But he was not there. As he walked another four metres further away from the rock, he shrugged his shoulders, and reached for his Winfield blues.

For the last second of his life, Brett wondered if his cigarette had caused the small, fatal explosion splitting his body into hundreds of pieces.

Ross heard the ear splitting sound from his vantage point high on the rock. Burnum continued to take him further away from another death at Uluru.

* * *

Gilam reached for his handgun.

Achban fired another shot into the rock. 'Don't even think about it!' The TSA leader stood awkwardly, his face dirty and bruised, his clothes tattered, his left calf wrapped tightly with strips of his t-shirt, now coated in blood. He pointed the smaller Glock, the one he'd kept hidden, strapped to his leg. 'Well, my friend, you nearly got away with it.' Achban tapped on the radio attached to his belt. 'But I heard the click when you switched to mute.' His lips parted to show his teeth. 'Traitor, I checked the book, but then looked on my wrist. No visible insignia. Now, where is it?'

'You'll never find it.'

Achban nodded to the hessian bag. 'You fool. It will be a pleasure to take it from your dead body.'

Gilam saw what was coming and couldn't keep the surprise from his face.

Alerted, the Glock still trained on the traitor, Achban's head whipped round to find Ross Taylor, running at him at full speed, all those years as a super-fit footballer coming into play. Achban instinctively raised his gun at Ross, taking his eyes of Gilam for only one second.

The distraction was all Gilam needed. He leapt, his hands folding over Achban's, closing over the Glock. The three men wrestled for their lives on the hard surface of Uluru until a pistol shot rang out.

Achban wrenched himself away. Dropping the gun in agony, he staggered, teetering on the edge of a ravine that ended up down at the Mutitjulu waterhole, hundreds of metres below. Gilam and Ross watched in a kind of mesmerised horror as the bloodied TSA leader lurched for the book, thrown loose in the scuffle, scrabbled for a foothold and slid empty-handed over the edge, rolling away down the steep rock face.

Gilam breathed a heavy sigh. 'Now, he's dead'

'Don't count on it,' said Ross, picking up the book. 'A few tourists have fallen from here and lived to tell the tale, a fat Texan idiot only three months ago. We'd better get down there and finish this off once and for all.'

0:00:64

Achban was located just above the base of the Mutitjulu Waterhole.

At first glance, Gilam and Ross thought he was stone cold dead. A faint pulse indicated he was still hanging onto life, unconscious.

Burnum's instructions on what to do with the Israeli surprised both men, though they did as instructed without delay, before all three men, along with the TSA leader, headed back into the Heart of Uluru.

Dania, Chonen and another unknown Israeli soldier were last spotted fleeing the National Park in a stolen four-wheel drive. Amazingly, they slipped out of the Northern Territory only a few hours later, although their whereabouts were still unknown months later. Mysteriously, they never returned to Israel.

The two last remaining Russian sailors from the Romanov, handcuffed to the power pole at the entrance to the Uluru Kata Tjuta National Park, lived to tell the tale of the dingo cries they swore they heard nearby, the two big thugs reducing themselves to quivering idiots in front of the slightly bemused local authorities.

Achban opened his eyes. His mind was still a little blurry, though he quickly established that he was on a stretcher of some sort, his legs and arms tightly bound, inhibiting him from moving all but his neck.

Oh, and his mouth.

'What is the meaning of this!' he roared in the darkness, bathed by at least three powerful torches.

Chris, Adam and Burnum came into view. Without any warning Adam appeared at the end of the stretcher kicking the Israeli so hard it sent a shockwave of pain right up his left leg.

'You bastard, you are now going to experience Spirit Land for yourself, first hand,' he snarled.

Burnum raised his hand, 'Enough son,' before Adam stood back and stared down at the TSA Leader.

Burnum muttered something to Chris, who walked over to Achban; the Israeli flinched, waiting for another kick or volley of punches. But they never came. Chris untied the rope holding Achban's arms, before loosening the one tied around his legs.

Burnum and Adam stepped a few metres away, talking in hushed tones before Adam embraced his father for what seemed like an eternity. Achban at this split second realised something was very much amiss.

He was no longer in any pain.

His bullet wounds had disappeared, along with the bruises and cuts. As if Burnum was watching him, he stepped closer and leant down to him.

'Now do you believe in the power of the Seventh?'

Before Achban could respond, a small torch fell into his lap from behind. He sat up and picked up the torch.

'What is the meaning of this?' he asked.

Burnum smiled in the faint light of his torch.

'You wanted to experience the power of the Seventh,' he looked off into the distant darkness and seemed to wink at something, or someone, 'well now you can. And I will remain here to ensure you do so.'

326

Adam embraced his father one more time before joining Chris, ready to leave the cave.

'You must be kidding,' Achban snarled, 'I will escape this place with ease, I remember the way out.'

A fourth man stepped from behind Achban and came into view.

Gilam.

'Well that's what you think, Achban, you were always so sure of yourself.'

Achban's teeth in both corners showed, as if he were a pit bull. 'Traitor, I will come for you.'

Gilam ignored the TSA leader, joining Adam and Chris before looking back over to Achban, now sitting up in the stretcher.

'Goodbye Achban, remember,' Gilam shook his head with a tinge of sadness, 'a few of your soldiers are now down here too.'

As Chris, Gilam and Adam began to walk off; Burnum cleared his throat in such a way as to get someone's attention. Adam turned around and looked at his father.

Burnum grinned before slipping the Akubra off his head and in a perfect motion, threw the hat in his son's direction as if it were a Frisbee. It landed in Adam's left hand a moment later. Adam looked at his father and before he could ask Burnum said, 'It is yours son, I no longer need it where I am going.'

As the men walked off, one now with an Akubra proudly sitting on his head, Burnum turned and looked down at the TSA Leader, who was making huffing and grunting noises.

'You restore my body and health so I can escape, what sort of idiot are you, Elder?'

Burnum shook his head from side to side, a grin momentarily appearing.

'Tell me Achban, can you see in the dark?'

Achban was nearly free of his stretcher; he scoffed at the comment and pointed the torch in his lap directly in Burnum's face.

'This is a torch, you stupid ma—'

The torch at that split second, ceased working.

Pitch black.

'No!' Achban howled, loud enough for everyone to hear. Even the dead.

'Burnum!' Achban shouted with disdain.

Silence.

And as the seconds grew into minutes, the TSA leader realised his fate.

And then, as if the voices were only metres away, a thread of horror trickled down the nape of his neck.

'Achban,' the voice whispered.

As the TSA leader began to fully experience vertigo, falling flat on his face and nearly knocking himself out, he realised the voice that had called his name, was one he once knew well.

Chasid.

0:00:65

As the minutes dragged on, Ross lay on his back, the book nestled on his chest; he held it firmly, not for one second wanting to open it, no way. Burnum had been quite specific. He was not to let go of the book at any time, and was to stay at the bottom of the first massive cave of the seventh, now with a gigantic hole exposing the night sky.

'What now?' His words seeped into the darkness, though with full moon overhead, there was enough light coming down through the enormous hole to distinguish shapes and even cast shadows.

He looked up and enjoyed the beautiful stars, far above, for nearly a full minute, the peace, the serenity, nearly sending him to sleep.

A distant, familiar sound quickly broke the solitude of the moment.

Rotor blades.

His mind spun as quickly as the rotor blades, which were growing louder by the second.

Shit! More bad guys – Russians, Israeli – who knows? He felt like a sitting duck, his nerves tightening up all the muscles around his chest and neck. He swallowed hard.

Ross cursed. He could probably escape into the tunnel system below, but Burnum's instructions were explicit – stay on this boulder – with the Seventh List in your arms – and don't move.

Ross's heart was beating in his throat. He cursed Burnum and wanted nothing more than to run. But he remained on the boulder.

The explosion of sound directly above the cave opening was frightening. Whatever the chopper was, it had made the distance from when he had first heard it in lightning speed. It sprang across the opening and then disappeared into the night.

Ross heard the rotor blades turning; he knew the sound in his sleep. The chopper coming back for another look was a sure thing.

The chopper came into view and halfway across the hole pulled a manoeuvre Ross had only managed once in his life. The chopper arced into a 180 degree turn and suddenly was dropping directly into the gaping hole above.

It then levelled back out, but continued to drop. Ross had never seen a chopper like it, or one dropping from the sky at such a blistering, rapid rate.

It dropped at least seven hundred metres in less than twenty seconds, before slowing with only fifty metres to go. Ross rose to his feet, the book still in his arms.

The rotors powered down. It had landed, no more than 60 metres away, on a flat chunk of Uluru just big enough to accommodate it.

Fuck it – whatever Burnum's original plans were, they probably didn't include this gatecrasher. Time to make a run for it, Ross thought.

The door on the opposite side of the chopper to Ross opened. What he believed at that moment was a man, obscured by the darkness of the night shadows, appeared from behind the sleek looking machine.

He seemed to stand there for a moment, contemplating his next move. Just as Ross was about to say something, the man moved to the side of the chopper, heading on purpose, to the darkness of the shadows nearby.

Ross had had enough.

'Who are you and what do you want, mate?' he shouted at the top of his lungs.

The man was now making his move. Still obscured by the darkness, he moved closer.

50 metres from Ross.

Ross clutched the book tighter, feeling it was his duty to defend it with his life. He cursed himself for not retaining the high powered rifle, or even a fucking handgun.

The man was now moving with intent.

30 metres from Ross.

'Shit,' Ross muttered, now he was really shitting himself. The stranger had no intention of revealing himself and was on purpose, remaining in the darkness, avoiding any hints of moonlight.

20 metres from Ross.

Ross contemplated his next move. He would dive off the boulder in the opposite direction and make a run for it. If this was part of the damn plan – Burnum would have told him about it, Ross surmised.

The man was now close enough for the adrenaline in Ross's throat to nearly choke him.

Ten metres from Ross.

The lone man then stopped dead in his tracks, as if waiting for something. For nearly 30 seconds, Ross felt as if he were in a nightmare Mexican Standoff.

And then, a small ping.

His watch. *His normal watch.*

It chimed at the sound of a new hour.

And at that split second, a new day.

12.00.01 … am, 21st December, 2012.

The small inconsequential sound did something else at that very moment. It was as if the sound was an invitation.

The man in the shadows stepped forward. For the first time since he had exited the chopper, the moonlight brought him into full view.

0:00:66

'You're looking good, son.'

'Dad?' Ross gasped, stumbling off the boulder.

Jimmy lunged forward and reached for his son.

'Dad, what the hell?' Ross muttered as he embraced his father, his mind a whirl with confusion.

'I guess I owe you one hell of an explanation Roscoe, sit.'

Ross followed Jimmy over to another rock and sat down with him.

'I told you once before, I was chosen to guard this book.' He touched it and smiled. 'And as I said, it was either guard this, or die.'

Jimmy looked up towards the stars. 'It wasn't that hard really, I fell in love with this place and I had John Kelsey as a boss. But, as you know,' they met each other's eyes, 'I could extend my life but ... and this is the kicker, son: not on this planet.' Jimmy's words hung heavy in the air.

'You've been ... on another planet? Jeez, Dad, are you kidding me?'

'I have been where the human race originated, Ross, where,' he touched the book once again, 'this little book was created.

'You see son, today, is a very special day. The day, the Human Race's Knock List, as I like to call it, is brought together, with its other two books, what is more commonly known as the Akashic Records.'

'The what?' Ross felt his mind going numb.

'Two other books exist, hidden on other continents. If all three books are not re-set together, every 26 years, the human race would cease to exist. Every single soul would simply vanish.'

'Hold on.' Ross sat up straighter. 'Today is the day many people think the world is going to end, the Mayan Calendar, etcetera.'

Jimmy placed the ancient book on his lap. 'The Mayan calendar was originally based,' he ran a finger around the circular glass dome on the cover, 'on this very book.'

Jimmy studied the glass dome for seconds before turning to Ross.

'You see, originally, this book was placed on Earth 52,000 years ago, two full cycles of 26,000 years to be exact. When more than 260 souls inhabit the planet, the book is required for the population to continue. It is the ancestors of the human race who set the cycle of this, and the original 5114 year Calendar, the Mayan calendar as we came to know it. Today is the day the books are reset, and' Jimmy afforded himself a little chuckle, 'by no means the end of the world.'

'So why aren't these ancestors of the human race, here with us, right now? Why don't we know of their existence, Dad?'

'Fair question.' Jimmy took a deep breath. 'The ancestors have hundreds of colonies across many galaxies, and beyond. Only when they believe a colony has come far enough in their progress, is that colony informed, as one society, of its ancestry...'

'And we're not ready yet.'

Jimmy's face turned serious.

'Ross, other planets have been in peace for thousands of

years. We,' Jimmy shook his head and looked downwards 'as a total human colony on this planet just cannot seem to achieve a sense of oneness. This is one of the requirements they seek, and we seem to be nowhere near it.'

Jimmy rose to his feet and nodded for Ross to hand over the book to him, which he did without delay.

'Today was supposed to be the day the Human Race was going to be informed of their ancestry, and the existence of hundreds of other colonies out there in the many Galaxies.'

Ross thought he'd heard a door on the chopper close shut, but for a second ignored the sound. He rose to his feet and met his father's eyes.

'So what happens now, we have to wait for another 5000 plus years before we are told about our origins?'

Jimmy shrugged his shoulders, in the corner of his right ear he heard the distant sound of light footsteps coming in their direction. He smiled at Ross and stepped a little closer, turning him in the opposite direction of the chopper.

'No,' Jimmy put his arm around his son and felt pride pulsate through his body and soul, 'they are watching, and if we one day find our true peace and realise we are one, they will then come forward.'

The other occupant of the chopper was now only 30 metres away from the two Taylors.

'Anyway Roscoe, let's not worry about that, for we have other issues to discuss.'

20 metres away.

'Nice flying by the way,' the younger Taylor said, not that was high on his list of questions; he just wanted to get it off his chest.

Jimmy scoffed; his laugh was a little sarcastic though Ross didn't register it as such.

15 metres away.

'Why did you not come sooner,' Ross waved his free arm around the enormous, now exposed cave, 'and stop all this madness?'

Jimmy could hear the footsteps getting even closer and knew he had to keep Ross pointing in the other direction.

'We could not come any sooner,' Jimmy said, 'although they are obviously extremely advanced, they are still a long way from here. In addition to this, I could not come within a few metres of the book until today. Don't ask me why, that's the rules we were given.'

Ross digested the answer and seemed to accept it, and it was at that moment he thought he'd heard something directly behind him. He tried to turn around although Jimmy held him tighter, not allowing him to turn.

'Besides,' Jimmy cleared his throat as if he was about to speak in front of the entire nation, 'although we lost close friends, and those bastards damaged this most sacred of places, they believed the book would remain safe in the end.'

'Why is that?' Ross said, growing annoyed and nervous at the same time, he could feel the presence of another person standing behind him.

'Because,' Jimmy smiled.

'Never in the history of hundreds of colonies, and the Akashic Records on each and every planet, have they come across such an anomaly.'

'What would that be Jimmy?' Ross was now getting a little agitated with the theatrics.

'That the offspring of *two* gatekeepers, would in the end be the leader of the resistance to defend and save the book.'

Ross caught his breath in his throat.

'I think it's about time I showed you boys *how* to fly a Helicopter.'

Ross had never forgotten the calming tone of his mother's

336

voice. She was now standing directly behind him.

Epilogue

'See what happens when you go away for a little while? Silly things happen.'

Ross smiled at Oxy, as he, Chris, and the new bartender stood behind the bar of the Old Yulara Hotel, all gazing at the two people who had just entered.

One was wearing a grin only a girl, deeply in love, with a new addition to the jewellery on her left hand would wear. The other, smiled as if he were the proudest man in the Northern Territory.

Adam and Erin.

Chris nodded as Gilam poured the perfect Schooner; Oxy was surprised at how easily the big Israeli had picked up the art of pouring the perfect beer. He knew employing him was the right thing to do, his skills of pulling a beer, being as strong as he was when Chris needed a little extra security, plus his newfound knowledge of the Seventh, more than enough reason to put him on the books, especially with Gilam deciding that he had no intention of ever returning to his homeland.

The two big men had hit it off, like most of the crew of the Seventh; they had all taken to the Israeli, who, as they got to know him better – had a heart of gold.

'Come on then, let's see it,' Chris grinned as the two engaged lovebirds stood in front of him.

Erin pulled her left hand up, the pink diamond shimmering in the afternoon sunlight. All three men let out a small whistle in perfect harmony.

'Whoa,' Chris muttered, 'that is the largest rock I have seen since—' he swung his head around and looked straight out the window towards Uluru. The small group of friends burst into unabated laughter.

After Ross handed Adam a schooner, and Erin a glass of champagne, Chris stood back and slowly raised his own beer. He nodded to Gilam to grab the beer the Israeli had just poured to join in the toast.

'To three of the greatest fathers to ever set foot on Earth,' Chris announced, ensuring he made eye contact with Ross, Adam and Erin separately. He then turned to Gilam and rested his hand on the Israeli's shoulder, 'and friends who, we miss and are no longer with us.'

Ross took a long drink from his glass. He looked over to Uluru through the pub window. He thought of all those souls, still trapped 1700 metres below, and wondered how soon that bastard Achban would join them.